T0208957

LUNA
THE GIRL FROM GLIESE 581D

P S Morningstar

BALBOA.PRESS
A DIVISION OF HAY HOUSE

Cover Artwork: Emily Miller Yamanaka

Balboa Press books may be ordered through booksellers or by contacting:

Balboa Press
A Division of Hay House
1663 Liberty Drive
Bloomington, IN 47403
www.balboapress.com
1 (877) 407-4847

Print information available on the last page.

ISBN: 978-1-9822-3880-3 (sc)
ISBN: 978-1-9822-3879-7 (e)

Balboa Press rev. date: 11/29/2019

CONTENTS

FOREWORD

LUNA is a very young non-classified resident of Gliese 581 d, in the Andromeda Galaxy. She knows through the Outpost history that her family as well as other volunteers left Earth on this spectacular voyage.

The settling of this small Outpost, over the last century, has grown and prospered. Yet, all the answers that Luna seeks, are consistently found in the Data Archives Center. The most important of which is "the Mission Statement." This document conveys everything relevant to their past, present, and future existence.

LUNA shares sixteen of her adventures with us. How she overcomes adversity, and invites others to join her. We are all pulled into these incredible experiences as she willingly questions and addresses her colony, as well as the reader. The designing Commission, before her, shared the stars and a new universe for others to follow. LUNA has the wisdom and ingenuousness to understand where she is. She will grow, share and go further with each adventure focused on the Mission Statement as her guiding light.

SUNSHINE

⬤

Luna hopped out of bed, so excited… today is the day! She could hardly sleep last night in anticipation. She was finally going to see real sunlight! The experience of a lifetime and she was going to be able to "take it all in."

Luna really didn't know what to expect; except this was a very extraordinarily special day. She decided to dress for the occasion by pulling out and donning her "Ceremonies" outfit. She felt that was befitting of this day of *"Sunshine."*

Mum hadn't called her for breakfast yet, so she sat on the end of her bed, swinging her little feet to release the excited energy she had and started thinking about all she had studied and knew of the Sun. Luna wasn't born when this Outpost was targeted, planned reached and built. This colony had successfully thrived for over 3 generations now, and she was part of the upcoming fourth generation.

As a tiny child, she always asked "why?" this or that- No one responded to her internal nagging questions of wanting to know… *Why?* Everyone who lived here had a position or job to which their education was tailored. To her- it seemed well and good. In her heart she knew and had researched that her home was the "Blue Planet," earth. From the time she was allowed in the Data Storage & Archival Studies Building, she would go there and check in with her tiny fingerprint and start looking. Looking for anything that would help her understand and learn about Outpost 621 and Earth. There were only 3 books at the Data Storage facility and Luna marveled at these, wanting to touch and hold them. What was in their secreted interiors? But that was strictly forbidden to *everyone*. All data- past, present, as well as projections was recorded for viewing on any one of the computer templates.

It took some years of reading, rereading and assimilating for Luna to understand that this project started over 200 years ago on earth, when various visionaries, humanitarians, astronomers, botanists, economists, and programmers came together and started the 621project. They asked for 200 volunteers from all walks of life with varying skill sets for this commission. Their lives would be changed-there was no turning back if they accepted this undertaking. This statement always excited Luna... the big adventure.

The "team" had found this planet in the Milky Way and had plans to colonize it. The one drawback was there was virtually NO sunlight. Every part of Outpost 621 was going to have to be supported by A.I.s and computers. The humans were required for social abilities, forward trouble shooting, and to create an environment for a permanent colony. And here Luna was- identified as fourth generation, female, age 8, occupation- not identified as of yet.

She felt so alone because her only kinship she felt was with the Data Storage of the Outpost's history and Earth, those that started this project.

She would ask her instructor in classes at various times about gravity, temperatures, survival, hybrid plants, vitamins and minerals only to have the rest of her class start howling and booing Luna. The instructor would quiet everyone, and then reply to Luna she would be taught about these things at a later time or the more devastating choice the instructor made was to tell Luna she had to leave class.

If that happened, Luna accepted the dismissal note from the instructor and headed to the Life Subsistence Wing of the Outpost. At least she wouldn't be laughed at for her curiosity, and usually she learned important information on plant and animal life, or about soil and air balances: The Botanical Wing. And today this wing was going to be filled with activity as the Botanical was designed with the translucent panes, and is where everyone will want to be *"when the Sun comes out."*

Luna had learned through her studies at the Data Archive Center that the sun only revealed itself on Outpost 621 every 99 years. This fact was barely mentioned in her instruction class, but everyone was excited, and knew something different was happening today.

Mum finally called Luna to breakfast, and she ate quickly and headed off to class. She did not want to miss a thing today! She felt so special. She was going to be one of the fourth-generation voyagers to witness the *sunlight*. When she got to her class, she was one of the first students there. As the other young classmates started coming in, there was a strange quiet and reserve about them that Luna noticed.

Finally, the instructor came in and addressed what was going to be the topic and lessons for today- *Sunlight*! Everyone turned and looked at Luna, and she didn't know why. She was excited, expectant, but as always, the perfect student. Today's topic and lessons was posted on the holographic board for accentuation. The whole Outpost would be lit by the sunlight for 2 hours between 11:10 and 13:09 today. Then the instructor began to give facts and historical data that she had gathered from the Archive about this wondrous phenomenon. Luna listened intently, absorbing information shared, hoping there may be a nugget or two of data that the instructor was relaying that Luna didn't already know about. But she was watching the clock also, as was everyone in the class. Time was getting shorter and closer to the *sunshine*. Luna's heart was about to burst with happiness. She *knew* today she could not call any attention to herself by asking questions. She knew what would happen. So, she sat stoic, with a smile on her face...waiting.

The instructor announced it was time for a snack, and then they would proceed to the Botanical Wing for the event. She turned and walked to the educational storage for food stuffs.

With the quickness and power of the planet winds- they ascended on Luna! She was grabbed by 2,.. 5,...10 of her classmates making it impossible for her to move, yell or escape their clutches. She could tell she was being lifted and moved.

Where?

Why?

They were quick, swift, and stealth. They put something in her mouth and threw her in the back-storage closet. They pushed the door shut, and heard it click as the lock engaged.

She was in the dark- alone. She heard feet shuffling across the floor and away from her.

The instructor noticed the students out of their seats and simply asked them to get their snacks and head towards the Botanical Wing.

Luna was so shocked she couldn't make a sound at that moment. Then she tried the door. It was locked. She couldn't get out. She listened...it was getting quieter and going to silence in her classroom. Luna started crying and pleading "Let me out!!" over and over. No one heard her, or cared to check out the commotion from the classroom. In exhaustion Luna dropped to the floor of the closet, sobbing.

How could they?

Why would they?

How come no one is missing her?

Then she could hear the reverberations throughout the whole Outpost of singing, dancing, shouts of glee, joy, and laughter. It went on and on. Time was passing-so was Luna's sunlight. She melted into a small ball on the floor to await her fate. There was nothing she could do to escape. She was left with only her imagination of what sunlight was. If she just stopped breathing right now, it really wouldn't matter. Tears continued to stream down her cheeks. All her heart and soul could think about was sunlight, and its brilliance. She had so wanted to be a part of this historical milestone happening in her lifetime- to share with others in due time. But it was not to be. It would stay in her dreams.

Finally, she heard noises coming up the hallway. People were returning to the Educational Wing. Luna didn't know at this point whither to stay silent or to start screaming again. She could hear shoes scooting across her classroom floor. They were back!

Luna stayed quiet, but could hear voices in the room asking each other if Luna escaped, but no one came to the door to check on her.

At long last, the instructor entered the classroom and asked what was going on, immediately noticing everyone staring at the storage closet. All was silent. This was Luna's chance! She started screaming- she kept screaming as she heard footsteps racing towards the closet that held her captive.

The door opened, and little Luna fell out of the closet onto the classroom floor, unmoving.

OUT OF THE CLOSET

The instructor stared down at Luna. What had happened? Where had this child been for the whole outing? The instructor looked around the room at the other students, and could not get a read on what was really happening right now, so she swept down and grabbed up Luna in her arms and headed to the Medical Repository, Health, and Wellness Lounge. Something was definitely wrong. This was not her area of expertise.

Getting to the Medical Area, carrying in a small child the instructor was quickly surrounded by qualified staff to start a diagnosis as to what was going on with her. An attendant gently removed Luna from the instructors' arms, and carried her a bit further into the lounge and placed Luna on an examination table in the evaluation cubicle. The head physician reached for the body-scanning device, and adjusted the settings for a small female child. This would limit the information the scanner had to pull up and analyze, instead of the whole population of the Outpost. He turned and asked the instructor two quick questions as he awaited the scanner to pull up the identification and first vital readings on Luna. With a very concerned look on his face he asked had the girl been over stimulated by the sunlight today. To which the instructor shook her head in a negative motion and replied "No." She thought about it. She had not seen Luna at all since departing for the Botanical Wing. The Doctor's second question was 'did anyone have an idea why Luna was pale, unconscious, and unresponsive currently.'

He then read the information from his scanner as he passed it over the microchip implant on Luna's right arm, fourth generation, female, LUNA, age 8, occupation- not identified as of yet. Parents: Katavon and Lux Grandiose Vite- Living quarters #162. The first set of numbers identified that she was in normal qualified good health, all body tests were to perfection, and had no chronic illnesses. The second set of numbers were all pulsing red or yellow that Luna was not breathing normally, she was showing all signs of shock, which was not normal at all, for residents of the Outpost. Not believing what the scanner was telling him, he began a physical examination on Luna, in each and every area of her body. As he begins this process, he called over his shoulder for someone to contact Luna's parents, find them and get them here... STAT!!

Doctor is confirming all data that the scanner relayed to him: Eyes, dilated; Skin, pale, clammy, warm to touch; Mouth and lips, dry; Pulse- rapid, Blood pressure- high. Scanner diagnosis was to start with Saline I.V. and cold compresses to relieve stress and cool skin and extremities.

A few moments later, both parents came running into the Medical Lounge, looking for Luna. The Doctor and Assistant stopped them and plied them both with questions. The instructor had completely forgotten about her classroom and students in concern over Luna. She started to back away and return to her class when the doctor stopped her, as she was the last adult to see Luna up and functioning normally. He called a Security Monitor Team and requested that they be sent to Luna's class to observe the other students, and his orders were to hold all students there until they could be cleared that they were not exposed to something to make them ill also, and to begin questioning each one- separately as to their day with the *sunshine*, and, or did they know what has happened to Luna.

Both parents and the instructor all reported that Luna was excited this morning, as the *Sun* was going to be in view for two hours, all noted that she had taken special care in her appearance this morning, and had chosen to wear her Ceremonial Outfit, though it was damp, frumpy and wrinkled now.

The Doctor was becoming more perplexed by the moment. Luna's parents were beyond words. What had happened to their ever creative and inventive daughter? They just looked at each other and were completely baffled by this development in Luna's appearance. Without seeming proud or boasting parents of this child, they both knew in their hearts Luna probably knew additional information and was excitedly ready to observe the *Sun*, than most anyone on the outpost. She had been reviewing and studying for weeks for this phenomenal event.

Luna started to stir on the table. First she saw Mum, then Poppi, then the Doctor, followed by the instructor and the Assistant, as her eyes came back into focus. She wanted to jump up and run, but was too weak to move, and for that matter, she wasn't quite sure where she was at. They all came rushing at her, frightening her, as she really didn't know what was happening. Last thing she remembered was screaming and pushing against the closet door.

Oh no! Not the closet. The doctor regained charge over his ward, and asked the three visitors to wait in the lounge seating area, while he spoke with Luna.

The doctor's work day had been a quiet one, as everyone that possibly could, had gone to the Botanical Wing to be a part of the wonderful celebration of genuine sunlight. So that was how the Doctor started questioning Luna. "Well young lady, what did you think of the *sunshine* today? Luna never answered questions or requests with falsehoods, as she had learned that honesty was the best answer, and usually, there were more facts behind the first truth admitted to. "Well, sir, I never saw the *sunlight*." The doctor thinking that Luna was still incoherent and confused asked her the same thing, rephrasing the question. The tears started flowing down her face, "Sir, I did not get to see the *sunshine*." This was totally inexplicable to the doctor. The doctor thought… everyone possible went to the event. Luna's parents saw her off to class this morning to go to the event. Luna's class was excused and reassembled in at the event for 2 hours. Yet she had not seen the sunshine. Sniffling at her nose, the thought of what she had been through, the tears now running down her face, and her breathing becoming quite irregular again; the doctor in a calm quiet voice asked her how did it happen she did not see the *Sunshine*?

Luna knew the answer to this question was going to cause big problems for herself as well as everyone in her class; her parents, and all of the current generations living here, her answer would call into question the Mission Statement for 621. What had happened to her was against all constructs of Outpost 621. This made her sad, and she sobbed harder.

This reaction made the doctor more puzzled. Once again he gently tried to pry the answer out of Luna. She looked straight at him with big open eyes, this time, took a big breath, and told him that she had been locked in the storage closet of her classroom by her classmates before they all left to go to the Celebration. The doctor was stunned and amazed. He got up and told Luna he would be right back to attend to her, she needed some rest; and he marched out of her cubical with a mission.

Luna lay back in the pillows and was shaking again. Not knowing if it was from cold or fear, but in her heart she knew what she said was going to have major ramifications. She rang the attendant, who came running this time to assist Luna with any need she may have. She relayed she was cold, so the attendant lovingly said she would take care of some food, drink and some warm blankets immediately.

The attendant stepped out to the lounge and saw the doctor speaking with the instructor, with the parents listening intently. She walked over as professionally and quietly as she could and asked if the mother could go be with her daughter. Wanting to comfort and support this small child, the doctor told the mother he would speak with her later, but please go be with Luna. The Attendant asked mother what was Luna's favorite beverages, and snack foods. She winked at mother and told her she would be right back with nourishment and warm blankets for her to take into her daughter, and they could be alone and let Luna recuperate. The Attendant brought back some sparkling water, manna, and crackers with 2 warm coverlets, handing them over to mother, and then disappearing down the hall.

Mother entered the room, looking intently at her daughter. She only got a few words of what the doctor was requesting from the instructor, but it wasn't good. Mum put the food on the small table beside the bed and took the covers, unfolded them and let them float softly down to cover Luna's shivering body. This was a favorite of Luna's, she told Mum on many occasions it felt like a cloud coming down to take care of her. She needed that now, her cloud and Mum. Mother had overheard the reply that Luna was locked in a closet. Oh, heavens no! Mum thought with a deep pain in her heart. She didn't say a word to Luna; she just folded her into her bosom. After a while Luna quit shaking enclosed in her mother's warm safe embrace. At that point Mum offered her some cool water, which she drank down eagerly; she didn't realize she was thirsty. Looking up at Mum, her first words were could she have some more handing her back the empty tumbler. Mum refilled it for her, then picked up a napkin, fixed her 3 crackers with manna spread on them, and handed them over to her daughter. It seemed a long while before Poppi and the doctor came to the cubicle, nevertheless, they checked on their small patient, and said they would be back later. The doctor suggested in his kind soft voice he thought it would be best if Little Miss Luna stayed the night here at the Wellness Lounge. Mum and Poppi looked at each other and then to Luna and replied with reassurance that would be fine, and they would stay all together tonight.

The doctor and Poppi then left the cubicle, now... out into the concourse, with a determined stride. Where were they going? Luna didn't know, but she was so tired right now, she just reclined back into Mum's security. She didn't want to say anything more, or to think. She just let her long eyelashes flutter down to her cheeks, and allowed her body to relax and rest.

The doctor and Luna's father headed straight to the Outpost's Leadership Commission Chambers. There was always someone on duty for monitoring or for calling in needed panel members. This was a tragedy. This was a huge setback. How were they, as the whole Outpost going to address this catastrophe? Nothing like this had ever happened on Outpost 621 before. They were into their 4th generation living here, in the honor of their credo. "Prosperity- There Was Always Enough, a Contract of Love"

The panel members had already been alerted and were starting to assemble. The smaller conference room was filling quickly. The Outpost population was descending on the Commission faster and in larger concerned numbers than the doctor and Grandiose Vite had anticipated. The residents were all coming, inhabitants from all four generations. The Primary, for this rotation of leadership immediately saw what was happening and asked the Security Monitors to direct and escort all the Commission and their descendants to the auditorium, a much larger forum to house everyone that was emerging.

The Doctor, the Primary and Grandiose Vite all just waited on the dais, not saying anything as of yet. The room swelled to capacity, with others overrunning the corridor wanting to attend this extraordinary event.

The Primary straightforwardly raised his hand to bring this assembly to order. Everyone quickly quieted and was hanging on the next words from the trio at the front of the room. The Primary asked that everyone in attendance to stay composed, and promptly deferred to the concepts or writs that the original "Commissioned" had ascribed to for this project. He asked this as a matter of Love, Higher Intention, and Complacency to which this Outpost had survived for the last 100 years. Simpler wording would have been their Utopia or Socialism ideology. All volunteers and commissioned had always thought of this Outpost with an even higher ideology. This philosophy had worked well, and been in the hearts of all, until today. All meetings of import always opened in this matter to keep the primary focus on the Outpost as the foundation and the epitome if ALL objectives and topics.

Without any forethought or organized intention, Dr. Dignita stepped forward to give a brief summary of his encounter with Luna today. He stated before today, she was a healthy child, and he could surmise she was well cared for and thrived here on the Outpost. Dr. Dignita stated she would remain in medical care overnight, possibly longer to assess the trauma she had experienced today, and her parents were with her in her recovery process. Dr. Dignita also stated that an investigation into what had happened to Luna today was going to be transferred to the correct authorities. The doctor was quiet at this point and lowered his head.

Katavon Grandiose Vite then stepped forward with tears in his eyes. His name held such importance on the Outpost, Latin in origin- Understanding the Grand Life. He had the respect of all of the Commissioned community, and he was third generation. The Outpost felt it was meeting its Mission Statements and Guidelines with such fine examples of current inhabitants as the Grandiose family.

Katavon spoke briefly as to what an extraordinary day it was and the expectations of all of the inhabitants on the Outpost, especially for his daughter Luna. He needed to go be with his daughter, and share the Love and Strength that all the citizens of the Outpost lived by. He really could not share more, as the truth of what happened to Luna was a simple statement she made, which is incomprehendable to all of us. She told the Doctor she had not seen the *Sun*. Katavon agreed, with a nod, that the Leadership Commission would be reviewing any and all information, statements, involved parties, and if necessary recorded data of the incident today. All he really understood was his daughter was almost lifeless, in the Medical Lounge this evening. He turned and stepped back into the small group standing above the assembly. He too lowered his head.

The Primary, Mr. Boreas, stepped forward again, trying to keep his voice in check and of authority, addressed the congregation. "Our ancestors came on this Mission, generations ago, and sealed a covenant for all of us to live by. We are living a Contract of Love. We Create Prosperity, and We Always Have Enough." "If there are any of you that have information as to what happened to a small child that belongs to all of us today, please relay the particulars and details to the Leadership Commission. We will stand adjourned this evening as there can be no assumptions taken. We have worked with facts and specifics on many challenges we have faced over the years. We will address this dilemma in the same manner. I am sure with all the resources we have at hand, we will be able to reconvene very soon, and use our pasts and futures to correct this impropriety. We have to remember at our cellular level, or atomic level, that this Outpost Is The 2nd Chance at Humanity. We want all to Love, Be Loved and to Thrive.

The three men retreated to a back anteroom. All three were quiet, engaged in their own thoughts. They said they necessary farewells. The Doctor and Katavon set their sights on heading straight back to the Medical Lounge, oblivious of each other, until they made the turn at the corner of the main Concourse. Neither still said a word.

The Doctor had to go find data, interviews, and witnesses to what happened to Luna. Katavon was only concerned about his daughter, Luna, right now. As they entered the Medical Lounge, the Doctor veered left to go to his office and start his own investigation. Katavon went to the cubicle where Luna and Lux were being accommodated. Lux took Katavon outside the cubicle to talk, as Luna was now sleeping lightly, but she kept waking up screaming and whimpering. Lux was worried. Mum relayed that the Attendant had brought both of them food and resting cots for the night, and was "on call" if they needed anything at all! Almost sensing Poppi was in the room; Luna woke up and cried out for him. This time, she fell into his strong arms and was held by her dad. She relaxed, and looked up at him with tired, watery eyes. "Poppi, please don't leave me." "I'm not, my little Luna."

Poppi knew his little girl was strong, inquisitive, and held a deep reliance on her parents. Luna would come through this incident with more questions and understanding of human nature and emotions. Tonight, though, Luna just needed to be surrounded with love, tender care, and support as she was just an 8-year-old little girl.

LOVE

—••●••—

Luna opened her heavy eyes sensing it was morning and time to get up. She instantly froze in her bed, where was she at? Focusing- she realized her "Moppet," her favorite stuffed toy, was there beside her, and she relaxed a bit. Then she peered off to the left side of the room and saw Poppi and Mum, each sleeping on a cot- holding hands. That helped Luna relax that much more.

She now remembered where she was and why. Her sleep was troubled all night, but Mum and Poppi was instantly at her side each time she had nightmares and started to stir to wakefulness.

Luna tried to stay still and not wake her parents, but this was too tempting to her. She figured out how to slide down to the end of the bed with Moppet in tow. She stealthfully hopped to the floor and quickly bounded the few steps to the cot and climbed over Poppi like a monkey and slid under the covers, safely and happily nestled between her parents. They woke up with her activity, but stayed still to see what she was up to. When Luna relaxed in the cozy make-shift bed, all three became less anxious, and just enjoyed this bit of intimacy and quiet together.

All three must have dozed back off to sleep, as the next thing they were aware of was the Attendant coming into the room with a pitcher of fresh sparkling water, breakfast juices, and several types of teas, nuts, mixed berries, some cheeses and toast squares. It looked tasty, and to the order of something Mum would have fixed for the family at home, Luna thought.

Well, no more sleeping now. Suddenly Luna didn't feel so well... Mum and Poppi saw the change in their little girl instantaneously. Mum, hugged Luna tighter, and suggested they go take a shower and get dressed. Luna looked down at her sleeping gown, and realized a lot must have happened; she just didn't remember right now. Mum had retrieved a fresh set of clothing for Luna and herself for today, last evening, when they knew they were going to be staying at the Medical Lounge. Mum- held Luna's hand tightly and said in a singsong manner "let's pretend we're camping, and we need a shower." With this, Luna was reluctantly led off to the shower room. Mum tried to lighten Luna's mood by suggesting they try some of the different soaps and oils available for their use. Mum found two herbal ones that suggested a calming, relaxing effect. She was glad that Luna found them appealing and agreed for them to use the ones Mum had selected.

Poppi had made hurried return to their living quarters and took a shower and put on fresh clothes himself, not wanting to leave Luna for a moment today. She appeared as if she was rebounding from her trauma, but Poppi wasn't taking any chances with his girl!

Poppi got back just as the girls were returning from the shower room. "I don't know which of you look or smells the best, so I guess I'll just have to eat you both for breakfast!"

Poppi played this game at times at home, so it was familiar, and made both Mum and Luna start giggling. Then Luna made her best imitation of Mum and replied "we're dessert, you have to eat your morning meal first!" Mum and Poppi nodded with a hopeful inward smile. Towards the end of the meal they were enjoying, Poppi swallowed hard, and softly opened the conversation he was dreading with Luna. She ran over to the bed and grabbed Moppet, squeezing it tightly. She knew she was going to be asked for information about what happened yesterday.

Mum, with tears in her eyes, had already relayed to Poppi the visual bruises that she observed on her young daughter as they were doing their morning bathing.

Poppi picked Luna up with Moppet, and sat her on his lap. He had a broken-hearted look on his face that was evident to Mum. He started with, "Luna, what happened to you yesterday is beyond the understanding of any of us on this Outpost. All of us are very saddened and upset as to what you experienced."

Luna looked up at Poppi with her big blue eyes, what was coming next?

"But do you know… what I know… about my girl? She is strong. She is truthful. She is full of love and compassion. She is a natural born problem solver! Poppi's face broadened into a big smile. "I know you, young lady, will be able to help everyone on this Outpost to process and come to a positive resolution about the sad event yesterday." Poppi had to choose his words carefully, as it was in the Commission's Edicts that certain words, actions, or activities of negativity, violence or abuse were not permitted in any form as stated in the Mission Statement that the Original Volunteers signed when they chose this commission, and it was a standing order for the generations that followed with the first voyagers.

"Luna, Mum and I will be with you the whole time today, or however long it takes, but the Outpost needs your assistance. Are you up to the task today? We can do this whenever you feel up to it, little one. And we can go as slowly as needed so you are comfortable with what you have to share with the Medical, Security and Panel Members." Poppi turned her to face him directly so she could see and know his sincerity. He gave Luna a wink and a tight hug.

Mum and Poppi had always encouraged her, told her the truth and supported her in trusting her own instincts. She had grown, so far into such a precocious young girl.

She answered Poppi "I'm ready!"

Poppi suggested that if it was in agreement with Luna, that they form a panel of all the Primary investigative staff, his reasoning being that Poppi would need to detail the significant and weighty questions she would be asked. Therefore, she would only have to answer questions once. She was also told she would also have to complete a full examination by the doctor today, to make sure she was healthy enough to go home. (But the examination was also to detail the physical harm that had been done to this child.) All the commission was at a loss on how to proceed as nothing like this had ever happened before.

Luna felt Poppi knew best on how to proceed. She grabbed Moppet and went to sit in a chair beside Mum while arrangements were being made.

Poppi went out of the cubicle and conversed with Dr. Dignita. They both nodded in agreement. Poppi set off down the concourse to find the members of the other teams that needed to be included in the interview. Two rooms would have extra audio and video to record actions, conversation, and questions asked. The examination room was the first room. The smaller room of the Commission Chamber was the other room. Everything was in place, and they wanted to keep Luna as calm as possible after ordeal yesterday.

When Poppi left, Luna hopped off the chair, grabbed her mother's hand and said she had to go home! Everyone within hearing stopped and turned around and stared at Luna, the doctor, Poppi, the Attendant, and Mum. Luna was excited and said she had to go home! Poppi walked back over to his little girl and gently asked why she needed to go home? He was afraid he had overloaded her with obligation and she wanted to retreat and hide from the situation. "Poppi," she answered, "I need my tablet. I need to review my oath before I take on such a duty for the whole Outpost." Everyone breathed a sigh of relief, and Mum knew her daughter's determination, so they set off for home to retrieve the tablet.

Rounding the corner to the wing their living quarters was on, Luna and Mum noticed piles of flowers, cards, toys and baskets of treats at their door, all addressed to Luna. Mum was one more time moved to tears; the Outpost residents really were worried about her little girl. Luna was surprised at all the gifts at their doorstep. This was to be a quick trip home, so Mum said they must move all the items into the salon, for now, and get the tablet and return, as it was going to be a very busy day.

Luna retrieved her tablet, but unhurriedly started examining the items that were left for her, and her family. Luna and Mum loved flowers, and many small tokens and varieties were offered, baskets of food treats for the whole family, small stuffed toys creating a whole new menagerie for Luna, and cards wishing her to be well, safe and she was loved. There were fancy engraved cards ranging down to ones, hand drawn with pictures and words from young children in pencil and crayons. Finally, everything was moved out of the hallway, and they could return to the Medical Wellness Lounge. Luna knew she had to do her best now.

When they got back, Dr. Dignita greeted them as they walked into the Lounge. He asked how Luna was feeling today, and was she ready to start with her exam and interviews. She smiled politely, and asked could she have a few minutes to review some information that was on her tablet. Once again the doctor was baffled by this child, but readily agreed to her wishes. She was all important today.

The Attendant asked Luna and her Mum if they wanted some refreshments as Luna crossed the room and climbed into an overstuffed chair that seemed to swallow her up. She had Moppet under one arm and her tablet in the other hand and she addressed her objective with her keen determination. The Attendant came back and put some fruits, tea, manna and crackers on the small table between the two lounge guests. Luna was lost in her tablet, looking in the correct directories for the information she wanted. She found them. The all-important notes on the Outposts edicts':

The Outpost's Honor Contract. "Prosperity- There Was Always Enough, a Contract of Love"

The discipline of the Outpost was always held to one's own self- correcting, and for there to be the highest good in learning, creativity, love, and intention. Create, support, and motivate all others to their highest good and creativity. Never impede or challenge new ideas. Never do intentional harm to a fellow human or resources that are necessary for survival. The Outpost intermingled their lifestyles, governing, and living situation into a utopian, socialistic, native/ aboriginal and communal blended style. It had worked well for generations.

Luna had learned all this structure from reviewing the data at the historical retrieval archives. She believed this. She lived it with her parent's guidance, and she could assist with the Committees today. She was ready. She picked up some fruit and nibbled at the little bites; she then ate 2 crackers with manna, and had some sparkling water. For some reason she was famished. Dr. Dignita walked over and asked if she would like to get started. He was being extremely nice to her. Handing her tablet to Mum, she agreed, and asked what they were going to do first. Doctor looking over to Mum suggested that they do the examination so he could compile his data for the meeting later on today. He also smiled down to Luna and said let's get her released from the Medical Lounge. He asked Mum and Luna to go with the Attendant, back to a cubicle so she could change into a gown and they start the examination, then afterward, he would ask her some questions if necessary. Luna took Mum's hand, and had Moppet in her other hand, holding each tightly. All three were starting the next part of this continuing adventure.

Luna, Moppet, and Mum came out of the dressing area, and this morning Luna was strong enough to be able to climb up on the exam table by herself. She sat there on the table waiting while Doctor and Mum talked for a few minutes. Then both came over and with relaxed smiles said "Let's get started."

Dr. Dinigla asked Luna to lie back on the table, Mum assisted by adjusting the gown for Luna to be comfortable, still holding her hand tightly. The doctor picked up the scanner and pressed buttons to retest her body vitals from yesterday. When this was done, doctor nodded to Mum and she adjusted the gown again to remove wrinkles and just lovingly touch Luna in assurance as the doctor reset the scanner program buttons to record pictures he wanted of skin abrasions and scratches he wanted documented from the incident. Mum was watching, and Luna's curiosity was piqued the whole time, so she was busy looking back and forth between the doctor and Mum. She had never had an exam like this, and she really wasn't at ease, but Mum and Moppet were there, and she knew Poppi would be back soon. All the testing and information was gathered with swift fluid movements. Luna heard a click each time the scanner changed position. Suddenly Luna looked to Mum, in fear. This wasn't like being in the closet yesterday, but this unknown information the medical team and Council wanted was beginning to frighten her.

They were near completion in gathering all the medical information needed, and the Doctor pressed the button one more time to press "send" to finalize and process the information, and Luna came up off the table and almost leaped into Poppi's arms, who had come in during the exam and was standing beside Mum. Poppi started stroking Luna's head and hair as well as holding her close, calming the anxiety and fear he never usually saw in his daughter.

The Doctor commented he had all the information he needed. He glanced at Luna then at Mum and Poppi. What further trauma had he just further inflicted on this small child? They were nodding again…. The doctor excused himself and Poppi carried Luna with Moppet to the lounge and Mum was right beside them. They sat there quietly for a good while, just waiting for Luna to express her inquisitive self, which was her normal reaction to life around her. The family unit did not get this chance this morning. After a period of time, Dr. Dinigla came to them with three questions. "Miss Luna, how are you feeling today?" She made herself smaller and cuddled even closer to Poppi. Her reply was straight forward, but in a small voice, the reply was she felt much better than yesterday. The doctor nodded, smiled and replied that was important, and healthy. With the doctor's second question, he reached for Luna's small arm, and gently raised it to where it was visible to Luna, her parents, and to him. Luna allowed the doctor to hold her arm since he actually had her arm resting over his open hand, there was no restraint. "Are you having any pain anywhere from these marks?" Luna looked down at her arms and legs- that were visible to her and she replied she was sore, attempting to give a positive response to the doctor's inquiry. "It's not that bad." Her breathing and body, much more relaxed now, since she was out of the exam room.

The doctor glanced at Luna's mother and father first, then asked, "Are we ready to go down to the LCC and chat with the panel?"

"Are Mum and Poppi going to be with me?" she asked with big, intense eyes taking in both her parents, since Luna had no idea of what was happening. This hasn't been too hard so far, Luna thought, but she looked up to both her parents for reassurance before she replied "OK." "Well, I'm glad Luna. Why don't you go with your Mum and get dressed and we all will go down to the Commission offices and continue with our evaluation." While listening to Luna's reply, and noting her parents' protection of their daughter; the doctor pushed a sequence of buttons on the scanner to process, evaluate, and forward today's information to the Panel's Computer network.

After changing back into her day clothes, Luna took back her tablet from Mum, walked rather tensely back to the lounge where Poppi and Moppet were waiting with the Doctor, and said "Let's go!" Poppi leaned down and quietly asked Luna for her to hear only.... "Are you sure you want to do this today?" Luna smiled broadly up at Poppi and said "We can do anything together!" She hoped her smile and words could fool Poppi this one time. She didn't feel brave or safe at all, but she knew her parents would protect her. She could feel their love.

Poppi picked up Luna, plopping her on his hip, as she held her tablet and Moppet in her little hands, wrapped around Poppi's neck, with Mum on one side, and the Doctor on the other they headed out of the Medical Lounge, and started down the corridor to the Leadership Commission Chambers.

It was decided last night, by the Council, when the assembly broke up as to how they were going to evaluate Luna today, with the least amount of added intrusion to Luna today. The Dr. Dinigla and Poppi made suggestions, and there was other input from Council members.

Everything on the Outpost had to be monitored constantly for the health, stability and welfare of the residents, so there already was Visual, Auditory, and if necessary other data available to be reviewed regarding the "incident," by the council, doctor, and Luna's parents. The objective that the council members wanted to address today was the demeanor of this child. How was she recovering and her response to what had happened to her yesterday?

Upon entering the inter Chamber room of the Council Hall, a medium size table was set up with chairs all around it. The furniture in the room seemed very big to Luna, as small children were not traditionally allowed into this all-important room of decisions and resolutions. Four men and two ladies were already setting at the table, leaving open four chairs, one for each of the honored guests that just came in. The Doctor went to the open chair on the far left, Poppi stopped beside of him at the next chair. He allowed Luna to slide down his body, allowing her to land on her feet beside the next open chair. Mum took the last chair. The Primary asked that they all take a seat, looking directly at Luna and smiling. Once again, Luna had to climb up into the large overstuffed chair and then scoot herself to the front edge of chair, so she could see everyone, and be close to the table. She laid her tablet on the table and allowed Moppet to sit in her lap while they were in this meeting. Everyone was comfortably seated, and a hostess brought herb teas with crackers and manna for snacks while they were in session. Luna didn't know what to expect. She sure wasn't hungry, but she leaned over to Mum and asked if she could have some sparking water to sip on. Mum relayed the request, and the water appeared before Luna in the blink of an eye.

The Primary, introduced himself, and the other distinguished people that were on this committee for Luna's understanding, and then he proposed how they would like this meeting progress, with Luna's approval.

Once again everyone seemed so nice to her, she was beginning to relax and really listen to what he was suggesting.

Luna readily agreed to the plan they wanted to discuss and how she could be of assistance, and so the questions began. They asked her all sorts of questions about yesterday morning. Why did she want to see the "Sunshine?" Who was in the classroom with her? Did she notice anything different yesterday? Was she supposed to meet her parents at the Biological Wing for the viewing of the Sunshine? Did she know who grabbed her and locked her in the closet? Did she know how many of the other classmates were involved in locking her in the closet? Did she know how she got out of the closet?

All of these questions were coming from various members at the table, and Luna answered as clearly and unemotionally as possible. They went on to the second part of the questions of her recovery and treatment in the Medical Lounge, again she answered as best she could, but she was beginning to feel small and overwhelmed again. Poppi reached over and took both Moppet and her hand and put them in his large secure hand to help her finish. The third set of questions were a lot harder for her, the council wanted her input on how she felt the Outpost should handle the discipline or correction of the offenders to her life. She sat for a few moments thinking, and then picked up her tablet, and went through the directories to exactly what she wanted. She replied "Honorable Council, please let us stay within the directives of our Outpost's Mission. There is Enough Love for All. Let us use this and move forward. If there needs to be an explanation, let it be oriented in a positive learning platform. We do NOT want to move into FEAR or negativity. All of us must learn from our mistakes."

It seemed like the questions were going on forever to Luna, but with that last answer, the Primary made a comment, he was truly sorry for what happened to her yesterday, and this sentiment was repeated by each and every person at the table to Luna. Luna was moved to tears. She looked up at

Mum; and Mum asked were they finished with this query; she could tell her daughter was exhausted.

The Primary replied yes, and looked around the table to verify that he was not overlooking any information they still may need to ask about. With that acknowledgement, Poppi, picked up Luna, Moppet, and Luna grabbed her tablet and they set off out the double doors to the larger assembly room, then into the corridor, and heading home, finally.

In the walk back to their quarters, Poppi allowed Luna to slide down his body again, and she landed with both feet hitting floor. He stopped her, and looked into her big clear blue eyes. She knew this was serious. "What Poppi?" He broke out in a bid smile, and said "Little one, I have a surprise for you, just for you!" "Poppi, I don't need anything. I am happy. I have you and Mum!" "Luna, I have arranged for you to see the SUNSHINE tomorrow! The Sun will come out for you, Mum and me, exclusively!" Luna didn't know what to say, or think. But Poppi can do anything!

So, they went home to have some leisure time and quiet for the rest of the day.

THE QUERY

Katavon (Poppi) had asked his associates if they could cover for him for the next few days at work. His fellow colleagues all readily agreed to cover his normal duties as he was needed in double capacity right now. His daughter needed support to process the trauma she had sustained a few days ago and Grande Vite was needed in his obligations to his post at the Commission.

Having the support of his division, Katavon went back to his quarters to gather his family and take Luna on her promised "Sunshine" day trip. Lux (Mum) and he had talked last night about asking if they wanted to include a few of Luna's friends for this excursion. The answer was 'yes!' Mum sent messages to the Instructor that Luna was still recuperating from 'the incident.' The reply came back to just let her know when Luna felt well enough to return to classes. Mum then asked a special request if Sonnet, Kai, and Oliver could join them at the Activity Holographic Pods in an hour. Again, the Instructor's immediate response was yes. Mum sent a group message to the parents of Luna's friends asking permission for them to join Luna in an important healing adventure for a few hours, as long as it was acceptable. They were to meet Luna at the Activity Holographic pods in an hour, and the children were being supervised by both of Luna's parents. If this was agreeable, please relay the request to their own children.

When Katavon got back to their quarters, Mum and Luna were in the salon going through all the gifts that had been left at their door. Luna never realized that so many people cared about her. The cards that the old and young scribes wrote to her were special. She wanted to decorate the whole salon with the artwork and words. Moppet was supervisor of all the new playthings that had arrived. Moppet was center stage, watching her new charges. Mum took the flowers and food stuffs to the food preparation area to be stored accurately so they would not spoil or lose their longevity.

When Poppi came in, Luna asked Mum if Poppi could have a few of the special eatables that were left for the family's enjoyment. Poppi grabbed a handful of nuts and refilled his water container he had attached to his belt. He looked up and smiled asking 'girls are we ready to go see the Sun today?' Luna squealed with delight because today Mum and Poppi were going with her. The other day both of them were in charge of their stations monitoring the changes that actual Sunlight would have on their precious vegetation for Mum; and Poppi had to monitor the inside and outside temperatures on how the radiant heat would impact the Outpost shell and environment.

Luna was so excited to go she was standing at the door with her little fingers ready to trigger the 'open' latch when her parents finally caught up with her. The three exited their quarters with Luna in the middle, twitching in delight. They headed towards the Activity Holographic Pods all holding hands. Mum was the first to see Luna's friends up at the AHP portal entrance. The buddies had seen all three of the Grandiose Vite family approaching. Mum quickly put an index finger to lips to signal to them that they were the added surprise, and to stay silent until Luna noticed them. Luna was chattering happily with her parents when she noticed her friends at the portal door awaiting their arrival. Luna again squealed with delight that her friends had come to join her. This was so special!

Katavon was so happy that the immersion of the Sun was captured by three different monitors for the Outpost archives and for study of this phenomenon at their actual living station. In his position and with the permission of the Commission he was allowed to expedite the processing of the "Sunlight" processional across the Botanical Wing for his daughter's enjoyment. Poppi went first and all the children followed close behind to see how the Activity Holographic Archive would be programmed this time.

Luna noted that this was the same 5 Panels that they used for their adventures. But this was different as they were retrieving an actual event for review .....and it only happened two days ago!

Panel #1 Planet Gliese 581d

Panel #2 Poppi entered the necessary date and time of Sunlight on Outpost 621, where the Sun was going to be appropriately visible and the 'replay' would engage

Panel #3 Retrieve monitoring tapes of Sunlight as seen from Botanical Wing. Two-hour window- Start to finish. This was a new type of entry for Katavon to put in the actual Outpost location in such proximity in the time continuum of only a matter of hours before.

Panel #4 Location- Outpost 621- Botanical Wing with full 5-D holographic projection capacity

Panel #5- Normal, current attire, and sandals appropriate for the celebration activities. The only change was Poppi modified Luna's apparel to be "her Ceremonial Outfit" that she was wearing originally for the Sun Celebration. The rest was easy as all were staying inside the Botanical Wing thus weather and exploits were not of concern.

Poppi pushed buttons to activate program.

All of them stepped into the first chamber. The door silently slid closed behind them and securely clicked shut. The next set of portal doors seemed to come alive once again to Luna. The entry beaconed them all. Kai, Sonnet and Oliver had gotten to see the actual Sun and participate in the festivities two days ago, but were now in trepidation, almost regretting this escapade. What would the adults think? What would the adults relay to their parents?

A strange glowing light was immerging, so this thinking was soon overcome by wonder in the first few steps they took into the Botanical Wing. This was very different than the usual illumination.

Luna's anticipation was almost more than her small body could contain. She looked at Mum, then at Poppi pleading with her eyes, could she go play? Explore? Did she have to stay in their company? Both her parents laughed.

Mum gave a broad sweep of her arm as to call all the children to her. They all responded to her motion. All four of them quickly huddled to her to hear her instructions. They were ready to experience the Sun! Mum said in her soft, gentle voice 'you are free to play, explore, observe and enjoy the sunlight. Please heed and pay attention to your viewing- look at the horizons, landscapes, or shadows around the Sun. I am reminding you not to look directly at the Sun itself, as it could hurt your vision. Also remember this is your everyday Botanical gardens, we are only visitors, and we must leave the trees and shrubs as we found them today. We do no harm.' Ooohh. That sentence hit Luna like a rock. She stood up, took a step back and looked at Mum and Poppi. They did all of this for her, and to show her they loved and supported her. She did not have to carry fear from the two days ago, or from the comment Mum made to the group; as this was created especially for her. And she was sure it was a 'mother' thing as she was chaperoning her friends as well as herself. 'Go, play, enjoy!' Mum said. Then Poppi tilted his head in amusement adding 'learn, experience, and remember!' With those closing comments all four of them were off running together at first, and then they quickly separated in different directions. Mum and Poppi were happy that they could provide this unique experience for their daughter to hopefully override the tragedy of two days ago. They started their own 'Sunlight' stroll through the trees and shrubs, arms entwined, each quietly reflecting.

Luna and the others went running between the trees, they would stop and stare out of the sky windows at the brilliance of the Sunlight, in contrast to the perpetual dusk-like illumination that they lived with every day. Luna knew this would be fantastic; yet it was more than she expected. Oh, how her heart loved this radiance over everything. She ran up to Mum and Poppi and exclaimed that she had not brought her tablet with her to take notes about the Sun. She was very exasperated with herself at this point at not being able to record this magnificent event. She knew it would be with her forever, but she needed to document her emotions that were engaged with the Sun in her presence. Poppi smiled at Luna, she was in her element, her best, wanting to know... and record... and keep everything. She didn't want to forget any of this wonderful day. Poppi reminded her that she was in the hologram of the actual even that happened two days ago, so she would always be able to go to the Data Archives Center and pull up any part of this day, and she could make notes or refresh any part of the sunlight she wanted to from now on. She really has experienced the Sunshine. It was hers now. The two hours was almost up and both Poppi and Mum wanted them to leave before the Hologram closed down. They wanted the experience to be total brightness for the children to remember. Poppi gave a whistle that got all four young ones attention, and they came running to him. 'I think we better go now', he said.

They all headed towards the portal doors, exited, happy, tired, and feeling oh so special that they witnessed the Sunshine. Sonnet, Kai and Oliver said they had to return to classes, yet they stopped and thanked Luna and her parents for asking that they accompany her on her visit with the Sunshine. Luna told them that she was glad she could share the experience with them, and in a sing-song way said 'wasn't it wonderful?' they agreed, and headed back towards classes. Luna looked up at Mum and Poppi inquiring as to what is next for today? Poppi immediately said he needed to return to work, and Mum said that she was taking Miss Luna home and giving her some luncheon and if she wanted to make notes on her tablet about the Sunshine, that would be a good afternoon task. Again, the group split- Luna and Mum heading back to their quarters and Poppi off in another direction.

Only Poppi wasn't going to work at all. He had to go to the Commission Chambers joining the rest of the committee about the 'terrible incident' that had happened on the Outpost. 'They must come to a positive healing resolution' was the only thought that kept repeating itself in his head as he walked towards the Leadership Chambers. When he reached the room, there were the normal eight attending panel members already there. He took a seat. The Primary, Mr. Boreas said they were just getting started. He told the group that there was video and audio that he felt they should all examine together. He pulled out an old book that he had retrieved from the Data Storage and Archival Studies Center. 'This is my personal opinion, but I believe we should read the whole Mission Statement for 621', touching the book with reverence and love; 'since we have never had such an incident in our existence here in the last 100 years. May this give clarity, help remind us of our responsibilities, and highlight our commitment to this Outpost- that our ancestors recognized was the 2nd Chance at Humanity' 'Our Credo: Prosperity- there is always enough, a Contract of Love.' Everyone agreed at once this was a good suggestion. 'While reviewing the data that we have, please bear in mind that there are three concerns we need to address: The 7 children involved, Luna, and the Instructor.

The Primary opened the book and started reading the Mission Contract. After reading a few paragraphs, the book was passed to the person to his right. Words flew off the page being read: Love, Higher Intention, Creativity, and Prosperity. They echoed in the room. The book was passed to the next person, more of the same ideology: Motivate, Support, Highest Good in Learning. Each person in the group kept reading: Watch over, Protect, and Shelter. "The Contract words" were reverberating, seemingly louder. Touching their hearts and the readers' voices' seemed to be dropping and becoming more gentle, loving, and quiet. Each person read their few lines of the Mission's Commitment, and the book's conclusion was with Katavon. His lines were:

Never impede or challenge new ideas. Never do intentional harm to fellow humans or resources that are necessary for survival. We do **not** want to move into FEAR or negativity. We are Prosperity- There is Always Enough, a Contract of Love.' The committee was so emotional with their pledge voiced in unison out loud, they could hardly move.

Mr. Boreas thanked everyone, and said after they all reviewed the audio and video tapes of the day of Sunshine; they would break for the afternoon. In the morning, we will then start with the personal interviews of each of the eight persons involved. The larger committee room will be set up so each of us can interview one person each. The questions will all be the same, and we will take their responses and evaluate them, for us to consider our next step. Luna is not to be present for this council deliberation. Then there will be the Outpost's Leadership Commission's conclusion and unanimous decision must be made for the resolution to this issue for all persons involved and for the whole population of 621.

Poppi sat in the anteroom with the other members of the board, and heard and saw what happened to his little girl. Once gain he had tears streaming down his cheeks, he could not help it. He briefly refocused and peered around at the other members. They were all weeping also. They all saw how Luna was captured and held against her will. She struggled for freedom, but that was not possible with 6 classmates holding on to her tightly. There was a look-out, one student was watching out into the hall to make sure they were not caught. This was planned, pre-meditated. They pushed her in the closet, scratching and screaming. They deliberately closed and latched the door. Why hadn't anyone heard her?

The monitors definitely picked up her voice and cries for help. The deviants dashed for their seats when it was signaled that Instructor was coming back with the rest of the class. For some reason, at this point Luna was silent. Why? The Instructor walked into the room, she dismissed everyone to go to the Botanical Wing for the 'Sunshine.' All the children made a dash for the door and to the celebration. No one looked back or checked on Luna. Then there was over an hour of her screaming, whaling to be released, in panic, in the dark. It could be heard that she was pushing, pulling, scratching at anything and everything to get out of the closet. Then the sounds from her became soft whimpers. Sometime later the class returned and Luna started screaming again. The students looked puzzled? They looked at each other with the thought processing that could be read on their faces- whom can I blame? The Instructor came into the room, from a very pleasurable activity, happy and relaxed. Suddenly she realized something was very wrong by the looks on the students' faces. Then she heard the screaming coming from the closet. Who was in there, she thought? What was going on? She ran over to open the door and release the shrieking, weak child. It was Luna. She was soaked. She was hardly breathing. She was non-responsive. All the students stood in the room as if stone, not moving or assisting in any way. The Instructor gathered up little Luna in her arms and rushed as quickly as she could to the Medical Repository, Health and Wellness Lounge. There was more following the actual episode with Luna, concerning the students' behavior and conduct after she left the room with Luna for medical care. But for right now, this was all that Poppi could take in and process, his little girl. Why? Katavon asked himself. He knew they were almost at the close of this intense session, so he excused himself from the meeting, and left the room.

Poppi knew he had to step into his dual roles at the Outpost, nevertheless, his heart and soul was really hurting right now. So, he set out walking. He had no direction, nor did he recognize or speak to any of his fellow residents. He was lost in thought, his daughter and the Mission Statement. Where had they all gone wrong? How could Love fix this? He walked and thought. He thought and walked for hours, it seemed. Then he went to visit with Dr. Dignita.

Upon entering the Medical, Health and Wellness lounge, so late in the day; both the assistant and Dr. Dignita both came from their cubicles deeper in the facility. Dr. Dignita saw the distress and disappointment on Katavon's face. He instinctively knew what was troubling him so deeply. Dr. Dignita asked his friend 'What can I do for you today?' He put his arm around his slumped shoulders and led him back to his private office, where he directed him towards a couch where they both sat down. The assistant knew comforts and nourishment were needed when most of their patients came here, so she appeared at the doctor's door with a tray of some fruits, cheese, and sparkling water. Since Mr. Grandiose Vite was such a highly regarded resident of the Outpost, she brought the best tea set the office could supply for them, and their private discussion.

Katavon opened the conversation stating a while ago, in the Leadership Chambers he reviewed the incident from two days ago, the both audio and video of that day. He turned and looked straight at the doctor. 'I watched and heard most of it, but I had to leave as my heart was so dismayed. I have been walking and thinking for hours. I haven't had a concrete positive resolution that I can offer the Committee tomorrow when we reconvene. I don't know what to do next.'

Dr. Dignita got up want walked to a cabinet and removed a small object, and brought it back to the couch returning to his seat. 'Katavon, you are a great leader! This was evident years ago. You were so named for this Outpost because you are the example that all of us want to exemplify.' 'Think of it: Katavon Grandiose Vite, 'Understanding the Grand Life' in daily English translation. Your family epitomizes what this Mission is all about. All of you go about life on this planet with grace, beauty, creativity, and Love.' 'My dear friend, do not become lost in this moment. A new colony is bound to make mistakes and forget themselves at times. This event involved 7 children, still growing and learning. It happened on an extraordinary day, where the focus was outside of our everyday reasoning. Most of us were thinking on "the outside" of our meager station.'

'But this happened to my daughter, and I am on the Leadership Committee in making decisions for the betterment of our colony. I feel I should excuse myself from this obligation. I am so emotional!' Katavon quickly responded, even though the words the doctor spoke told the collective truth about his family and was representative of the totality of the Outpost residents. Dr. Dignita took Katavon's hand and placed in it the small crystal he had gotten out of the cabinet. He said, 'This is a precious gift that came from earth and has many lessons in it. I am going to loan it to you in this time of discerning love and the need to correct errors.' Katavon looked down at the crystal in his hand. The doctor went on with the story, 'this came with my ancestors on this voyage. It is so simple, but so complex. If you look at it from one direction, light will pass through in only that one direction. If you chose, you can turn it over and a totally different light will shine through. This stone has many sides, so it will give you many options.'

'You are a born creator and leader. Observing this total incident, I already want to praise you on one issue, giving your daughter care, love and inspiration.'

'Luna.' Katavon said quietly.

'I am sure that in the future, that she is going to remember with a tender place in her heart, the support of her parents, the love, and Sunshine. She will heal quickly. You gave her the Sun today. That was much more powerful than the poor actions of those that held her captive.

'I know you have more information you need to review and process before Leadership makes its final decisions. But my dear friend, be strong, be who we know you are. Do not let our colony down. Show us all how this one small incident affects all the residents, and how we will use the Mission Statement to address and self-correct errors, now and going forward.'

Katavon and the doctor stood together, and the doctor put out his hand and Katavon responded in like. The doctor squeezed his hand with intention and a shared strength. He quietly blessed them with his usual, 'Namaste,' letting go of his hand then.

Katavon Grandiose Vite walked to his quarters to be with his family feeling much better. He knew the evening meal would be ready, and he had not intended to be late, yet he knew Lux would understand what was transpiring and would be patiently awaiting his homecoming. When he opened the door to their home, Lux met him at the door today, not Luna. She took him by the hand and headed to their private rooms.

Lux (meaning Light) didn't have to inquire about the day. She knew it was beyond their normal challenges and setbacks. As Lux studied her life mate, she saw that he still was working on his own personal opinion about the dilemma. At this point Lux took both his hands and wrapped them around her waist and she wrapped her arms around his neck tightly in a big hug of support. They were together, and she trusted him. Lux started to then share a truism, 'If a pebble is thrown in a pond- it makes ripples that spread and creates more movement. The ripples do not necessarily mean there is trouble or disaster, just that there is change.' Katavon looked up, paying more attention to what Lux was relaying to him. She continued with her second adage, 'If a stone is thrown and shatters a sheet of glass into a million pieces, is it still not the sheet of glass, only the stone has changed its appearance. He knew once again what she was inferring. She smiled sweetly, embracing the man she loved so much. 'We all need to remember the three constants in Life: Change, Choice, and Principles. This is an exercise that tests us in all three areas.' The "light" itself seemed to emanate from Lux as she finished her commentary. He gave her a kiss and then asked where Luna was. She told him she was doing her 'Sun' project in her room, and was waiting for the evening meal. With that Lux went off in the direction of the food preparation area to put out their evening food. Everything had been made ready for Poppi, when he arrived.

Poppi went down the hall to Luna's room. She was sitting on her bed with Moppet and her cozy blanket around her. The Sky window was open, so she could view the stars, and she had made room for all her new playthings on a shelf. They were lined up according to size and color. Poppi was amazed, once again. Luna looked up intently from her tablet when Poppi walked in. She bounded off the bed into his arms, with zest. 'Poppi, I saw and played in the Sunlight today! I have been making note of the different observations I took in with the actual sunlight. I know I have more I want to write about, but I'm hungry. Aren't you?' 'Oh, Poppi! Today was so wonderful. Thank you so much.'

They sat down to their meal, and today Mum said a prayer of thanks for all the blessings they had. At its close, they all ate with relish, and neither Mum or Poppi could get a word in edgewise as Luna was talking so fast, skipping from one subject to another. Poppi was lighthearted for the first time today. Luna was giving him a distraction, and he had the love and support of Lux. He felt much more optimistic that everything was really going to work out now. The Mission Statement will be upheld, and they all would grow from this slip from their true commitment.

The next morning Poppi ate some fruit, nuts, and tea before his girls woke up. He wanted to be at the Commission Chambers early to see what the intended plan was for the day. He was correct in coming early, as the rest of the members and the Primary came in shortly after his arrival. The Primary wanted 16 chairs to be placed in two's, at 8 different places in the main chamber and the anti-room, as distant from each of the other sets as possible. The committee did not want any of the other persons to overhear an answer, and attempt to duplicate it to placate the committee. The Primary wanted to be fair and just, so after the review of the tapes yesterday, he and the committee had created a list of questions that they would have each of the students and the Instructor to answer for them, where the tapes did not reveal answers that were necessary. All involved were asked to be at the Leadership Chambers at 09:00. It was easy to send for each of them, as they all were visible on the monitoring tapes. They were to be asked the same questions. The Primary asked Katavon to step out into the hall as he had a few requests of him. First, would he please send a message home to make sure Luna did not come to the Chambers and have to relive this episode again. Also, Mr. Boreas saw how upsetting this whole skirmish was for Katavon regarding his daughter, and asked if he wanted to be relieved of the questioning.

But Mr. Boreas did want him present when they were compiling the answers they received. He also wanted Grandiose Vite present for the decision on how to handle this as a learning experience for the whole Outpost, with love and care. Katavon was much more grounded and sanguine today. He asked if he could be excused from the interrogations, as his daughter was involved. He could wait for a Security monitor to retrieve him from the Concourse salon when they were ready to discuss the information they received from the interrogates.

09:00 came and the Instructor and the seven students all made their appearance at the Chamber doors. Katavon slipped out the back door of the anti-chamber, messaging Mum to keep Luna at home this morning as he walked to the Concourse salon. He found a seat, and tried to stay as calm as possible, chatting with residents he knew passing by. The wait seemed like forever, but he knew it wasn't really that long. The Security monitor finally came up the hall and asked that Grandiose Vite please return to the Leadership chambers.

The monitor escorted him into the anti-room, where he had exited about an hour before.

All of the members were sitting at the table with tablets in front of them, and a large work board turned on for the group to post their findings. The committee worked quickly and efficiently noting commonalities and the exception. One of the committee members had interviewed the Instructor. All of her answers were true. The committee was in agreement on that. But did she follow the Credo of keeping her charges safe? Was she aware and being watchful of her charges, especially on this very active and unusual day? Was she creating support and motivation for her class as a whole? The members agreed that all of these requirements of the Instructor resident, in particular were not met. The committee brought the Instructor into the anti-room and asked her to be seated. The members started by asking if she had reviewed the Mission Statement in the last few days, since this incident. They then asked her questions that were inquiring about her duties as an Instructor, and how she felt about her charges she was educating for the upcoming generation. The members realized that she had fallen into a complacency. She knew she had very intelligent students, but overlooked a reality, they were 8-year-old children. She knew that the Leadership Committee could transfer her anywhere, and relieve her of her teaching students all together.

Grandiose Vite spoke. 'Our Instructors are very special and we hold them in highest regard with honor and trust to educate our youth; taking on the responsibility of this growing and flourishing colony to its next level. That said, we live here by a commitment and a Mission Statement that allows for freedoms and creativity. We always must have a

44

discipline and self-monitoring that is acceptable for the Mission of Outpost 621 to survive.'

The Primary spoke next. 'We are sorry that the Committee as a whole feel that there is a current deficiency in your classroom of the Mission Concepts and Statement.' 'We have an idea to suggest to you, but first would like to hear your response to our conclusion.'

Instructor had been in anxious, depressed and in shock since this had happened. She answered as such. She shared with the members that she even went as far as to speak with Dr. Dignita about her situation in the last few days. Before the Sunshine, she felt she was allowing the students to be creative, but she realized she had been negligent the instant she walked back to her class with Luna locked in the closet. She had been reviewing her attitude, activities, and class structure, and she was not upholding her duties to the Mission and her students. The Primary asked did she want to continue as an Instructor. She was shocked and amazed at his question. Her response was 'yes' she did. No further comment was made because there was nothing she could say justify her neglect in her position as an educator.

The Primary looked around the room, and they had already made their decision. 'You will have two weeks off duties as an Instructor, this is to verify within yourself that teaching is what you want to continue with, then you will be reassigned to a new class as a co-Instructor, until the Commission feels you are ready to conduct a class un-supervised again. We do expect you to take the two weeks and spend time in the Data Archives Center and review and examine your teaching skills. This will also include special consideration of traits and skill sets of students you will be working with in the future.' Instructor was so relieved her shoulders finally relaxed. She said 'thank you, and she would become an exemplary teacher for the Outpost.' Grandiose Vite spoke a few words as she was excused from the meeting. 'Luna, the day this happened, relayed before the whole Commission, 'This Outpost is the 2nd Chance at Humanity. We all want to Love, Be Loved, and to Thrive.' The Instructor, humbled, bowed and left the room. She was smiling, thinking 'This will never happen again!'

The chairs were rearranged for the seven students to come into the anti-chamber to speak with the Members. They already had their answers of what happened. They had already made a decision to allow for self- correction. No one had noticed that the back door of the anti-chamber had opened and Luna had slipped into the room. She wedged herself into the corner, in a shadow where she hoped she would remain undetected. She wanted to know what had happened and why she was put in the closet. She deserved the same answers that the Council was seeking on her behalf. She was not attempting to draw special attention to herself, or expect any considerations.

The Security Monitor brought each of the 7 children into the anti-room and asked them to have a seat. They were astonished at this room as Luna was a few days ago. Children were not allowed in here. Mr. Boreas spoke first, greeting them, and thanking them for their corporation in this matter. We, he nodded at each of the members, have reviewed the class monitoring from the day of Sunshine, and we have read and discussed the answers you gave this morning before this current interview.

The students were squirming in their seats. All of them dreading what was going to happen to them. A few were very familiar with the Mission Statement, as it was practiced by all on the Outpost, others of the group, not as familiar, but followed the 'rules,' and had not given the Mission Statement much serious thought. Grandiose Vite spoke next. 'We as members of the Leadership Commission would like to engage all of you in an exercise of what the true story is behind Luna being locked in the closet on the day of Sunlight.' Now all of them were really worried as what was going to happen. Grandiose Vite continued, 'The truth is the truth, so we would like each of you to tell us this event from beginning to end. 'We are going to play this story out, like a game of Roundabout. You were all there, you all know what happened. All of you will relay one or two sentences of the episode.' Luna could hardly stay quiet or believe her ears, they wanted each of them to admit to their participation of her closet lock-up. She leaned out of her corner a bit to see who was going to speak first.

Mr. Boreas looked directly at the boy with red hair, and pointed at him to start. He blurted out.... 'It was to be a joke, or a game! We had got together the day before and all of us had planned that whoever came into the room first, was going to be nabbed and held captive. But released before the Sun Celebration.' The next member pointed to another boy sitting in the group. 'Luna happened to be the first person in the room that morning. We had to wait outside the room until all seven of us was at the classroom.' The next member pointed to a little girl that had tears in her eyes already, she readied herself speaking softly. 'It was to be a game, like hide and go seek. But we needed a look-out, and Logan was elected.

He just had to tell us when any other class members or the Instructor was coming. We all closed in on Luna. We were actually sneaking up on her, unnoticed.' The next member pointed to the boy at the end of the row. He tried to clear his throat and started, 'the six of us took our positions around the room. Luna wasn't paying attention to any of us.' The next committee member pointed to the girl at the far end of the row. She swallowed hard and added to the story, 'We reached out and grabbed at anyplace we could get hold on to her. We didn't know how heavy she was, and she didn't know we were playing a game.' The next member pointed to one of the boys that had not responded yet. He too had tears rolling down his cheeks nevertheless, he spoke up with all the volume he could muster, 'Suddenly it was clear that she was scared and fighting us like a wildcat! We had hold of her, and what do we do now? Harrison said let's put her in the closet. So, we did.' Logan, now spoke, 'In a panicked voice, I said they were coming to class. I ran across the room in time to get to my seat. I saw Harrison latch the door, and everyone else was quickly running to their seats. Instructor did not notice our frenzy.'

The red-haired boy then commented that the Instructor dismissed class to go to the Botanical Wing. We all were so excited to see the Sun. It was to be a day of fun and games. 'All of us escaped. I don't think any of us thought of Luna again until the closet door was opened hours later. And then we were terrified that we really hurt her.' He lowered his head, with tears now running down his cheeks. The girl sitting on the end, Lucinda, spoke again, 'Instructor had unlocked the door and Luna fell out. She grabbed Luna and left the room. None of us moved, a little while later a Security Monitor came to our class to make sure we didn't leave, and just keep a watch on all of us.

Mr. Boreas had a serious look on his face, but his voice was not as harsh as his facial expression. He asked that all seven of the children adjourn to the main Conference Room, so the committee could finalize their decisions. They all staggered out of the room, not having any idea of what to expect next, finding seats all together on one wall of the room. Lucinda quietly started repeating the parts of the Mission Statement that she remembered. She knew they all had messed up; however, the resonating of the Credo was in her mind. Prosperity- a Contract of Love, there is always enough.

All eight of the members and the Primary came to the same conclusion. They all told the same story, even when the Primary broke the retelling of it down where they could be tripped up. The whole committee was glad they told the truth about their poor decisions in this event. It made deciding their consequences much easier. Grandiose Vite was in agreement with all his fellow members. Katavon shared the wisdom of Dr. Dignita and Lux from last night. He went on to suggest whatever their consequences were; they would all have the same task. That was quickly agreed on also. Mr. Boreas put out a suggestion to help bring clarity of the Mission Statement to each of his young residents. He even added Luna's first statement to the Council after the event, "We do not want to move into FEAR or negativity.'

All the members agreed on the task for the students. They were called back into the anti-room to hear their fate. They each took their seats again. Mr. Boreas thanked them again for their honesty and cooperation. 'I, or I should say we have come up with a task of restitution for each of you for your acts against the Mission Statement.' Poppi was glad he could be a part of the bigger plan, and he wasn't called on to single out or correct any child. He had enough to do with caring for his Luna.

Mr. Boreas went on to deliver his missive, closing this incident, with high expectations this would become part of the 'Outpost lore,' and it never would happen again. He spoke with authoritative eloquence representing the lead post he held. 'It is the decision of the Leadership Committee that each of you will spend at least two hours time, individually with Luna Grandiose Vite doing a constructive, creative activity of your combined interests. Each of you will have a plan of activities on my desk tomorrow, and the committee will verify that you carry your task to completion.'

Luna stepped out from her corner, into the light. Everyone in the room stared at her, especially her father. 'I have an admission; I have been here for the deliberations. I felt it was important that I know what happened to me. I want to honor the Mission Statement and not be in fear or negativity, as I affirmed the other day. Thank you all for assisting me to heal today.'

The students didn't know how to respond. They were relieved, they were happy, and they were challenged, because none of them really knew or understood Luna.

FISHING

Luna was patiently biding the time for classes to close for the day. She was awaiting the downtime so she would be able to be free to go explore and create. Yesterday she decided she wanted to go fishing again. Poppi taught her to fish. What an extreme amount of fun, excitement, patience, reflection, and skill it took! Over the last few years this was a favorite pastime of hers.

Poppi was busy today with his occupational duties, so Luna asked her friend Kai if he would like to join her. He wasn't in the mood and squashed up his nose with a resounding negative head shake and verbiage to match.

Well- he was missing all the fun! He didn't get it. So, Luna would do as she often did- go off by herself. Her thoughts were... "it's probably for the best" because last time Kai went fishing with her, he was insistent to stay on the water's edge, determined not to get wet. But he really made an annoyance of himself by stomping up and down the shoreline with his heavy boots on making big splashes and certainly scaring away any hopes of catching a fish or two. He was attempting to get Luna all wet with the water as it sprayed out from under his feet. This was *his "fishing activity."*

Luna wanted to attempt to teach and share with Kai the joy fishing brought, but fell silent as she turned to see many iridescent rainbows the water sprays made as the drops fell back to their home in the stream. What beauty!! The Colors!! How can this be possible? With quizzical amusement Luna realized – oh- another topic of research in the data- studies archive.

Luna was amazed at the Blue planet, no sadness or isolation. All its magic and mysteries, in truth, helped her be where she is today, just a constant source of questions and imagination and being able to continually create.

Classes are finally dismissed by instructor. Luna could now go anywhere on the Outpost her age would allow. Therefore, she was off to the Activity- Investigation Pod Headquarters. She ambled up the concourse, not to draw attention to herself.

She was so proud of her parents and the freedoms they allowed her to have at her age. They were gifted and they allowed her to bloom into her own talents and realities. At a young age, she gave each of her parents' special names that came from the Blue planet, and she has seen cultivated in the Botanical Wing. Mother- Mum is a flower. Tough, but it encapsulates her essence- fragrant, colorful, with soft inviting petals making everything witty, always challenging and definitely containing a lot of information, if you dared inquire. Father- Poppi a different kind of flower. He offers healing-medicinal and recreational. Poppi also brings a symbol from the 20th Century that stirs her mind, *remembrance*. And they just nicknamed Luna- Blossom. What was she going to mature into was yet to come.

At the Activity Pod Headquarters Luna checked in with her fingerprint. Her parents or anyone else for that matter knew where she was.

There were 50 Pods located here, so everyone regardless of time or duties always had access to assimilate where they imagined, needed for recreation, or a research project.

Walking over to POD H42, Luna got a big smile on her face as she remembered the first few times Poppi brought her here to begin learning the system operations. Poppi would ask "Where do you want to go?" With that Luna would start slapping all the buttons on the 5 Panels that she could connect with. She gleefully turned to Poppi and replied "Everywhere!" Well that didn't happen.

The Intel system of the Bio-Genetic Holographic chambers had overrides that only allowed certain assimilation of data points in the activity or area of interest. Systems didn't crash. The Activity System replied in a gentle voice" Not able to interpolate all information provided. Please start again." Poppi only smiled thinking "That's my girl!"

The 5 Panels were full of so many options.

Panel #1 was for Stars, Planets, Black holes, Milky Way, various Galaxies, and one special button whose exclusive use was for the Blue planet.

Panel #2 was for era, age, year, or some semblance of time

Panel #3 was for Life (air, water, soils, or terrain) Colors, definition points- necessity or opportunity

Panel #4 broke into the real idiosyncrasies of the Bio-Genetic and the Holographic properties of recreating and solidifying the total experience of the adventure. The Data Archive uses and retrieves an exurbanite amounts of data from the 20th and 21st centuries of how DNA was discovered and identified. The Blue plant has paired sets of stranded Genetic markers of DNA. One set of the twined strands will create a fish while another set of strands will create something completely different, like a tree. These set markers are infused with the 5-D Phase Beam lasers to create smells, sounds, depth, movement, and tastes of the experience. This panel projects animals and plants. It is kind of painful to review the logs of the Bio-Genetic PB Holograms of animals or life that is known to be extinct. Poppi explained all of this to Luna. It was an extremely important responsibility and honor to work in this department and be part of this division of Outpost 621. Poppi also explained to have this much detail in all phases of the exposure was why there was a time limit of 70 to 120 minutes of virtual reality. Poppi is so smart! He shares and teaches Luna so much.

Kai, Oliver, and Sonnet always just shrugged at the adventure- not caring how precious these POD experiences were.

Panel #5 was for necessary apparel and or gear needed for this adventure. Since clothes, utensils transportation modes or other sundry items created from different time periods- each item is micro chipped with touch activation as to purpose, and usage. WOW! When you can go anywhere, with anything you have to be prepared- even if in *observer mode.*

Poppi and Luna went on adventures all the time when she was younger. Now Luna is acceptably knowledgeable to operate the Chamber herself.

At first when she went alone, or with her friends, there was a bit of fear. Fear was really something alien to the Outpost. If there was an anomaly in some structure or function, everyone used their intellect to resolve the situation with reason and positive acknowledgement, and then moved forward. Luna had developed fears in the chambers. Her exposure and curiosity reported data of actual, emotional or regional fears of animals or societies, with documented scientific data included and verified at the Data Storage & Archive Studies

Center. Luna addressed this with Poppi. He explained so much to her with respect, integrity, and love. This was the grassroots perspective of Outpost 621; if it would survive.

There was no fear today! Luna wanted to fish on the Blue planet- Panel #1. Panel 2- North American Continent, Rocky Mountain Foothills, year 1955. Panel 3- request gently flowing water current, clear, blue, cold. Late spring- warm air: 21degrees Celsius. Panel 4- Trees and flowers in bloom. Supply appropriate animals, insects, and livestock. Panel 5- Supply and match apparel and fishing gear to time period for escapade.

Luna's energy and enthusiasm increased with each set of buttons she engaged. Time to step into vault one.

Opening the first door and stepping in immediately triggered the closing and sealing of the second immense door. The doors seemed huge, overwhelming, heavy and unimpressionable. But with the touch of a hand, the doors were light and easy to move, obeying the travelers command. The doors even seemed to change into a type of window where the visitor felt safe and invited to journey through to the next door.

In this first chamber, as Luna moved to the next door- she was being offered apparel, gear, shoes, supplies and any other objects that A.I. computed the visitor would want or need for full enhanced experience. No longer was she in her daily attire and sandals. Luna was a fisher person. She always broke out giggling at this point because she donned a brimmed cloth hat, a soft cotton or fleece shirt (depending on the climate she had set) Poppi called the pants she had on "waders" made of a rubber material, and they were attached with suspenders.

The outfit was complete with big waterproof boots that came almost up to her hips.

Nearing the second entry door, she picked up a pocketed vest, to put many little gadgets in. She now knew in the water, you had to be self-sufficient. The vest was outfitted with a sundry of items foreign to her normal life, but definitely needed to fish with. She put on her vest, picked up a wire fishing basket, a fishing net, and 2 poles with appropriate line strength for doing stream fishing- 2 to 2.5- kilogram test. Poppi made sure she knew what line strength she needed so when she caught her fish, the test line would not snap and she would lose her fish and the lure she was using. Luna became partial to certain shapes and colors of lures she had in her tackle box. She didn't want to lose any of them, or her fish... and disappoint Poppi. Last item she picked up was a rattan wicker tackle bag. It was so quaint, made with reeds and had a lid and straps attached with leather pieces she called solid, sturdy, and dependable. Luna liked the appearance, even though she was a novice fisher person. Luna reached for the second door and it glided open so she could step into her afternoon activity. The door seemed to change from the solid chamber door to an inviting clear faceted gateway to her transitioning experience. She noted the digital timer by the door. 120 minutes. It didn't matter; she was at her and Poppi's special place.

Luna could instantly smell earth and trees- pine and maples- sweet. Birch a heavier aroma, but they liked being close to the water's edge. She waddled along a path through the trees towards the sound of moving water. She stopped for a minute to take in this wonderful kind of quiet. The water bubbling was along on its way over the stones and sand. She heard birds call out in song, then silent- who was approaching? Then they sang again when feeling no threat. There was a warm breeze Luna could feel on her face that was beckoning her to the shimmering water with gleans of silver light and small sounds and movements on top of the water that announced the goal she was close to.

Luna found a downed tree log to place her gear by and proceeded to test her line attach a lure (one of her favorites) and make sure net, pole, her boots, hat and clothing were ready for the water. She walked to the water's edge, bent over to feel the cool, brisk movement of the water. What a joy! Then gently and quietly stepped into the stream as not to disturb or alert the fish she sought. Luna carefully moved through the water, feeling the smooth stones under her feet and the gentle push of the current against her tiny body. With this different apparel, she had to stop several times to adjust her balance and be in control of her efforts and purpose.

OK, she looked back at the bank where she just came from, then to the sky, blue and clear- focusing in on the leaves of the trees fluttering as if in applause that she was here. The stream undisturbed or distracted by her attendance. Ready. Set. Go. Luna pulled out 2 arm lengths of line, took her pole back over her shoulder and casted the tiny lure and line through the air at a 45-degree angle into the downstream flow of the water, just like Poppi had taught her. A bird swooped past the line and lure as it traveled to its liquid resting place, bobbing successfully, resplendent with shimmers of light reflecting off of the tiny crests of water and line. Attractive to any fish!

Be patient, be with nature, just look and observe.

In a little bit Luna's lure started dunking under the water. The line grew taut. Luna's moment was here. She braced and balanced herself in the stream, she started carefully pulling at the line winding it gently back onto the reel. This is the art! Let the trout think he has the prize and is sneaking away, and all the while Luna has the prize and is bringing it into herself. This is a game of craft and skill at both ends of the line. The line is getting more tension and sway with it as the fish must realize his prize is fighting as much as he is. Luna makes sure her wire fish basket is ready at her side.

They both tussle some more, but Luna brings in her prize, a nice trout about 34 centimeters long. Poppi taught Luna extensive skills so she would win this competition with her fish. Put him in the basket, and then remove the lure hook that brought him to her. Do not hurt the trout- it has feelings just like her.

She held her prize high in high in the air to gaze in amazement at this creature. Then so the trout would not die, she made sure one end of the basket cable was securely attached to her waders and let the cable out with the flow of the stream, the trout safely in the basket, to swim around.

Luna repeated this process numerous times. Adjusting her stance, the length of line, even switching lures once, and which way she wanted to flex her arm as she cast into the water. She was so happy.

It must be time to leave. Luna stared at the 3 trout she caught and she knew she must return them to their natural home. Poppi taught her the terms and rules: "catch and release". She did not need food, this was education.

She reluctantly turned the basket sideways in the flowing water and watched as her 3 new friends for the afternoon quickly disappeared amongst the foam and bubbles of the stream. Luna felt sad, but a quick breeze had all of the trees and stream brush moving and swaying, applauding her in her endeavors.

Luna left the water, gathered her gear and went back up the path to the archway. By the time she was at the door, she beamed in happiness. "Just wait til Poppi hears about my day!"

POPPI'S WILDERNESS ADVENTURE

Poppi had wanted to take Luna on a weekend camping adventure, but had been waiting until his workload could do without him for a few days, and Poppi was not going to excuse Luna from classes when she was in this new learning program.

It seemed that things were quieting down now in both arenas, and the opportunity could come up soon. Therefore, at breakfast, Poppi asked Luna if she was ready to go camping as they had lightly touched on earlier in the year. Luna's face lit up, and she asked when can we go? Poppi responded in that he would make arrangements and they would go soon. This overjoyed Luna to be out of classes, outdoors on Earth, and doing an adventure with Poppi again. It had been a long time since they had done such an activity.

Luna excused herself from the morning meal, ran around the table and kissed Mum and Poppi, grabbed her tablet, and said she was off to classes. She started up the corridor on the way to class when a thought came to her.

She still had to deal with the incident of the Sunshine and its repercussions with all seven of her fellow students that captured her. Luna knew that each of them had written ideas of restitution activities to participate in with Luna and sent them into the Primary. When he had all the suggestions, Luna was called to the Primary's office to discuss them. She had reviewed the suggestions, scrunched up her face, and felt that nothing was being resolved, as each of their ideas was childish and a waste of effort to correct the situation. Luna looked up at the Primary; and they had a bit of a discussion. Luna apologized for her intrusion to the closed meeting, and knew she had to be held accountable as well as the seven other students at this time. She had disobeyed. After looking over the ideas that the seven had proposed to the Primary, Luna asked a question; more of a request to him. 'Sir, I feel as though this whole incident has been the failing of the communities understanding of our Mission Statement. I say this humbly, but I possibly know more about the Mission than others in our colony due to my family's services and occupations.' 'Sir, I would like to know if I can plan the activities to which all of my classmates have to attend for their restitution.' Mr. Boreas was stunned at such an idea. This girl has gone too far! But in fairness, he left the conversation open and said he would think about it. Luna had been reflecting on the situation for a while. She only liked to hang out with her friends she knew and trusted. But she was in this spot where she knew she had to interact with each of these peers, one on one regardless; Luna then challenged herself that they would do an activity, she would initiate it, and it would be a co-learning session for them both. Now, to come up with seven activities, she had to go back to Mr. Boreas for that opportunity and permission. Then Luna had to talk to Poppi about her idea.

Luna thought about her idea off and on all day while in classes. She thought the best approach was to talk to Poppi first. She wanted to know if Poppi would allow this to be part of her amends for her disobedience to both the Primary, as well as her parents. If Poppi agreed with her idea, was it then acceptable for one of 'them' to go on an outing with us. She thought that would be the best way to test out her idea. Must talk to Poppi first!

That afternoon after classes, Luna hurried home, gave Mum a kiss and hug then grabbed some cheese and fruit for a snack, and went to her room to do her home studies. She wanted to be sure she had her class work finished so after the evening meal, she and Poppi could discuss her idea. Neither Poppi nor Mum had brought up the violation she had committed since the Query. She didn't know how they felt about her behavior. But she reasoned if they were really upset at her actions, she was sure she would have been reprimanded about it by now.

When Poppi came home, Luna ran to greet him as usual and hopped up, hugging his neck and quickly asking if they could talk after the evening meal. Poppi was intrigued. He was sure it had to do with his asking his daughter about his inquiry this morning if she still wanted to go camping. He asked if Mum could sit in on the chat. Luna always discussed her problems with both parents, but this time didn't think of including Mum. Luna let go of Poppi's neck and slid down to the floor, she was distressed with herself that she had not included Mum in their discussion. She thought a second, and gave Poppi her biggest smile and said of course Mum could be a part of the conversation. She had been thinking of all the implications she wanted to make in her talk with Poppi, she absently excluded Mum. That was not good, hopefully Poppi and Mum would understand after their meal, when she could express herself. Mum said the food was ready, and to wash up for dinner. Poppi put his work things away, and both of them got back to the dining area at the same time. Dinner was rather quiet as Luna just listened to her parents talk about their day, they always interacted as if they loved and cared about each other so much, it was amazing to watch them. Luna was trying to think about what she wanted to say to Poppi in just a little while. They finished their meal with a custard Mum had made with berries mixed in. Luna wanted to learn how to prepare food like Mum. She always made such wonderful dishes for her family.

Poppi took Luna's hand and they headed towards the salon for their chat. Mum raised her head and said she would join them in a few minutes, as soon as the dishes were cleared away. Luna hopped up on the couch, scooting in close to Poppi. This was her favorite place to be. She wasn't sure if it was proper for her conversation with Poppi this evening, but she felt safer and more secure sitting so close to him. When Mum came into the room she dropped herself down in a comfortable chair close to them, where she could relax, and still be a cozy part of the conversation. Mum thought this must be big news if Luna asked for a formal setting for this discussion, instead of their usual chatting over the evening meal. Luna wasn't quite sure how to start, so she was quiet for a few moments. Mum got up and went to the food preparation area and brought back a tray with three tumblers of sparkling water with her, and sat them on the small table between them. Luna still had not started talking.

She took a deep breath, and charged into her ideas she wanted to talk to Poppi about. 'Poppi, I really want to go camping with you, whenever we can set up a time that is convenient to your schedule.' 'Ok, I'm glad you still want to go,' was his reply. 'Would you like to make a weekend of this event?' At this question Luna burst into tears, she was not even expecting herself to be this emotional and cry, but here they were, dripping off her long lashes, and rolling down her cheeks. 'Luna, what's wrong?' Poppi and Mum asked simultaneously. She looked up at her father and sniffled out her response, 'I didn't think you wanted to take me camping any longer, because of my disobedience at the Query.' Mum and Poppi looked seriously at each other, not realizing the ramifications of the whole ordeal was still so overshadowing to Luna. 'No, Luna that is not the reason we have not gone camping yet. There are two things that have prevented our outing. First and foremost, the special classes that you are in. Your participation in these are very important to the future of the Outpost. And the second one, is I have been working on some upgrades needed for equipment we work with daily in our research center.' Poppi quickly reassured her.

'However, since you brought up the private meeting that you had direct instructions to avoid; and you disobeyed three of the people that I know you have the highest regard for, the Primary, Mum, and myself.' Luna could see that Poppi raised his right eye brow in question as he was speaking, through her tears. 'What have you got to say for yourself?' Luna recovered somewhat, and earnestly asked Poppi 'Why didn't I get an explanation as to why I was put in the closet?' Mum felt the deeper hurt that Luna held about being barred from the meeting that was all about her welfare. Mum rushed over the other side of Luna on the far side of the couch, and clutched her daughter close to her in a big hug, squeezing her tight. Mum said she was so sorry that Luna herself had been overlooked. 'Nothing like this has ever happened on the Outpost. All of the residents and council have been in such concern over how to handle this unfortunate event, that my dear, dear child, we were trying to protect you from further harm.' Luna looked directly at her father and started 'Fear comes from not understanding something. If I was not given the opportunity to learn about the whole closet incident, I think that could set me or anyone else up for fear of unknowns, or environment, or peoples. Do you agree Poppi? Mum? I came across how the earth people were set up and governed by fears in the Data Storage and Archival Studies Center. Have you learned about how bad fear can be?' Luna looked questioningly back and forth to both her parents. 'I wasn't trying to be disobedient; I wanted to comprehend how this happened to me, and for what reason. I did not want to be fearful. I do not like what happened to me. I have briefly spoken to the Primary about the punishments that each of my classmates suggested to the Council.'

Poppi came out of his trance of what his daughter was saying to him. He was being part of the problem also. His heart fell. 'What did you talk to the Primary about? Why didn't you talk to me first before going to the Primary?' Luna responded, 'He asked me to come to his office to see what the students suggested as their penalties. Poppi, it was awful! They wanted to play games, or do my homework, or go assist in the nursery or botanical wings. That was not going to help them learn or correct their errors!'

'Poppi, I think the Primary was upset with me at my noncompliance of his, your, and Mum's instructions to stay away from the meeting; and at my dismissal of the suggestions the students made.' 'I think the Primary is going to want to speak with both of us about the consequences that all eight of us are going to have to address over the incident, and our punishments.'

'Luna, what have you done?' Poppi asked.

'I just told you most of it....' Luna answered. 'The second part is that today I was thinking. If I'm going to have to spend time with each of these seven pranksters, why can't I create activities for each of them, to help teach them something about the Outpost, or the Mission Statement, or how we all need each other, teaching Love and not fear?' 'Poppi, Mum this is where I need your help. Do you think this is a good idea?'

Mum and Poppi looked at each other once again. Luna always seemed to come up with a positive point of view. She had such wonderful creative ideas, and her belief in the Outpost and their Mission was amazing to them. They both nodded that they felt she was correct with her ideas and objectives. Poppi asked 'What do you have planned? How can we correct this situation for the betterment of the whole Outpost, my dear little Luna?'

'Poppi, I was thinking that I, if it was OK with you maybe one of the students could accompany us on the camping trip. But first, we both need to speak with the Primary and see if he likes my idea and agrees to my suggestion for helping these students pay off their obligations. Poppi, I need your help because I don't really know these students, and now you know more than I do of what they are capable of. I don't want to be alone with them and allow them to have free reign over me ever again.' Poppi nodded in agreement, 'That's a very good idea. We will see what Mr. Boreas thinks. No one was given a time period that we had to complete these amends to the outpost. And I truly think you're having permission to create healthy learning tasks is awesome. If Mr. Boreas agrees, we will adjust the camping trip to include one more, and really make it an adventure!'

Luna was so happy with her parents' response to her idea. She started giggling, hopped down from the couch giving each of her parents a big hug and kisses and headed off to her room where she grabbed Moppet, and after she opened the sky window, just sat on her bed for a while. Maybe this was going to turn out alright, she thought. Then she readied herself for bed, snuggled under the covers with Moppet, and her favorite blanket she thought, Poppi would definitely help her now with this big project. Luna drifted off to sleep, knowing Poppi would invent some creative adventures for her and her "protégés."

A few days later Poppi met Luna at the door of her classroom, at the end of the day. This was a surprise to her, but she was always happy to see and be with her father. Poppi stooped down and gave her a hug, and whispered, 'we're going to have a chat with Mr. Boreas.' Luna looked closely at Poppi and noted that he had a relaxed smile on his face, so she smiled brightly back at him. As they were walking up the concourse, Poppi stopped and turned to face Luna. He had previously been to talk to Mr. Boreas, and they talked about the situation. 'Luna,' Poppi started, 'The Primary and I have already discussed the decision of the Council, and the conversation that you two had before you spoke with me.' Poppi took a breath, and with an intense look on his face, he continued, 'I wanted you to know what we deliberated over before you and I join him in a few minutes. First, Mr. Boreas is not used to anyone defying his authority. And then you stood up for yourself when he wanted to speak with you privately. You really shocked him, Miss Luna!'

'I originally agreed to you being coupled with another student on a task, as your penalty for your disregard for an instruction that was given to you by the Primary and both your mother and me. I know that this is not your usual behavior or response to any of us. I was glad that we talked about the issue together, before meeting with Mr. Boreas.' In our conversation, Mr. Boreas showed me the papers that the other seven students had returned to him as their penitence tasks. After reviewing their suggestions, I could see how you would have quickly rejected them. I understand your distress at what was being offered to the Primary. I went on to suggest your idea of assignments, to Mr. Boreas, that you would fashion. Then, engaging and educational assignments would be set up for each of them. I even suggested the first student participate with us on the camping venture. Except that I didn't give away our camping event, I made it a wilderness outing.' Poppi looked down at Luna to take in her expression. She was deep in thought. 'Luna, what do you think?' She looked up and smiled, 'that is a great suggestion, Poppi!' 'And I will help you build six other activities in which you can be the lead. Luna, I know and trust that you will show the character and exemplary behavior I know you have, and you will make great friends of these seven fellow students.' Luna felt peace in her heart, and kept smiling, 'I will Poppi!' So, they continued their stroll to the Commission Chambers, and Mr. Boreas office, holding hands.

They knocked on the Primary's door, and were instructed to enter. Mr. Boreas waved his hand towards two sets in front of his desk for them to be seated in. Once they were comfortable, the Primary greeted them both and said he was happy that they were all working together towards a resolution of "the sun light incident."

Luna chimed right in saying, 'Please Sir, can we not refer to this mishap in connection to the Sun.' I know the event happened on the day the Sun made its appearance, but it was human naughtiness that all of us are dealing with now.' Poppi and Luna could see the expression changing on Mr. Boreas face, and his knuckles turning white.

Holding the leadership office, Mr. Boreas, used his diplomacy that was sometimes necessary, and calmly replied that Luna made a good point. He forged ahead asking if Luna and her parents had discussed Luna's idea for the adapting of tasks for the seven students. Luna looked at her father, then back at Mr. Boreas, not knowing if she or Poppi was to respond to his question. Poppi opened the conversation with information that all three already knew. The tasks that were turned in by the perpetrators were not enough to give credit for their serious errors. And this needed to be an example and learning experience to the whole Outpost. Poppi even noted his own error in judgment in this situation. Poppi then looked to Luna and as a complimentary introduction, conveyed to Mr. Boreas the wonderful idea that Luna had of constructing different events for each of the seven involved that would lead to educational, engaging experiences for all involved, including Luna. Each event would help the young persons' to understand much more about the Outpost, how we all are interdependent on each other, and The Mission Statement of Love.

Mr. Boreas had been thinking about what Luna said to him on the day she had come to office at his request. Then Katavon came and spoke to him at his appointed time and they discussed this matter further, he was gaining insight! Now this was the third time that the same proposal was before him. He knew the final decision was his, except the Grandiose Vite family kept coming back to him with the true tenets of the Mission statement. In his mind he was thinking that this Family has been hurt and violated, yet here they are offering leadership and education for the whole community. Now he must reevaluate his own prejudices and attitudes. Mr. Boreas looked at Luna and asked with a much gentler voice, 'Do you think you and your family can come up with events that would be as described, educational and engaging?' 'Oh, yes sir!' Luna replied. 'Poppi and I wanted to go to Earth's wilderness to learn and explore. Luna eyed Poppi on the sly. 'We would be happy to have one of the libertines accompany us. If you wish we could even have the person, as well as father and I send you a small report back, and possibly set up other excursions we could take, with my fellow classmates.'

Mr. Boreas knew they were heading towards an agreement, and he did approve of these tasks, so far. Mr. Boreas was gaining a huge respect for Luna over this incident. Maybe by the fourth generation we all need to review and renew our commitment to the Mission statement. We can't allow what was crafted so carefully for our survival to become faded words on a monitor to read over, forgetting to take in every sincere word that is part of our Mission for survival and expansion. 'Luna, I'm going to give you the Council's approval for this first task. After it is completed, we will call meet again and decide if this is appropriate, and will proceed forward. I will relay this meeting to the other Council members to be added into our meeting notes, as a trial.' 'Luna, I want to apologize to you for the Council's and my inconsideration of your feelings and hurt over what happened. I do appreciate your insight and assistance in wanted the outpost to grow and be safe and stable.'

With this, Mr. Boreas asked if there were any other questions or concerns for today. He then said that Poppi and Luna were dismissed. Luna turned around to Mr. Boreas and smiled brightly saying 'Thank you for this opportunity.' She then turned back to her father, took his hand and they started walking towards their quarters. Luna had her approval to start these assignments, and she wanted to do them, and get them over with, so she could continue with information she really wanted to study. Now Luna was full of questions. "Poppi, when do we and to do this first adventure?' 'Poppi answered, 'as soon as you select one of the classmates.' 'Poppi, how long will out Outdoors Wilderness adventure be?' 'I would say at least three to four hours. We have a lot to learn about and explore! Do you have an idea of which student you would like to start with?' Squeezing his hand tight, 'Yes, Poppi. I want to start with Logan.' Poppi looked at her in surprise. He didn't have to ask why; he knew his daughter had her reasons; and probably had all the tasks and other students all lined up already. Poppi knew what he needed to do to fulfill his responsibility to his daughter, and to educate and encourage each of the seven students; however, he knew this was Luna's project. He was there to assist and guide her through this process. He smiled as they reached the door to their quarters, this was going to be educational for everyone, and quite dynamic he felt.

Mr. Boreas sent a message to the parents for Logan to meet Mr. Grandiose Vite and Luna at the Holographic Activity Pods at 09:00 this coming weekend. The parents already knew that there was a punishment that was coming up for Logan due to his misdeeds a few months ago. Not much else was on the message for the requirement for attendance, other than he would probably be there all day. Logan was going into melt down, he was so afraid, as he knew this was not part of the suggested punishment he had turned into the Primary. Luna was almost bouncing around she was so happy and full of energy.

The weekend arrived. Luna and Poppi got up and dressed, they went for their morning meal, electrifying the energy in the quarters. Mum thought that both Poppi and Luna glowed they were excited about their outing today. Both of them were dressed with cotton turtlenecks, Luna's a Sapphire Blue and Poppi style matched in a Honey Yellow. Both had on dark blue khakis, and light weight boots that laced up. They definitely appeared the Father and daughter team.

Katavon had gone ahead earlier in the week and spoke with Ms. Emagine about securing a Pod for their use today. He had also inquired if there were any special requirements in applying a "reset" for their adventure for today. Poppi had never returned back to back to the same program settings in a Pod adventure before, so he wanted to make sure that it was possible and the Pod Monitor knew what they were going to do. All was approved.

Luna had been attentive in class all week, as usual, but she had to excuse herself from activities for the weekend with her friends, Oliver, Kai, and Sonnet. This somewhat distressed her, but she was going to be with Poppi, so everything would work out, and she felt sure she would come back with some amazing information to share with her friends. Logan seemed lost. He attempted to chat with Luna but he knew he would be blunt because he was afraid of what was going to happen this weekend, if he said much of anything to her. No one knew what their activity was going to be, so Logan was in the spotlight as everyone in class went to him asking questions, once more making him feel inadequate.

Saturday morning, Logan dressed in his school class attire, left his quarters alone, heading to the Activity Holographic Pods. As he neared the entrance to the Holographic Wing, he could see Luna and her father up ahead of him. He was a bit puzzled by their attire, but he kept walking towards them. When he was within hearing range, Katavon greeted him, and inquired if he was up to an adventure? Luna just stood there and smiled at the moment, watching this very serious interaction. 'We are going on a wilderness adventure on Earth today.' Poppi announced. "If it is Ok with you can we be on a first name basis for this trip Logan? Logan hadn't moved or spoke as of yet, but at this point he nodded yes to his elder leader. Poppi continued with, 'It is a pleasure to meet you Logan, and I'm glad you are accompanying us today. I am Luna's father, please feel free to call me G.V., and I know you are acquainted with Luna. We have decided to go to planet Earth today for a Wilderness Adventure, and learn basic skills about environments that we haven't been exposed to, but are rich with beauty and discoveries that our ancestors had easy access to.'

Luna could see the tense expression on Logan's face, and Poppi saw it too, so he asked the young boy, 'Have you ever been on a holographic trip to earth guided by your parents or your instructors?' Logan replied in a very small voice, 'No, sir.' This concerned Poppi, but he asked the follow up question, 'Have you ever gone to the Data Storage and Archival Studies Wing and done research or searched out some topic of interest you may have?' Again, Logan replied in an exceedingly low voice, 'No, sir.' G.V. tried a different avenue to see what type of student he had accompanying them today by asking if he had ever spoken to Luna about her various adventures that she had taken with her family in the Holographic Pods. Once again the answer was the same, 'No.' Poppi knew his daughter was taking all this in, and he was almost positive that she already knew about Logan's non-exposure to anything outside the Outpost's physical environment. At this point, the one very important question that G.V. had for Logan was 'had he even been in any of the Holographic Pods for recreation, activities, or a learning experiment?' He lowered his head and nodded no for the last time. Logan was being overwhelmed with questions of exposure that he had never been involved with. Luna heard the answers he was giving and felt very sorry for him, and was so grateful for her parents. Luna then chimed in, 'We're going to change that today Logan. This will be your first trip, and I'm sure you will want to return. We have plenty of advisors to help us, and everything is at our disposal for us to learn and grow to be better citizens on the outpost.' Luna's voice was rising in pitch as she was excited at what they were about to do.

G.V., not knowing this child's prior life experiences, wanted him to enjoy and embrace this journey they were going to take today. He did not want to frighten or overwhelm Logan with the very strange surroundings. G.V. had to acknowledge, both of us were strangers to him also. 'Do we need to sit down and talk about our adventure today, and what our intention is, before going into the Holographic Pod, Logan?' G.V. could read right through the child's fear of these unknowns, but Logan replied with a bit of a smile, 'No, sir, I am ready to proceed!'

Luna watching this interaction between the two, jumped right in on that comment and said, 'Poppi, let's go! I love the Blue planet, and can't wait.' Logan was still very concerned and perplexed by today's activities that were to be his punishment for his misbehavior.

The three walked over to the programming panel, and G.V. turned to Logan and told him that they would start out slowly with learning how programming went for the activities pods, and what he would expect in the next few minutes. There was silence in their few steps to the control programming panel as all three were deep in thought. Katavon was thinking with overwhelming gravity as to how the Mission Statement and credo was slipping away, unnoticed by the residents until this incident. It must be addressed by the Leadership Commission immediately. He was so used to Luna's inquisitiveness, that it escaped him that other children were somehow not getting the correct instruction as to their living situation and how fragile it was. Luna was now intrigued with Logan. She was in deep thought as to why didn't he explore their outpost, planet and how they got here. What did he do when he was not in classes as he definitely was not a wiz in his studies? Today should be interesting. Then there was Logan; he was still nervous about today's activities, nevertheless he was certainly curious as to their activity. He looked at Luna, sideways, with a deep uncertainty, questioning 'what was she up to?'

It did seem as though it was going to be an exciting day for him, and he was starting to relax and enjoy their company.

When they were standing in front of the programming panels, Poppi told Luna that he had reserved Pod #24 for their use today. G.V. looked down and addressed both children. 'Since Luna is familiar with using the Activities Holographic Pods, I am going to give her the programming instructions for the adventure, and then I can explain what we are doing to you Logan. Is that OK with you two? Luna eagerly responded yes to Poppi. She wanted to show both Logan and Poppi her skill at being able to properly use the Holographic Pods, and she could go anywhere she wanted to, with her programming. Only today this was planned, so she must follow Poppi's direction, because she knew she still had six other classmates she was going to have to create tasks for.

G.V. looked directly at Logan and said as gently as possible that their day was planned to go to earth for a Wilderness Adventure. Luna already knew this, but was amazed at how Logan's eyes became wide with interest when Poppi announced their destination. G.V. waved his hand towards the five panels on the wall. Luna had placed herself in front of the panels. G.V. continued with each of the panels was a specific part of the series to give a comprehensive, life-like experience for the two hours that were allotted for the scheduled program's use. He went on to accentuate that the programs included all five senses.

Poppi looked up at his daughter, excited and ready to start their day. To help make the workings of the Holographic Pods clear, nodding his head at Luna and told her: 'Panel #1-location –Earth' As Luna was pushing the exclusive button for planet Earth, G.V. explained that this button was the beginning of the journey and you could program anywhere in the universe you wanted to go. Quick as a flash, that button was activated. Luna moved a little to the right to the next panel. Poppi knew she was ready and instructed her with,

'Panel #2- year 1956.' Logan watched Luna with keen interest as she had to do a bit more detailed programming as G.V. explained that this was the panel that was specifically for the semblance of a certain date, or a wide range of time. With that completed, Luna looked to Poppi for her next directive. Poppi told her that information she needed was to program Panel #3 for Earth, and mountain foothills. Luna was curious about this data input, but followed Poppi's instructions because he had the day planned, and she knew that this was going to be a new experience for her also. G.V. briefly explained that this panel set the idiosyncrasies for the type of soil, water terrain, and air of their venture. Things were going well, so far, Poppi thought, Luna was definitely handling her task with ease, as Logan looked on with stunned amazement; she worked so efficiently and quickly at her father's direction. Luna was now ready for the next programming endeavor. G.V. gave her the programming for Panel #4. 'Fort Nelson Park, British Columbia, Canada,' Luna turned around and looked at Poppi in question. He nodded back to her and said, 'we're going on an adventure and someplace new!' With this answer, Luna eagerly followed Poppi's instructions and was hoping they were going to arrive at their destination very soon. G.V. peered down at Logan and told him the fourth panel activated the 5 d Phase Beams for the creation of smells, movement, sounds, which included animals, vegetation, water, and winds or storms. He was not sure if Logan understood the complexities that he was telling him about right now with this programming, but hoped he would feel safe enough to question anything he did not understand. This child was so different than his Luna. Luna inched over to Panel #5. They were almost ready. G.V. quickly looked up to Luna then back at Logan. He gave his instruction to her to program this panel for their adventure. Necessary accessories and utensils they would need for the day. Logan overheard this, and did not need further clarification, but G.V. stepped over to the panel pushing some extra buttons to be included, Poppi made no further comment about it. Luna didn't care. Their program was set, and she was ready to go.

Luna reached back to take Poppi's hand and then reached out to take Logan's hand as they entered through the first door. This wasn't necessary on her part but she was protecting Logan as he had no idea of what was to come. Once through the threshold, the first door activated the automatic closing and sealing system, slid shut; also duplicating the process for the second door. Luna turned and looked up at Poppi, and asked, 'Do these doors seem so large and overwhelming to you?' Poppi knew what Luna's intentions were, so he answered, 'The doors to the Pods have to be strong and secure so the Holographic imaging and creations can function to full capacity. Luna, they are exactly what you observe.' Logan was holding tight to Luna's hand, wide eyed and wordless. Luna went on to the next process that always impressed her. She voiced her observation of how the doors seemed to change into a type of looking glass where she always felt safe and inviting to enter, for the beginning of her journey. Logan noticed this also, and finally made a comment, 'Gee, that's neat!'

They moved through this entry into the next chamber, and the doors slid closed behind them. This was the area where they dressed and gathered their gear for their adventure in the wilderness on Earth. Luna and Poppi were almost outfitted, they only needed to put on some light weight vests, and pick up their backpacks that had essentials for their day. G.V. looked to Logan and pointed out that they had assembled an outdoors hiking wardrobe for him. He was very surprised at this phenomenon, and quickly replaced his clothing and footwear for the excursion. He felt ready for the next event when he picked up the backpack that was still laying there awaiting him to retrieve it. Before opening the next set of doors, G.V. said they all should take walking sticks with them as he reached for one leaning up against the wall. There were various sizes and shapes, made from a variety of woods. Luna and Logan both examined a few of the staffs, not sure of what was the proper use or purpose of the utensils. Poppi realized they were both perplexed. He then informed them that the walking sticks served the purposes of supporting their balance as they walked, making sure ground was solid, and they made a reverberation in the ground that would cause any unwanted animals or insects to retreat from them. Logan looked at Luna for affirmation. Luna understood what Poppi was saying and investigated the sticks further. Poppi then added to his instruction to make sure the sticks were not too heavy and felt a comfortable length to walk with. Logan took all this information in and promptly found a staff he felt would accommodate him. G.V nodded in approval. Luna was the last to find a walking stick she felt worthy of her needs. Poppi giggled under his breath at her precision in finding an accessory. Outfitted, and with all gear in hand, the three were ready to open the door and enter the next chamber.

The door opened on command, and they walked through. Poppi led the way demonstrating the use of the walking staff. After they had entered, the doors slipped silently closed and disappeared, leaving a full 360-degree panorama of their

Wilderness. Luna giggled enthusiastically, jumping up and down, spinning so she could see the whole vista. Logan stood for the first few moments transfixed by the gurgling sound of the clear blue river flowing by. He slowly changed his view to all the dried dead wood, bleached white with age, mixed in between the rocks on the shoreline ranging in size and colors from about 5 millimeters to 4 to 5 meters across. Luna was starting to slow down and closely observe her surroundings with shining eyes. G.V. just stood there and watched the two children take in this beauty of Earth for the first time. He had visited this place before himself, when he was younger, and could relate to their absolute wonder of it. He did a full scan of the area they were in seeking any native animals that may be out hunting their next meal. All three of them looked at the hiking path with wild grasses growing tall on either side of it that stretched in front of them; and then they looked south. They scanned up the ascending hillside populated with various coniferous trees that seemed to be growing out of the smaller boulders that covered the slopes. After taking in the whole vista, Poppi plopped down on a good size rock to address his children accompanying him.

It took a few more minutes for Luna and Logan to realize that Poppi was sitting there waiting on them. But he wanted this first impression of wilderness earth to settle in their hearts and minds before they did any other activities. Logan, for the first time spoke up today saying he never imagined Earth was so beautiful. Luna returned with her comment that Earth was beyond glorious! That she had come here many times and she was always coming to a new place that seemed grander than the last. G.V. smiled and spoke to them with tenderness, but with authority, 'I have a hike planned for us today, some fishing, building a campfire and a sleeping shelter. Not sure how we are going to identify the materials we will need in what order, so let's just set off on our hike and see what we find.' Luna once again started hopping up and down with joy, this was going to be so special; a treasure hunt, exploration, and learning experience all rolled together for Logan and her today.

Logan was totally enthralled at being here. Through classes or with his family he had never used the Activity Holographic Pods to visit Earth. He was humbly asking himself how he got this special venture, when he had unwittingly caused Luna such harm and suffering. And here she was happy, excited and willing to share part of her experiences. Logan, still being anxious about today looked up at G.V. and asked, 'How long is this activity? Are we spending the night?' G.V. was sensitive to the situation, and replied, 'No.' he went on to add that any Holographic venture could only last for 2 hours, but he wanted to complete certain educational tasks so they would have a second session after a break for a midday meal. G.V. and Luna were glad that Logan was finally starting to get his voice and express himself.

'Let's be off!' G.V. said standing, and heading onto the sandy path by the river. Luna was following her father with Logan bringing up the rear. He didn't like that, so he scurried ahead and was walking beside G.V. Luna liked that idea. That way she didn't have to constantly interact with Logan and she could take in the terrain and vegetation as she came to it. While they were walking, G.V. asked Logan did he have an idea of which task he wanted to attempt first. They walked for about 20 minutes in this beautiful, living landscape that was ever changing but constantly staying the same. The visitors noticed the indigenous wildlife of deer, rabbits, a raccoon, and fox scurrying away from them as they did not want to interact with humans. The three were embracing the fresh air that had the scent of pine trees. Relaxing into a steady pace they enjoyed a soft, gentle breeze that caressed their faces. They could feel the mixture of river spray with hints of dust in it reaching out and touching them. G.V. knew they were coming to an area that widened out where they could undertake at least one of their missions. He also knew that the 2-hour working window would fly by very quickly.

Luna heard the question and asked could they build a shelter first? G.V. looked at Logan and asked what did he think? He nodded in agreement. G.V. then went on to say that was a good idea. They stopped and leaned their backpacks up against some of the mid-size boulders in the opened area. Poppi signaling to Luna not to answer, asked Logan did he have any idea of how to make a shelter from the materials that was around them. Logan looked around and replied that all he had ever made was a hut in his sleeping quarters with furniture and some bed covers. G.V. understood Logan's dilemma, and then made two further comments to him, before he wanted Luna to participate. The first was what he would choose to use in the wilderness for a substitution of the furniture and bedding from his home. The second was if he was camping, or in an emergency situation how fast could he build a shelter for safety? Luna knew how she would answer these questions, but remained silent looking at all the different colors of nature that were native to Earth.

Logan thought for a few minutes looking at the landscape and said he would use larger branches for the shelter and put grass over the top and on the inside. He was smiling expecting approval from G.V. for his decision. G.V. gave an affirmative nod, but nudged him on, how fast could he build this shelter? Logan looked stumped, and didn't know the answer. Poppi looked to Luna and asked her, what she would do. She immediately responded that if she was part of a group, all of them would work on the task together. Some clearing a building space and taking inventory of their supplies of useful items they may need to make the shelter sturdy. Then have some looking for branches, and others gathering grasses. Poppi was proud of her retained knowledge he had shared when they had gone on other outdoor excursions. Logan wasn't upset, but thought, 'How did she know to use more than one person?'

G.V. suggested that they get working, if they wanted to do the shelter first. He said he would look for a spot to safely build their shelter, and that Logan could look for branches and Luna could gather the grasses. At first Logan had a bit of trouble identifying branches that were usable for their shelter, but he soon realized what adjustments in size and length he needed to take. Luna looked in her backpack and found a knife and took it with her up the trail and began cutting the grass stalks and brought back several arm loads of them. Poppi had found a good flat spot without any rocks under it for them to work with to build their hut. He had also pulled out his own knife, and some string. He had looked around and found a weighted stone they could use if they wanted to tie down their structure. Soon Logan was coming up from the river bank with some good choices of branches for their refuge.

With all their materials sorted out on the ground around them, G.V. glanced at everything and inquired about what to do next, looking directly at Logan. He was somewhat surprised that he was asked to guide the next step. Logan went over to the branches and started looking at them, on the river bank he had a plan for each one, now he must remember where he wanted to place each one. It was like putting together a pieced puzzle. Luna went over to the branches and bent down to either pick up or separate one from the set, awaiting Logan's instruction. She smiled sweetly and said that this task would progress much faster if they all worked together on it. Logan agreed and then remembered the branches he brought up for the base of the three walls. They both pulled and pushed the branches into the suggested clearing that G.V. had made. The two worked together using the smaller, lighter wood for the shelter walls. Soon the frame was done, and Luna picked up the picked-up handfuls of grass and started weaving it in between the openings of the wooden walls. Without a word, Logan followed suit. He then suggested that he would work on enclosing the roof, if Luna kept working on the walls. She replied that was a good idea. G.V. stood off to the side and watched how the two were constructing the shelter from their own imagination. He only made a few suggestions, and found that they both either accepted his ideas or dismissed them as they had a better plan. They were quickly to the point of putting the last of the grass into the shelter for mat flooring. G.V. walked over to examine their structure closer as they started giggling as they crawled into the shelter and sat down. G.V. started laughing also, but called them outside to gather their gear, as it had to be stowed in the shelter also. Both Luna and Logan looked surprised as G.V. stooped down attempting to crawl into the shelter with them, with his back pack. All three were nestled in the structure, laughing, and looking at their handy work.

G.V. was pleased with their interaction and independence on the construction project. While seated in the shelter, G.V. asked Logan what he would like to do in the way for the next task of the day. This time Luna remained quiet and looked at Logan wondering what he would suggest. He had a big smile, and inquired if they could go fishing. Only he confessed that he had never fished before. This was right on target, and both Luna and Poppi were happy at the prospect of going fishing. Luna looked at Poppi with the question, 'How are we going to fish? We didn't bring any fishing poles.' Poppi turned to Luna and Logan and said that they were going to make their own fishing poles. They had plenty of wood branches to make poles with, and they had brought string and hooks with them in their back packs. When ready, they could dig in the soil for worms as bait. This was an exciting learning experience for both the children. G.V. gave them some instruction as to what type of stick or branch they must find as the first step towards going fishing. The crawled out of their shelter, and happily went in search of their "poles" on the river shore. G.V. followed them so he could make a pole of his own. Everyone was being treated as an equal today.

They all found adequate sticks to use for fishing poles, and they walked back up to their beginnings of a campsite. G.V. retrieved his back pack, then sat down on the ground and propped himself up against a good-sized boulder. He suggested that the young people do the same in gathering their supplies and then coming close so he could instruct them on how to make a fishing pole. When they had gathered their materials, and found suitable seating, G.V. started a small instruction for them.

'It is of the upmost importance that as humans we learn how to be independent and can quickly learn and adapt to a situation, very important skills. Today we are challenging ourselves with what is called "minimalist survival." We are only doing a few small tasks, and only going to be here for a few hours, but I believe that each of you will learn from this experience about how important it is to work together towards a goal and benefits that are reaped when doing so. I came here as a child with my father for much the same education. We live in a highly interdependent environment on the Outpost, and this fragile... Luna, what's the word?' She quickly responded with 'ecosystem.' Then Poppi continued, 'can strive or be very easily destroyed by the simple inappropriate action of as little as one person.' 'When we learn basic life skills that was used by our ancestors on this planet, we can certainly appreciate the advances we have achieved and are maintaining and developing on the Outpost.' G.V. took a deep breath and looked at the sky. 'Can you imagine how you or a whole colony of people could get to Gliese 581d, when you are sitting here, like you are today, with nothing around you? Well we, our ancestors did it, and they had a whole dynamic global community that was behind the greatest adventure ever, going to a planet in another galaxy and colonizing it.' 'Logan, have you ever gone to the Data Storage and Archival Studies Wing and done any type of investigation as to Earth inhabitants and their daily hardships and struggles for their survival?' the attentive Logan, hanging on every word, now had to respond with 'No' as his answer. 'How would you feel if this was your life? This wasn't an exercise.' G.V. pressed on. He did not start speaking again for a few minutes. Poppi just kept looking at the beauty of where they were today, and letting his commentary and interpretations soak in to both Luna and Logan. He wanted them to start understanding how extraordinary they were. 'I know that Luna has a huge curiosity as to this planet versus the planet we live on, and for years she had gone and researched situations that she did not understand or she would go and hunt out residents that could explain certain activities or regulations to her.' 'This is of critical importance to the survival of Outpost 621, we are on that planet, alone and we have to depend on each other, and support each other at all costs.'

G.V. bent down and picked up his stick and examined it, and was back on track for making a fishing pole. He showed the children how to examine their sticks to see if they could be flexible enough to cast out onto the water, and then have the internal strength in them to pull in a fish, once caught. When the sticks were approved, G.V. told the students to hunt in their back packs for the string, hooks, and knife that should be inside. All three of them pulled out the necessary items. Luna was amazed at this experience. She and Poppi had never done anything like this before. Luna was just as engaged as Logan, in listening and learning what was being taught by instruction and creating today. Their next step was to take the string and learn how to make two different knots to be able to tie the string onto the stick. Logan and Luna quickly mastered the ways to fold and weave the string to make the knots. G.V. then took his own stick and ran his hand up and down the length of the thinner end of the shaft feeling for the place to notch out the locking hold where the string would be attached. He found such a groove just behind where another branch once had started to grow out of this stick. He demonstrated this to both the astute children, and requested they find such a place on each of their sticks. Without too many mistakes, both Logan and Luna had located the special needed spot on the sticks for creating their fishing poles. G.V. then showed them how to notch out a small groove for the string to be attached in as he worked on his own pole. Just a tiny wedge cut out. Once they observed this next step, they both carefully and quickly cut the needed notches. G.V. picked up his string and reported they needed approximately 1 3/4 meters of string for their line. He took his string and held one end in his fingers of his left hand and kept spreading his arms apart, unfolding the string as the sting lengthened. When his hands were extended as far as possible, he held the string tightly between two fingers of his right hand and proceeded to cut the appropriate length for his fishing pole. Logan and Luna marveled at this unique trick, and immediately imitated G.V.'s measurement technique. When each of them had a length of string, Poppi leaned in over his stick that was resting across his legs, and took one end of the string and held it close to the notched spot on the pole. He stopped, and his students mimicked his actions without question. G.V. then said, 'This is the important part of inventing your fishing pole. You must make sure you use a small amount of string, but the knot you make has to be very strong and tight.' And with that said Poppi went about attaching his own sting to the pole. G.V. locked his string into place, giving the string a couple of tugs to test the knot and position of the string. Luna and Logan were experiencing more difficulties at this task. G.V. gently said to them to relax and think about what they wanted to accomplish. They hadn't realized they were working so fast that they were unable to achieve the required outcome because it took fine, delicate, deliberate movements to achieve the required fitting. Once they each started working with the string again, they had a lighter, calmed intention, and they both soon had the strings properly attached to their poles. The children both watched closely at G.V.'s next movements for making a fishing pole. In one hand he held the stick with the string attached, close to the middle of it, and with the other he held the other hand he walked his fingers up to the tip of the thin end of the pole, and held it there, freeing one of his hands. Logan and Luna both began this same process and awaited the next direction when they had each reached the tip of their poles. G.V. lowered his voice at this time, as if he thought the fish could hear him. The students leaned in to make sure they hear and carried out the instructions to be given at this point were clear and understood. G.V. took the string and used the second knot to secure it at the end of the pole. Tying a knot in the middle of the string and at the end of the pole was indeed tricky, so G. V. demonstrated tying the knot at the appointed place on the string where it could be slipped over the tip and pulled tightly. Logan and Luna managed this task with a little bit of inaccuracy that they quickly corrected. They each held their fishing poles up for examination to G.V. at the same time. Both started laughing. Poppi was very happy with their focused interest in the day's activities.

G.V. looked at them and calmly said, 'I want you to lightly wrap the rest of the string around the pole and we will complete the fishing pole and go fishing when we come back from our break. Our time for this session is just about over. Both of the youngsters followed his example with wrapping the string. All three of them leaned their proud possessions they had created on a larger boulder at the side of the path.

They gather up their supplies and returned them to their back packs, and they started down the path that had brought them to this place. The only walked a few meters when off to the right, G.V. noticed the chamber door had appeared for them to exit through. Luna and Logan followed. Poppi put down his accessories and clothing that he acquired for the venture. Luna, dropping the back pack and shedding her vest, told Logan that all Holographic property must stay on premises. So, Logan, not understanding the procedure did as he was instructed. He replaced his clothing with his school uniform and took off the boots and put his sandals back on. G.V. assured both children that they would be returning to this event in a short time, after they had a noon meal and some refreshments.

When the next doors opened Katavon went quickly ahead to reset the adventure and put the program into the 'save mode.' He needed to follow the directions Ms. Emagine had informed him of, to allow so them to continue where they had stopped. When this was accomplished, he turned back to his protégés and asked if they would like to go to the Concourse Salon for their meal and refreshments. They both gleefully said yes. They were exuberant with their experiences so far today, but realized they were hungry, so the eatery sounded wonderful to them. Luna took to heart that this was part of their whole plan for the day, that they stay together, and Logan's thought was he didn't have to go home and then return. Upon entering the café, they found a table and Katavon told both of them to order whatever they would like for their midday meal.

When their food arrived, Luna and Poppi had decided on salads with nuts and fresh fruit slices mixed in, flat bread, and sparkling water for a beverage. Logan on the other hand had ordered 3 poached eggs, manna, a variety plate of dried fruits, a small salad of greens and tomatoes, and a large fruit shake. Everyone ate with relish. Both Poppi and Luna noticed the caloric intake and how much food Logan had ordered for his mid-day meal. Poppi noted maybe he was a growing boy, or maybe it was something else.

Katavon wanted to keep the conversation light and unstructured for their break, but wanted to ask Logan some questions about his day so far. He ventured by opening with a simple question, 'What do you two think of our adventure so far today?' Poppi looked directly at Logan, eating with enthusiastic relish. Luna knew to wait before answering Poppi about their adventure. Logan looked up at G.V. over a forkful of salad he was about to put in his mouth. Luna and Poppi continued munching their salads while awaiting his answer. He finished the mouthful of food he had stuffed in and gulping it down to clear his mouth so he could answer the question. 'I've never experienced anything like it before!' Logan replied. 'I have never had use of the Holographic Pods to go to earth! Is all of Earth this beautiful and dynamic?' G.V. answered that this was only one small adventure of the magnificence of Earth. Luna couldn't stay quiet any longer. She started enthusiastically voicing her discoveries. 'I have gone on adventures to our home planet many times for years. 'My father' nodding towards Poppi, 'taught me how to use the Activity Pods; and Earth is such a wonderful place to visit.' 'Poppi today is amazing! We have never been on an outing like today. I am learning so much, and seeing a different part of the Earth's Wilderness than where we have visited before. I'm seeing different animals and Logan and I built lodging for us! Logan, that was so helpful you already had the basic idea of how to build our shelter.' Logan was blushing at Luna's comment, but he then became engaged in their conversation about today's activities. 'I've never seen wild forest animals before, only pictures from the Data Archives. I can't wait to catch a fish! We are still going to go fishing, aren't we?' Logan asked questioning G.V. Katavon smiled and said yes they were going to finish their project of making their poles and getting bait and going to hopefully catch some fish on this adventure. He added that they still needed to build a campfire so they could enjoy the warmth and peace the setting would give them, as well as being able to cook their fish.

All three of them were about finished with their meals, and G.V. asked them were they ready for the next part of their expedition. Logan was getting excited and was totally embracing this adventure. Both of the children with a resounding yes! So, they gathered up their belongings and headed back to the Holographic Pods.

Katavon went over to the panels to reset their program for entry, and at the same time reminded the young adventurers they only had two more hours allotted in the Pod setting. This time the youngsters knew what to expect, and were dashing ahead of G.V. as if their speed would somehow extend the two hours. They all quickly entered through the chambers, stopping to don their appropriate attire, and gather their needed gear to return to their camp. When they stepped through the last door, and it slid closed they were on the sandy path, only about one hundred feet from their fishing shelter. Logan and Luna raced ahead to pick up their fishing poles and then they edged close to the water's edge looking to see if there were any visible fish.

G.V. laughed and called them back and said they still had work to do. Luna knew there was a lot she didn't know about the environment she was in, so turned to go back and get instructions from Poppi. Logan was inundating himself with this special expedition and was now holding on to every bit of the adventure. He looked up at G.V., but did not return to their guide at first request. G.V. was happy to see Logan investigating and actually being inquisitive about their surroundings. G.V. opted to pick up his own fishing pole and back pack and start with further instruction on attaching the needed hook on the line to catch the fish. When Logan realized he wasn't included, he scurried up the bank to grab his backpack and start rummaging around inside of it for the necessary hooks. Luna was quietly sitting by her father mimicking his every action, because this was a new way for her to go fishing. G.V.'s students were quick and astute. All three of them expeditiously had their poles ready for fishing. G.V. deliberately held his pole up in the air so the string wasn't reaching the ground. 'Now we have two tasks to do. We need to start making our campfire and we need bait to fish with.' 'Luna which one would you start with?' Poppi asked her. She thought for a moment, and replied to Poppi, 'If we catch some fish, we will need a cooking fire that is already hot and ready to use. If we catch fish first, it will take time for the fire to get built up and hot enough to cook with.' G.V. Nodded in approval. Logan's eyes popped open wider, 'Gee, I didn't know that. I would have thought we should catch the fish first.'

G.V. propositioned that he wanted Logan and Luna to work together on both of the upcoming tasks. Building a fire pit for their site, as well as digging in the earth for worms was a new experience for both of them. Luna's partner for all of these excursions had always been Poppi. Today he was broadenings her experience by having Logan as her partner today. Today was definitely turning into a win-win program, Poppi thought. 'Let's start with building a fire pit. Do either of you have any ideas of how to do this?' G.V. asked sincerely. Both of them shook their heads from side to side, answering 'No.' G.V. took a small stick and made a diagram in the sand of what they basically were going to construct, and what it would look like when finished. He went on to inquire of both of them the reasoning behind the structure they were making. Since Logan did not have any outdoor experience on Earth, he looked to Luna for a possible explanation. G.V. was closely watching their interaction. Luna looked at the diagram, and thought about fishing, and about safety. She had examined data that was stored in the Data Archives about disasters on Earth hundreds of years ago. She thought about different outcomes and suggested to Poppi that the stones arranged around the actual place of burning wood was a safety precaution for the humans as well as to contain and control the burning fire. G.V. nodded in agreement, and inquired further, 'how about the preparation of the ground beneath the fire?' Luna was attempting to figure out what Poppi was eluding to. Logan at this point reverted to being agitated and impatient…why was this important? he pouted, but didn't offer any suggestion because he didn't have any idea of why it was important.

G.V. took his stick and cleared a circular area of about a meter across, and leveled out the inside of the area, picking up any sizable stone and removing them from the area. "This is our base, and we have created a safe place to start construction.

Now we need smaller stones to construct a circle that will be our fire wall.' G.V. drew a circle of approximate size in the middle of his cleared area. 'Can you both find stones for our fire pit?' Luna was already heading down towards the river's edge to look for stones, and this request got Logan's interest sparked again, so he followed Luna. They picked up some stones, evaluating them, and had some discussion between them, and brought back as many stones as they could carry. G.V. showed them how to place a few of the stones, starting the circle. They realized they were going to have to make a couple more trips to the water's edge to get enough stones to complete the circle. When that was completed, G.V. told them they were almost finished, but they needed dry wood to put in place to start the fire. Logan caught on this request immediately, and went back down the bank to start picking up sticks that were smaller and away from the water's edge, so they would be dry. He picked up as many as he could carry and brought them up to the fire pit. Luna stood watching as G.V. kneeled down beside the circular area and started placing the sticks in a lean-to order. Logan followed G.V.'s actions with the other random sticks he had brought up to their camp site. G.V. then asked did they feel that was enough kindling and firewood to sustain their campfire, especially if they were going to cook some fish. Logan had no idea, and Luna was unsure, as she had never done this before, but G.V. responded immediately that they were going to need more wood, and asked Luna to go get another armful. She was learning. She happily did as Poppi requested of her. G.V. turned to Logan and said it was time to dig for worms to go fishing with. He broke out in a big smile as Luna came back up the bank with another armload of dry sticks.

G.V. dug around in his backpack and found some matches. When he pulled out the small packet, both Luna and Logan stared at the item. They had never seen anything like that before. G.V. started handling the small pieces of paper with the phosphorous tip with ease, explaining how they worked. He stood up and picked up a few dead, dried leaves and stuck them into the bottom of their arrangement of tee-pee stacked sticks. G.V. went on to teach the young ones about the invention of matches and how they had been so important through history on earth. He adeptly struck one against the flint scrap that was supplied and he instantly had flame. As he placed it under the tee-pee of sticks, igniting the leaves, the twigs began to burn, giving off a good bit of smoke at first, subsequently settling down into actual flames coming from the wood. Logan and Luna had never seen anything like this at all. Both were staring and smiling at this wondrous magic. The wood they had chosen was solid and burned readily. G.V. said, 'Now on to the worms for fishing.'

G.V. took another stick and took a few steps across the path into the grasses. He bent down and started poking into the dirt digging a small hole. Luna and Logan followed, and G.V. laughingly told them if they wanted to catch fish, they needed to dig for the worms like he was. They each went back and found small sticks and came back to the grassy area and started poking around for worms. G.V. went back to his backpack and got a container to put some worms in. The one that G.V. had dug up had slithered away while he was retrieving his container. And now both Logan and Luna had found worms. G.V. told them to handle them gently, but both of them were making faces and almost gagging over handling the worms. They both deposited their worms in the container for safe keeping. G.V. dug around and found himself another worm. He declared that that was enough for them to start fishing with.

They all walked back over to the campsite and Poppi poked at the fire they had built, to make sure it would keep burning while they were fishing. Each of them picked up their poles and headed down the bank to the river. G.V. took his pole and stretched out the string, and as an instruction, cast his line out into the water, just to show both the youngsters how to cast a fishing line, in a very old-fashioned way, on Earth. He repeated the gesture, and asked did they grasp what was needed to be done to get the line as far out in the stream as possible. They excitedly replied 'yes.' Now to add in the worms. G.V. nimbly mounted his worm on the hook, it was gooey and messy, but this was fishing. Logan almost backed out; he wanted no part of this after all. But he thought better than to not participate. He knew he was committed for the day, but at the moment, he wasn't happy. Luna didn't like the stabbing of the worms and placing them on a hook either, but this was a different kind of fishing than she usually did with Poppi, so she accepted the challenge.

G.V. instructed them to go to the water's edge and find a good stable place to stand, and cast out their string into the water, and hope for the best. After each of them had cast out their lines, they watched and waited. Luna knew to be quiet, but Logan wanted to talk all of a sudden.

G.V. advised him they would have better luck with the fish, if they remained quiet and calm. From the shore they could see a few fish leaping from the water in hopes of catching a tasty fly or bug that was dancing around above the water. When Logan saw the fish, he exclaimed 'Why won't they bite at my worm, he's moving around!' G.V. chuckled and replied 'No one could ever figure out the logic of what interests a fish.' They all had nibbles on their lines, which excited the youngsters, but they were not so lucky at hooking them, and bringing them to shore. G.V. finally was able to snag a medium sized fish, and gently pulled him to shore. Raising it up out of the water truly amazed Logan. 'Now, what shall we do with it?' G.V. asked Luna and Logan at the same time. Luna said 'Poppi, we always do catch and release.' Logan inquired what did that mean. G.V. explained that unless you intended to use any living thing, you did not destroy it. It was perfection, and you leave it for others to enjoy. Logan thought they were going to fish for a long time, but G.V. reminded them that their time in the Pod was coming to a close. He suggested that they go up to the campfire and just talk for a while before they returned home. Logan and Luna conceded that G.V. was right, and they could inquire and discuss their activities today.

Walking back up the bank, Luna grabbed Poppi's hand and said she was having a wonderful time. Logan looked on at this interaction, it seemed strange to him. Did girls just do this? G.V. told them both that the hooks had to be removed and the string taken off the stick and returned to the backpack. All of them stowed the items. Then G.V. sat on the ground and leaned back against a larger rock at the edge of the campsite. Luna and Logan found rocks and sat down also.

G.V. stared into the comfortable fire, flickering and dancing. He opted to put a few more small sticks on it so the blaze would hold true. He now was relaxed and acted as a sage wise man wanting to extract the deepest feelings from his charges. He looked and gently leaned over toward Logan, and asked 'how do you feel about you experience today?' Logan had many emotions running through him about the day. 'Sir, I'm happy to be able to join you and Luna.' 'I have never had use of the Holographic Pods before, and come to earth.' 'Everything is so fresh and alive; I don't want to leave.' G.V. inquired further, 'Have you learned anything today that helps you understand our lives on our planet where we now live?' Logan staring at the bouncing flames from the fire, thought for a few minutes, searching the day's events. He really didn't understand what the question was about. He was having fun, and this was a Hologram Adventure. Home was a limited environment, but there were all kinds of activities and opportunities for study and growth. Logan sighed in defeat as he could not answer the inquiry that G.V. had requested of him. He really did not understand the correlation. 'Sir, I have experienced many new things that I have only read articles about in the Data Archives. I have seen animals that we have no contact with at all currently. I have thought through and learned about safety in walking into the unknown, our trip up this path' he said pointing back to the natural sandy path they traversed to get to this spot. 'With your guidance and suggestion, I have learned how to build a shelter, make a fishing pole and have gone fishing for the first time. We are now sitting at our last task of building a fire, which is beautiful and magical.' Logan took a deep breath before surrendering he didn't understand the connection between the two places. It was foremost in his mind today, that this was his punishment for his part in the egregious scheme against Luna. He was having fun and learning; this activity today did not seem a penalty at all to him. They had left Luna alone, abandoned, and scared, yet she had come back with this wonderful experience for him. He was quite perplexed.

G.V. turned his line of sight from the flames to Logan, accepting his answer with graciousness. He nodded he understood, then slowly turned back to the wisdom of the flames. When Poppi was ready, he freed his thoughts, and turned to his daughter and asked her 'How do you feel about you experience today?' He returned again to the mystic wisdom of the flames to be able to hear and digest Luna's keen insight that she was going to give Logan, as well as himself; a lesson to think about and digest.

Luna was bursting with energy from her experiences today; the captivating flames stirred her heart and soul. Usually she saved her accounts of her encounters and learning until the evening meal, but Poppi was asking for her commentary here and now. She understood her obligation to bring this exploit to a close. She was transfixed as well as energized by the flames of the fire as well as the vast wilderness they were sitting in.

Luna felt as if she was in two different dimensions. She started, 'Poppi this was to be an outing that we usually take as a family. Sharing, learning, and experiencing something that our ancestors left behind in hopes that we could establish and create a new safer, more loving hospitable place for humans as well as any other space travelers we may encounter. Our ancestor's long history did live here in this place, on Earth, having to do tasks as we have done today. Fashion a home out of whatever was available. Be able to survive and live in harmony with wild life, use but do not abuse nature. They had to be creative and learn how to thrive with whatever was available. You were able to catch a fish today, but it was pointed out that we don't take or harm what we don't need. The two things that were magical out in this extreme wilderness climate were the hooks for fishing, and the matches that were provided. Both were invented many decades later in history.' Luna knew where she was going, so she continued, 'Poppi with your gentle guidance we took on our adventure as if this was our reality, and that it was going to be ongoing, not just a Holographic amusement. I noted that Logan quickly adjusted himself to this situation and was actively participating with us. Logan and I were put together today with basic survival tasks. You supplied aid to us, I was aware, because of time constraints. Logan and I, as the upcoming generation of our Outpost, are currently, almost opposing forces. But today we had to work together, side by side learning and creating the environment of safety and survival for all of us. I am so pleased, and am sure both Logan as well as myself shared life learning information, as well as collaborative time saving, effective strategies for task completion.' Logan was gazing into the fire, listening to Luna and was stunned by her insight and evaluation of today's endeavors. He turned from the fire to watch her more intently. What was she going to share next?

'Our ancient ancestors had to come together and live this way for the Earth's population and peoples to survive. Something went wrong in that there was constantly fighting and bloodshed over who had acquired more supplies or any assets available. As the centuries passed, it became evident of the divide and ill will that was developing across planet Earth. Some factions of philanthropists attempted to help restore balance and mutual support among all the earth's population. It wasn't enough. By this time there were many inventions and avenues of human improvement available. Humans were still imagining and creating.' Luna looked to the sky where all the millions of stars would shine through at night. 'Space travel sparked; and the humans wanted to get closer to the stars and galaxies they have only viewed and marveled at for thousands of years. They wanted to know how we related to these marvels of light pulling us to them.' Luna lowered her head, and quietly continued. 'Things were not looking good for plant Earth. If it was a galactic experiment, it seemed to be going dramatically awry.' She paused, adding 'All of this information I have studied and reviewed in the Data Archives Center.'

'Then the Commission was formed of outstanding progressive people from all the countries of Earth and they decided to formulate and set into motion colonization on another planet. They were careful, and examined each aspect of the voyage and colonization they wanted to establish. It was 20 years in creation and planning. They had to go into history annals to decide where life interests advanced and where things went astray. The Mission Statement was established.' Luna went silent for a few moments to reflect what she was saying? Was it important? Did it matter to Logan? Was Poppi bored with her babblings? She just peered into the flames. To her they were peaceful knowledge.

Poppi smiled at his daughter, and asked her to continue. 'Why was this relevant to today's activities?' Logan was totally fascinated and lost in Luna's narrative of human life from where he was sitting right now to where we were heading, to our new planetary home. Luna's face lit up, and she was happy to continue, but her demeanor went deadly serious 'The Mission Statement was strategically planned and sent forth as a blueprint for a new successful colony on another planet, showcasing humanity at its best. Its credo is Prosperity: There is always enough. It is a sealed covenant of a contract of Love. The guiding premise is it is a second chance at humanity.' The Outpost's Statement is a commitment to the discipline of always holding to one's own self- correcting, and for there to be the highest good in learning, creativity, love, and intention. Create, support, and motivate all others to their highest good and creativity. Never impede or challenge new ideas. Never do intentional harm to a fellow human or resources that are necessary for survival. There is Enough Love for All. Let us use this and move forward. If there needs to be an explanation, let it be oriented in a positive learning platform. We do NOT want to move into FEAR or negativity. All of us must learn from our mistakes.' She went into further detail,' 'We may need to be reminded by continual review of the Original Statement to gain clarity for us to remain true to our responsibilities, and highlight our commitment to this Outpost- that our ancestors recognized that is we are the 2nd Chance at Humanity' 'Our Credo: Prosperity- there is always enough, a Contract of Love.' 'We live by the ideology: Motivate, Support, Highest Good in learning, Watch over, Protect, and Shelter. We work within our credo these are the three constants in Life: Change, Choice, and Principles, and to what do we want to aspire.' With that, she lowered her head in humble reverence to what she has witnessed and what she proud to be a part of with the new Outpost's Mission.

'Poppi, I think that today was an example of how wonderfully unique and talented humans are and what we can achieve when we set out minds on doing something positive.' Her bubbly spirit was returning and she was lighthearted again. 'I think our visit today strengthens me in my commitment to my family, our leaders, and to our Mission Statement.' Luna swung around with an intent point focus on Logan, she asked 'What do you think Logan?' G.V. did not have a chance to refresh his intentional question to Logan. Luna was already on him. Today had to be a success. Logan was following what was being expounded upon and replied to both G.V. and Luna.

'I am grateful for this amazing endeavor that I was invited to today. My life will never be the same. I have a lot to process within myself and my intentions, but I know all of it will be for the Love, Growth and Support of our Outpost. I realize how fragile our small Outpost is in the Universe now, and how blessed and special we are. I will work with Luna and any of the Committee for realigning and recommitment to the truths of our Mission Statement so we can continue on and thrive. We do not want to be an experiment gone wrong again.'

All three of them knew it was time to leave, and they stood up quietly. For some deep reason in their hearts, they each reached down and took a handful of dirt and pitched it into the fire, as if sealing their lifelong promises.

They walked about fifty feet up the path and the chamber door was opening for their retreat. Still silent, they each reflected what a wondrous day it was.

After exiting the Activity Pod Center, when they were parting, G.V. asked Logan 'How do you feel about going to the Data Archives to learn more about the planet Earth and our ancestors. They were once where we visited today, and as much as that place has great beauty, it also holds great dangers and isolation. Survival was of the upmost importance. Each of the ancestors that lived grouped together so they could share and thrive. Protecting and dividing the workloads and foods. Without them, we wouldn't be here. I'm sure you can get guidance or any assistance you need for your inquiries from some of the second or third generation residents or from Dr. Otago and Dr. Sohan. It was a pleasure to have you join us today Logan. With that, they all turned and headed to their prospective quarters.

Luna was so happy she couldn't help but pull on Poppi's arm, and when he responded, she jumped up and put her arms around his neck tightly to be carried home.

COOKING WITH MUM

Heading home from classes, Luna was wondering what snacks were going to be today. She felt famished! Mum always fixed tasty treats for afternoon snacks. The idea of spending time with Mum and possibly Poppi made her little feet move a bit quicker towards their living quarters, and it wasn't even supper meal time yet. For her that meant pretty much any topic could be talked about. Luna loved talking with both Mum and Poppi. They were so intelligent! What may start out as a general question or comment about the day, usually sent Luna on an educational expedition. She wasn't inquisitive enough to ask if this learning game was shared by her classmates with their parents. So, she made the most of what she had available to her. She was proud of her family and how they interacted. She did not want to create any ill will or 'sense of lacking' if she happened to ask an innocent question to the 'wrong' person. Learning something new each day was so delightful and freeing; she did have a deep wish that all of her classmates had this opportunity. She sometimes wondered though, with the way they responded to life and circumstances around them.

Luna went through the front door and headed straight to the food preparation area to seek out Mum. She looked at ease, with a teal cotton shirt and cut off shorts on, toiling at the counter slicing up some fruit. Cheese had already been put on a small plate, and some sparkling water was awaiting them at the table. Luna peeked up over the counter tops to see what else Mum was preparing for the meal later this evening.

She looked up with her big blue eyes to face Mum and asked was Poppi home yet? 'No, he won't be home for a while, closer to the evening meal time. Why don't you go change from your school dress to your comfy house clothes and slippers? Moppet can even come have snacks with us.' Luna then giggled that Mum recognized Moppet as a member of the family and danced in a circle heading towards her room to do as Mum requested. Returning to the dining table, with her silver slippers in one hand and Moppet in the other, adorned in her lavender caftan with silver trimmings at the neck, sleeves and waist, Luna felt majestic.

Mum turned around to set the food on the table for them and smiled at Luna's creativity. Mum joking said to 'Luna how can I put you to work in the kitchen when you are so elegant?' Luna's eyes popped open in surprise at Mum's comment to her. 'Mum…really? Can I help?' 'Well I was thinking about you assisting me earlier today, but I think in my current presence of Royalty, I will tell you a story instead. Would that be Ok with you my Blossom?' Of course! Luna virtually inhaled every fragment of a narrative that Mum or Poppi shared with her. It came to both parents attention several years ago that they could no longer tell their little girl a bedtime story. The realization they had was Luna became more fully alert and wanted to hear more, instead of relaxing into a soft slumber. Luna's parents moved time for edifying stories to casual lounge time or the evening meals. The stories were of the Blue Planet's history, the travel to the outpost where they all lived now or maybe an account to make Luna laugh about her parents and their lives, but she would still go seek information verification. That's what made it all fun.

Mum took a sip of her water, 'and said I think we should start at the beginning.' Luna had no idea what type of story Mum was going to tell her today. Had to do with food, Luna understood...and in association with survival. Luna put her snacks on her plate and offered some to Moppet. Mum chuckled at her antics.

Mum, still holding her tumbler of water, spun it in her fingers and said I think we should start here. 'My mom, was taught about how precious water was from her grandmother who actually saw free flowing waterfalls, rivers, brooks and more when she was a child on Earth. 'Earth' is called the Blue planet because of water. If humans don't have water, we can't exist. The main chemicals that are necessary for air and water are on this planet, and that is why Gliese 581d was chosen for our galactic voyage. You will learn more about chemical elements in the next few years. Right now, I want you to experience water. 'Where is your tablet? Would you please go get it? I want to show you water... that was on earth.' Luna hopped down from the chair and ran to her room to get her tablet. She was back as quick as a flash. 'I'm going to show you natural flowing water from three different places, and then I want you to go to the PBS Research Pods later and see each of these in 3 dimensions was Mum's directions. She helped Luna look up each set of falls since the word spelling was so unique to each place.

Victoria Falls in Zimbabwe, Africa

Angel Falls in Venezuela, South America

Niagara Falls in New York, USA & Ontario Canada

Luna quickly sourced the pictures of this magnificent water. It sure looked different than the water sources we have here at the Outpost.

Mum spoke lovingly about how this was very special water as it was moving, had energy and life in it. 'The water on earth actually carried an element in it, such as we have here with the water we drink and use on the Outpost that makes it very healthy. We make our own composition of water. H_2O + CO_2 = H_2CO_3. It keeps our bodies healthy by allowing more oxygen into our lungs. Humans age because they do not have enough oxygen in the cells of their bodies. OK, enough Bio-Chemistry and Geography for today.' 'Your great, great grandmother knew this secret, and knew we would survive if we used the basics that we learn from the past.'

'Now on to our food stuffs. There are different levels of information you will need to know about the foods we eat that is critical for survival.' There is education you must have for a healthy diet that fall into six categories. This is pretty much the end product- planning and eating meals. If you get out of balance with any of these six groups by eating too little or too much, your body will become diseased. Simply put: dis- ease. 'Body is ill at ease.' Not happy.

Luna was listening intently. Mum went on to explain that the six food groupings were: Proteins, Vegetables, Grains, Fruits, Dairy, and Oils or Fats. 'Mum stated that we could work together on making balanced meals for each day, a little later. It's like a mathematical equation. It wasn't hard, just needed some practice.' Mum suggested for Luna to just take notice of what foods and what food group she thought she was eating at each meal or snack, for the time being. Luna readily agreed that should be easy.

Mum went on to illuminate how hard it was for there to be the necessary foods that needed to be grown and stored for travel, as well as once the Outpost was established.

Great-grandmother had shared this knowledge with her daughter. This was much harder than the Commission at first thought it was going to be. The engineers had to invent and build imitation gardens and crop fields in zero-gravity. The hydroponics gardens were not sufficient to supply enough nutritional food for the population of the voyage. This worked on earth, but soon the systems started to fail once they were in flight. There had to be a new committee pulled together quickly to correct for the non-gravitational atmosphere they were in, and what basically they were going to need once they got to Gliese 581d. The Food Storage Monitors and the Cooks had to work hard to use available foodstuffs to keep the travelers healthy and well fed, and at the same time relay their needs to the new committee as to nutritional foods that were necessary currently and for the new planet habitation.

'Luna, have you been out to the gardens and observed the goats and chickens we have?' Mum asked with sincerity. 'Your great- grandmother used to start laughing the way her mother said the voyagers had to think and come up with a way that these poor little animals could survive and be happy on this flight.' 'Only it wasn't funny then. Can you imagine a goat or chickens floating around in what was supposed to be their secure, grounded, safe quarters?' 'This was a mandatory part of the voyagers' survival, and everyone on board the vessels became involved in how to normalize the living situation for the farm animals.' 'The Committee had put years of research and testing into what animals should come to the new planet so humans could be provided with healthy sources of proteins that we need. The best choices were the goats and chickens.' 'With extreme efforts and modifications, we now have goats and chickens that survived space travel.' 'They have been here on the outpost with us for the duration, and now seem happy and settled. We have fresh eggs and milk for cheese and yogurt.'

Mum went on. 'Once the volunteer voyagers arrived here, at their destination, they had to again create a plan for the food stuffs growth and storage- to prevent spoilage. Everyone needed to be fed. The Cooks hopefully wanted all the residents to have their choice and variety of edibles, allowing them their autonomy, and to maintain optimum health. It was quickly realized that at first communal dining was the best choice since time, equipment, personal and available space for moving around was minimal. Everyone had tasks to work and strategize on. How was the Outpost to be built? All prototypes worked great on Earth, but manufacturing materials issues came up as they progressed. New Computer systems needed to be assembled and put online as quickly as possible. The residents needed A.I. robots activated to spend time outside their vessels to move materials around and do construction. Each specialty crew had their assigned projects and objectives. It is amazing how far we have come on this Outpost in the time we have been here.

'My Great-grandmother worked with the Cooks and the Life Subsistence groups to establish growing new food sources meaning the gardens and crops, they also invented ways to preserve edible foods. Their group needed to find water or the chemicals to make water and then take on the task to design purification and stabilizing systems for the Outpost to have plenty of water to drink and use. But... my dear Luna, water was precious. It could not be wasted at all; which meant it had to be saved and recycled for the crops, cleaning, or other chores. The volunteers came to this planet with the clear intention that they wanted to use "Non-Disturbance Practices" to be an example of how humanity had evolved and moved past the carelessness that was evident by the way things had gone awry on earth in centuries past.'

Mum looked up at the dining area time piece and said that they needed to go finish the evening meal preparations. Luna felt disappointed because it felt like Mum was half way through the adventure of food and water on the Outpost. Mum picked up Luna and they headed off to the quarters food processing area. 'We'll continue this food adventure tomorrow, but you can help me this evening, if you want to?' 'Sure Mum! What can I do first?' showing her usual enthusiasm. 'Well how about we learn the proper use and utensils we have in the food area?' Luna felt frustrated again. She wanted to know everything! Mum walked over to the cold storage unit, placed her hand on the door an asked Luna 'Do you know what this is and how it works?' Luna looked surprised at Mum's question, but answered her brightly-'This is the cold storage unit for quarters. This is where we keep food that needs to be cold or frozen; this size unit is for family quarters and stores foods for 3 to five days.' 'There are much larger units in the Life Subsistence Area and the Nutritional Supply Distribution Center' 'Great! This evening we are going to have a salad with yogurt dressing and crackers with Sparkling water.' 'That's what I planned for the evening meal. Would you like to come over here and help me get the items we need to make the salad and dressing?" Luna was beginning to feel better now that she was actually invited to help fix the meal. Mum opened the door and Luna peered inside. 'What would you like in your salad tonight?' 'Go ahead and get some things out and put them on the counter. You need a mixture of vegetables, protein and fruits. Color, shape and sizes of pieces are important.' Luna froze, what did she need to get from the cold storage? Then she took another look and picked out some lettuce, tomatoes, acorn squash, corn niblets, a bowl with broccoli in it, and a dish with some fresh boiled eggs. She grabbed two apples for dessert. Mum asked her what she wanted to make the dressing with. Luna got out the bowl of yogurt, and knew the salt, pepper, dill and garlic was sitting on the counter to be added in. Mum smiled. 'Very good planning, Blossom.' Mum went to a drawer that held cutlery, and took out two knives, one a bit larger than the other. With one knife in each hand Mum told Luna that every piece of cutlery had its own purpose to get the food preparation done quickly, safely and efficiently. Mum got three plates down from the shelf. She then asked Luna to set the table with the other dinnerware they would need, as at this point the evening meal was running late.

Poppi was just coming in the front door as Luna finished setting the table. Luna beamed up at her dad. 'Poppi, Mum is teaching me to prepare food.' 'Well that's wonderful, maybe then I won't be hungry all the time' Poppi replied.

'Blossom,' Mum asked, 'will you get some crackers of your choice and put them on the saucer with the apples, and put the plate on the table, then we should be ready to eat.' Luna turned to Poppi and said 'You and Moppet need to wash up for the evening meal, I will come help you.' They came back and started eating their food. Mum and Poppi were chatting about something, but this time Luna was thinking about the foods she was eating and what Mum was teaching her.

After their meal, Luna hopped down from the table with Moppet and started off for her room. Mum stopped her with temperate words; 'You're not finished with today's food lesson.' Luna turned around and wondered what Mum was referring to. What had she missed? Mum calmly said that the table needed to be cleared, and the dishes needed to washed, and the table wiped clean. Luna returned to the table and gathered the dishes, stacked them and put them in the basin. She picked up the cloth for cleaning and returned to the table and wiped it clean, then went back to the counter and cleaned it. By the time she had rinsed the cloth, Mum was beside the machine that cleaned the dishes. She placed her hand on the front of the domestic device and asked Luna her next question about the food preparation area. 'Luna, what is this piece of equipment and what is it used for? Luna looked at Mum and Poppi and replied that 'it was identified as a dishwasher and used to clean and sanitize the dishware and cooking utensils. It was a robotic machine that would minimize time spent in the food preparation area, aiding the residents of the quarters by cycling and cleaning the cookware once or twice a day as the residents needs required. You only had to push this button, to which Luna pointed to a blue button on the top left of the dishwasher to activate.' 'Very good Blossom. You are a dedicated student and observer.' We will continue with meal planning and food preparations tomorrow. Now off to bed with you and Moppet!' Luna came around and gave Mum a big hug and kiss and told her thank you for all she was teaching her and for their evening meal. It was wonderful! She picked up her tablet and Moppet. She skipped a few steps over to Poppi and gave him his hug and kiss also. She started off down the hall to her room and was thinking, what was so special about THIS evening meal? She smiled because the answer was that she had actually helped Mum prepare the food. In addition, every time Mum asked her a question, she had a correct answer ready for her.

Changing into her sleeping pajamas, Luna commented 'Moppet, time for bed and some sleep. Wonder what we will do tomorrow?' It didn't take long for her sleepy eyes to close and slumber to come soothingly over this busy little girl.

Next morning Luna woke as the lighting was triggered into 'dawn' mode. She was rested and continued her morning grooming with a shower, cleaning her teeth, dressing for classes and then she heads to the dining table for her morning meal. Mum had prepared a bowl of oatmeal, mixed berries, and nuts. On the side were a shaker of cinnamon and a small pitcher of milk with an empty tumbler beside of it. That way Luna could finish her cereal the way she liked it. She ate with relish, as if she never had had food before, yet it was the same food she had always ate. Luna was once again learning and appreciating her existence. Everyone had worked so hard to create all the amazing things in her life that she had taken for granted most every day... up to now. She and the Outpost were blessed. Mum and Poppi made sure she knew these things by many small ideas or details they took time to explain to her. Mum peeped around the corner and asked if Luna would meet her at the Gardens and Nursery wing after classes. They would continue their Provisions discussion there. Luna agreed and headed off to class for the day with her mid-day meal and snacks with her. Luna thought 'provisions' was a strange word to use, but was sure Mum would explain to her later that day. The other idea that popped in her thoughts as she neared her education area was- Mum was spending all this time with just her. Mum was not requesting or mandating her to go to the courses and lessons she taught to the group of other non- classified young residents. Wow!

Lux decided that if she were going to spend the afternoon with her daughter and educate her about how the Outpost grew, processed and handled food for all the residents, she had better prepare their evening meal, so it would be ready when the whole family returned home late this afternoon. She had decided on Spaghetti Squash with almonds mixed in, topped with Pesto Sauce; sliced small Tomatoes with Garlic oil, and Peach Sherbet. It would take a few hours to prepare this meal the way her family liked it, so she set about her tasks. Lux even set the evening dinner table so everything would be ready, and all she (*and Luna*, Mum thought) would have to do is warm the food.

Lux finished her work in the food preparation area and went on to review what food stuffs she would need for the next few days. She took out her food planner and assessed what she had on hand, and what she needed fresh. It always made her happy that she could share her knowledge with other families, assist them if they didn't understand how food stuffs were accounted for and distributed on the Outpost and how to be creative in times when it was between crops or a crop didn't produce as well as hoped. By the time she completed her review, she knew she needed to go into her wardrobe to choose an outfit worthy of her position and the divisions she was visiting with her daughter. She brushed her hair til the natural curl in it lay in place like a professional styling. Lux decided on an eggshell tailored long sleeve blouse with a medium mauve colored slack suit with matching suit buttons to be conservative. She opted for matching footwear with the required non-slip soles. This will do nicely, Lux thought admiring herself in the mirror. She went back to the food preparation area and checked to make sure everything was finished and put in its proper place for cooling or freezing. She picked up her list of needed provisions she had made and clicked on the data entry key. Lux fed the list into the slot of the appliance to send for her requests to the Nutrition Supply Distribution Center. She and Luna would pick up the food later. Lux usually had their food delivered to their quarters, but she was going to be at the Center later this afternoon, so she marked her list requests that she would personally pickup, do not deliver today. Everything looked in order, so Lux set off towards the Garden Wing to wait for Luna. She was *excited* to be educating, explaining and instructing her own daughter of how important all the aspects of food were to the Outpost existence. Lux wondered if her own mom had felt this way, even though she happened to be included in the normal group of Outpost Food educational seminars, when she was age appropriate.

Lux got to the entry doors to the Gardens and Nursery wing a few minutes early and was speaking with two other residents that worked regularly at the gardens. It felt good to be around botanical associates and to be close to the living plants that were always lovingly cared for. They were life. Lux could actually observe some of these young trees change each time she saw them. On the various days, she visited the younger plants that were still guarded in the nursery they too had jumped in size.

Luna showed up quickly, but stood there quietly until Mum and the others discovered her awaiting attention. Luna was also astonished at her mother's appearance. She very rarely saw her in one of her instructional uniforms. Lux introduced her daughter to the staff standing in the hall with her. Lux went on to share with them the different divisions and the explorations they intended to make today. Luna smiled and greeted each of them.

Mum smiled down at her daughter and with one hand on the door, said her adieu to the associates. They both took a few steps into the Nursery, and the door slid closed behind them. Mum just stood there for a few minutes looking around, and this caused a curiosity in Luna that compelled her to do the same thing. This was amazing! This was one more area of the outpost that in general non-classified young residents were not allowed in. Then it struck her. The aroma! Besides all the young trees and shrubs on one side of the gardens, Luna saw the nursery on the far other side. No wonder Mum was always speaking about the 'life' that the plants gave us. Luna now, could even smell and see it herself. There were many scents mixed together. All kinds of colors and shapes of the young trees and shrubs attracted Luna's attention. Mum was watching Luna's expression change as she was experiencing the gardens.

Mum didn't want to disrupt her daughter as she was digesting everything that her sight and sense of smell was encountering. Luna instantly understood what Mum had been sharing with her family over the years. There was much more on their venture that they needed to cover, so Mum said tenderly, as if for the plants to hear also that they must trek onward.

Luna, mesmerized, took her Mum's hand and they headed toward the larger trees. Mum chatting all along the way, 'There were no trees on the Outpost when they arrived. Everything had been cultured from seeds they had brought from earth. Then some trees were grafted to give more choice of tasty apples or other fruit. The real trick was bringing 'bees' on the voyage. But they were deemed less troublesome than the goats and chickens, due to their adaptability and hibernating cycles. This amazed Luna even more. 'How old were these trees and shrubs?' she asked. Mum didn't miss a beat in her reply that some of them were third and fourth generation plants also, just like the humans. To grow a tree to the size needed for reproduction, depending on the fruit or nut is anywhere from 10 to 20 years. The Outpost has had the most talented and creative Botanists and Horticulturists that started the nursery that developed into the gardens and now we even have the whole botanical wing. But you must know it takes special care and attention so that the trees and plants don't cross pollinate into something that is unusable for food or supplies for the colony. They kept walking in all the aisles. The fragrance of the plants and trees changed as they moved from one area to another. Luna wanted to reach out and touch many of them they were so enticing, but knew this definitely was not allowed.

Finally, they had ambled over to the nursery division. This was where the new seeds and sprouts were housed til they had the stability to be moved on to a bigger more open world. Walking thru the doors, into the nursery, Luna once again could smell the difference in the baby plants. Mum was observant to Luna's body language, so Mum would start telling the next narrative that was pertinent to where they were on their tour. An interesting project, that came out very well was the Geologists working with the nursery volunteers to create 'soil' that could be used for plants from earth, and hybrids of soil that this planet offered that could be mixed in with the earth soil so all the plants could grow and thrive. This meant that the Geologists had to do chemical breakdowns of the composition of this planet's ground, soil, dust, or whatever they extracted, to make it usable for our baby earthly plants. Tests of the dirt that was sparingly brought from earth had been already broken down and analyzed before the Voyagers had lift off. They also knew the optimum chemical structure for each plant to grow in. Some plants or trees needed more acid ground, some more alkaline. Some of the nursery had to be started with much more moisture in the soil than others. There was constant monitoring and testing to make sure the plants survived. This is why there are over 50 residents that have occupations that take care of our plants. They had strolled through the wing and were back at the doors they had entered over an hour ago. New occupation Luna wanted to be instructed in, she thought.

Mum guided Luna around a few curved hallways to the next entrance they were going to access. Life Subsistence Wing was boldly printed in three languages on the doors. They walked in and the doors that once again glided closed behind them. This was a huge processing area. Luna never had any idea of what this wing functioned as, but knew both Poppi and Mum were involved with it.

Mum said they were not going to walk thru this wing as there was a lot of work that could not be interrupted. If even she needed to speak to one of the leaders or scientists about a project or critical testing they were doing; she had to make an appointment or send a message. Luna was taken aback at this operational wing.

They walked up three steps to a small dais where you could look out over the whole wing. Mum pointed out an area to the left that was filled with plants and all kinds of bags of dirt. There was a lot of robotics that were separating this area from other parts of this wing. Mum told Luna that the machines could perform certain sets of tests and analyses. After they were performed, the botanists or nutritionists could review data quickly. Gathering a quorum was the next step that could modify or confirm information, allowing the department to move forward or address how they wanted to adjust projects. Mum pointed to the back of the wing where there were a lot of computer monitors and keyboards and tablets visible. She said this was where the Observatory Supervisors ran various algorithms of where they wanted to transmit messages to Earth and the other Triads of ships. They had the original coordinates calculated from earth, but as yet, were not sure if their calculations from the Outpost they were sending were correct. This group has had negative results in hearing anything incoming to our Outpost. They work in here, as they want to other astronomers not to be disconcerted by no communication as of yet. They also want them to keep creating new coordinates they have access to currently, and hope this will open up a communication with another planet or other planetary inhabitants. The smaller area up here on the left is for holographic updates and 5-d Phase Beam development. The area in the center of the room is for medical and nutritional evaluations. The computers run algorithms of all of the residents, and their health in comparison with their diets, occupations, and exercise. As of yet, none of the residents have had any issue with foods we currently eat, and no one has had any health alarm that had to be circumvented by the medical department. We are staying true to our genetic heritage of our ancestors with which who were chosen so carefully to be in this Mission. Mum swept her lower arm across the room at the assignment area that was directly below them. This area she reported was critical to all the plants, animals, and food on the Outpost. This area was designated for the Nutrition Supply Center. Luna looked down and there were three distinct areas of computers with touch screens. There was video monitoring of both the botanical and garden wings. There were smaller digital read out screens at the lower level of each of the much larger sets of computers. Mum explained that this was how all edible foods were monitored. The first set of systems data reported on daily amounts of edible food on hand for the outpost. These evaluations were computations of produce and how nutrient rich the crop was. The next set of analyzed data separated foods into usage: to be picked, processed and/ or stored. Perishable- needed to be used soon, could remain in cold storage for periods of time, frozen, or dehydrated. The third set of data processing was input and requested orders for individual families to be filled. The assessment of food on hand was quickly identified by the computers' computations of stock, and if there wasn't enough fruits or vegetables on hand, the order is flagged, and division staff investigate the requests, and offer other suggested foods, or send information back to the family and ask if they want to wait for that particular vegetable or fruit, or resubmit their order for something that is easily in stock. The requested orders were then sent over to the Nutrition Supply Distribution Center, where they could be picked up directly by residents or family; or the A.I.s were in full service to deliver groceries to residents' quarters at designated times. All the Outpost's inhabitants realized quickly that accounting for the food by a non-biased entity was the best way to assure equity, gratify, and please the populace.

The other part of this wing was the expansion and supervision of the Outpost's Operational Power Center. Their desks, supplies and monitoring screens took up limited space in this wing, but they were so important to make sure all systems disbursed maximum uniform energy flow to the whole Outpost, and if there was a power lag, they could identity and rectify it quickly and usually from the Life Subsistence work area, without disrupting other areas of research or activities in the post.

Luna was fascinated by what seemed to be the 'brain' of the outpost. But she did ask Mum one simple question. "Why did they walk up three steps when they came into this wing?' Mum answered that 'first it was to give the visitor the small amount of height to overlook the whole wing to scan and see if the supervisor or leader they needed was present in section. The second reason was what the outpost had put in place these stairs as minor security. Anyone working would notice if another staff member from somewhere else in the Outpost had entered the Life Subsistence Area unescorted.' All personnel honored and respected this protocol, so there had not been any security issues nor did they foresee any.'

Mum and Luna walked down the steps and went out the doors and further around some corridors to their next stop, The Nutrition Supply Distribution Center. Mum joked, 'this is our grocery store!' As they went into this huge echoing vault, Luna once again saw the basic set up for processing and monitoring the food stuffs. There were a good many staff examining the produce they had gathered today, entering their daily information by way of touch screens. Two other groups that were inspecting the days intake of eggs and measuring the quarts of milk the brought in from the goats. Standing by another set of touch screens, they entered the basic daily collection of dairy and poultry into the computer by way of the screens again. The supervisor had been brought over to join the conversation about the milk. Mum took Luna's hand and they walked over to the *evaluation area,* after they had donned hair coverings, smocks and booties to prevent contamination of the valuable goat's milk. The conversation was how they were going to utilize the collection of milk today. The goat technicians knew that their herd was not going to be in the 'milk' producing phase of their cycles much longer, and what would be the best use of the milk for the next 3 months, with so many dependents relying on their products. The technicians had been accounting for the milk for years, but usage responsibility always had to be signed off on by a supervisor before going to the next step, or the most beneficial processing of milk for this cycle. When Lux walked up, she introduced her daughter, Luna, and said she was on an educational visit today as to how the Outpost can grow, feed, and supply food for all its inhabitants. Lux asked one of the technicians to explain about the collection of the dairy products and how the Nutrition Supply Center with the Life Subsistence division used their knowledge and computer calculations to optimize the usage of the milk, as milk as a standalone product, or by processing it to make cheese, which takes weeks, and the longevity of the cheese made; as well as making yogurt from the milk, and its expected longevity. One of the men caretakers of the goats did a simple explanation of these processes for Luna. The one thing they did not want to happen be there was spoilage of the product or it to become inedible. The supervisor suggested that they send their milk quantities gathered for the last three days, and for their next three-day projections to the Life Subsistence center and have computations run on each of the milk products they wanted to produce and preserve. Lux wholeheartedly agreed with the Supervisor, with a wink. Mum looked down at Luna and told her though, with the day getting late, she would personally bring home the results of how the milk dilemma would most favorably be resolved.

The Dairy Supply team with the Supervisor trusted each other implicitly, but they were going to use their full data system to further educate their young un-classified visitor. Lux and Luna thanked the team for their information; and Luna told them that she enjoyed their excellent products she received at her home.

Mum took Luna over to the small cubical where they could remove the booties, smocks and hair nets they had been required to wear. Mum now said they had one more place they needed to go to here at the Nutrition Supply Center. Having a full day of classes and no snack this afternoon, Luna was getting tired. But smiled up to Mum and agreed as to their next educational stopover.

They walked down the corridor, past the large freezers and cold storage units. They went past the great bins of fruits and vegetables that needed to be stored at a stabilized 20 degrees Celsius, room temperature. Finally, they walked up to counters where there were employee residents that were available to assist them. Lux smiled and asked if the food order that was sent in by message for the Grande Vite family was ready to be picked up? The lady was wearing a red smock over her top and slacks, that had a name tag on it shaped like a tomato saying 'Hi, I'm Vicki.' This was amusing to Luna, and she started looking around the delivery center and there were various color smocks that the employees were wearing with color matching vegetables or fruits with their names on them. Vicki brought three bags of groceries out to the counter for Lux to take home. Mum picked up two of them and Luna picked up the third one, and they moved to the exterior doors that put them out in the Concourse hall and they started home.

'Luna, I hope you enjoyed yourself. I know you're tired. I already have dinner ready; it just needs to be warmed and we can eat and you can go to bed.' With this information Luna gathered all the energy she could to carry the package home and not go into despair over how exhausted she was.

They entered their quarters before Poppi had arrived, and Mum took all the packages to the food preparation area to store them away. She turned and softly requested that Luna go to her room, wash up for their evening meal, fold back her bed, and put on her pajamas. Mum quickly went to the cold storage and got out the Spaghetti Squash with Pesto and Almonds and popped them in the microwave. She set the sliced tomatoes on the table with a small cruet of garlic oil and set the peach sherbet out at each of their place settings.

Poppi came in the front door from working all day. He went straight to the dining table and sat down. Luna came out from her room dragging Moppet behind her, and hopped up on her chair. Mum filled tumblers with cold Sparkling water for their beverage with their meal. The microwave dinged, and with hot mitts Mum placed the two dishes on the table, and she sat down. They each filled their plates and ate heartedly. Poppi asked Mum how their food and cooking outing had gone, and Mum tipped her head towards Luna across the table, who could hardly keep her eyes open. Luna was sleepy but happy. Mum had made one of her favorite desserts- peach sherbet. She ate slowly, not wanting to make a mess or spill her food she was so exhausted. Luna left Moppet on her chair as she gathered her dishes and set them in the basin. She asked Mum was it ok for her not to wash the dishes tonight, and Mum replied that was 'ok' by her. Luna shuffled up to Mum and kissed her good night, and thanked her for the wonderful afternoon, and then picked up Moppet, and shuffled up to Poppi and gave him as kiss and hug. She felt sad asking Poppi if she could tell him all about the food on the Outpost tomorrow. But his response was cheerful and lighthearted. "Of course, she could."

With that, she ambled up the hall to her room with Moppet, and within minutes of getting under her covers, she was sound asleep.

OUTPOST 621 AND
THE WORKERS

Outpost 621 (Planet Gliese 581d)
200 volunteers, 200 years ago

CHARACTERS & HISTORY

The Volunteer Voyagers leaving Earth, total 200, Occupations- varied, highly trained, broad thinkers and wide range of interests and studies, inventive, biogenetically selected

Poppi- (Father) Proper Name: <u>Katavon Grandiose Vite</u> Grand Life Occupation: Engineer

(Greek (Italian) Nickname: <u>Poppi</u>- Understanding, Think and Remember

Appearance: Tall, Slender, Warm inviting features and manner (3rd Generation)

Luna-(Little Girl- Main Character) Nickname: <u>Blossom</u> What was to come, Confidence, (Latin, Spanish) Light, Blessed, Altruistic, Imaginative (4th Generation)

Appearance- Slender, Long Dark soft wavy hair, large inquiring intense blue eyes

Mum- (Mother) Proper Name: <u>Lux</u> Light, Nickname: <u>Mum</u>- Flower Challenging, Educational

(Latin) Occupation: Home Economics (3rd Generation)

Appearance- Slender, Light brown, short wavy hair, Large Blue intense eyes

Grandpapa Sebastian- (Poppi's father) Proper Name: <u>Sebastian Grandiose Vite</u> (2nd Generation)

(Romania, French) Esteemed, Admired Grand Life Occupation: Commanding Engineer

Appearance- Tall, Robust build, Thick, silver hair, Compassionate blue eyes

Oliver-(Luna's M Friend) Peace, Dignity, Strength Occupation- Non-classified 4th generation

(German, French, Latin) Dad- Observatory Hobby-Study this planet Appearance- Tall for age, slender, dark brown straight hair-side parted- neat appearance

Kai- (Luna's M Friend) "Keeper of the earth [sea]", Pure, Chaste Hobby: sketch /build rockets

Occupation: Non- Classified 4th generation (Welsh, Greek, Hawaiian) Appearance- Shorter than Luna, Dark hair w/ boxed haircut, Large brown eyes

Sonnet-(Luna's F Friend) Divine music, serenity, Little song Occupation: Non-Classified 4th Generation (Italian, English, French) Appearance- Slender, fair skinned, long sandy blonde hair, likes to wear flowing clothes

Dr. Dignita- (Doctor) Dignity, Occupation: Head Physician in Medical Center Repository (Latin) (2nd Generation) Appearance- Tall, Slender wears a tunic/ slacks, sandy light hair- gentle mannerisms & speech

Mr. Boreas- (Mission Principal) Occupation: The Primary "Master of Ceremonies" (German) ((2nd Generation) Appearance- shorter than Poppi, dress & stance as person of importance- listens, thinks, and speaks w/ depth

Security Monitor Team
The Commission
Instructor (M) Occupation: Class teacher for students non-classified (Latin, French) (3rd Generation)

Appearance: Tall, blonde, handsome

Mr. Rotan (Botany Caretaker [M]) Rotan- Occupation: Lead Botanist for trees and shrubs in Botanical Wing Reed or cane (Mayly, Greek) (2nd Generation)

Appearance: Medium height, soft brown complexion, brown eyes. Shirt and trousers with gloves poking from pocket. Carries a small pouch with tools to check on health of the trees and saplings

Ms. Emagine (IT Engineer [F]) Occupation- Computer and hologram and lasers monitoring

(Old French, Latin) (3rd Generation)

Appearance: Tall, thin, younger than most department leads. Light Brown hair, tied in bun. Eyewear to assist in verifying numbers she was inputting and calculating. She dressed in a purple two-piece tunic suit with a white under blouse.

Dr. Mackenzie Otago (DNA Botanist and Paleontologist) Occupation- Studies and Analysis of DNA (Old European, Scottish) (3rd Generation) Appearance: Tall, Fair skinned, Dark hair (pulled back in a knot), Quick comprehending green eyes. Dressed in Dark Green light wool lapel colored pant suit.

Dr. Inga Sohan (Genetic Studies Doctorate) Occupation- Works as major Support to Life Subsistence and Medical

Repository departments (Scandinavian, India, United States) (3rd Generation)

Appearance: Petite, Tawny skin tone with a Bobbed haircut. She was dressed in a long off-white flowing lab coat over a light brown, a high collar, fitted blouse with matching slacks.

Harrison (Student- has younger brother) Occupation- Non-classified 4th generation

Controlling leader personality (Old English)

Appearance: Medium height for age, strong body build, Brown hair, Brown eyes Usually seen in class activities school attire.

Lucinda (student) Occupation- Non-classified 4th generation Intense personality

Meaning: 'Light,' Roman Goddess (Spanish)

Appearance: Medium build, Long black hair, Brown eyes, Usually seen in class activities school attire

Logan (student) Occupation- Non- classified 4th generation Personality: Very mild mannered

Meaning: 'Hollow' (Scottish) Appearance: Tall, lanky, fair skinned, blue eyes, soft wavy red hair; Usually seen in class activities school attire

Mr. *Tomohiro* (Senior Systems Engineer) Occupation- Docent of the Data Archives Center

Personality: Exultant, astute, dedicated Meaning: Knowledge (Japanese) Appearance: Short stature, Black Hair, Dark Eyes, Happy relaxed mannerisms Attire for work- professional and polished (3rd Generation)

Levi Pranay (Voyage Leader) Occupation: One of 6 of the Mission Flight Committee Principals, Supervisor of Primary Manifest Meaning: Harmony, Leader (Jewish, Indian)

Asher Dalton (Voyage Support) Occupation: Systems Troubleshooter, 2nd of 6 of the Mission Flight Committee Principals, Records Management of Equipment Log Meaning: Blessed, Inventor, (Hebrew, Old English)

Gatlin Altair (Voyage Support) Occupation: 3rd of 6 of the Mission Flight Committee Principals Records Management of Flight Travel Manifest Meaning: Fellow Companion, Flyer (Old English/German. Arabic)

Luljeta Sage (Voyage Support) Occupation: 4th of 6 of the Mission Flight Committee Principals Records Management of Human & Population Condition Log Meaning: Flower of Life, Wise One (Albanian, French/English)

Aaden (Voyage Support) Occupation: Theologies and Philosophies, 5th of the 6 of the Mission Flight Committee Principals Meaning: Theologist (Algeria)

Alva (Voyage Support, Grandpapa's grandfather) Occupation: Master Engineer of Robotics and Computer Coding, 6th of the 6 of the Mission Flight Committee Principals Meaning: Highness, Exulted One (Arabic, Hebrew)

Callan Zale (MBS Exercise Activities Director) Sonnet's Father Appearance: tall, athletic build, dark curly hair, quick reflexes and thinking. Attire: Light Sport's apparel for various activities

Meaning: Callan- Rock, Zale-Strong (Gaelic, Polish)

Annalise Zale (MBS Division Director) Sonnet's Mother Appearance: tall, poised build; sandy, wavy mid-length hair, agile; graceful reflexes and quick thinking. Attire: Light-form fitting professional apparel, suitable for various duties and activities Meaning: Annalise- Graced with God's Gifts, Zale-Strong (French, Polish)

SOCIAL STRUCTURE VS. THOUGHT FORMATION

It was a nice day to just wonder around the outpost and not have responsibilities. Luna was comfortable in her blue overalls with a pink tee shirt on, and of course her sandals. The last few weeks with the project that she and her group had finished and presented to the class had left her exhausted in one way, but in other ways it opened her thinking to the Outpost and where she lived. For the last few days, whenever she was with anyone outside of her parents she noted their personality, occupation, family structure and what made them happy. Luna hadn't had a chance to really compile a full list as to her thoughts about these people, and how she was breaking down the general categories. That would probably come to her later. Her concern was would their Outpost survive? Were they too "sterile" or "focused"? For that matter was she that way too?

This all started the first day that they were going to work on the "Galaxies Project." Oliver made the comment when they first gathered for discussion of this project that this was a behavioral test. When the others looked at him inquisitively, what was he talking about? He went on to explain that the Mission Commission was now using different projects with the growing 4th generation students to observe their interests, aptitudes, and assimilation of information. This was one of the guides to focus or lead the upcoming age group towards occupations that they could and would excel in. Luna had never given this a thought. Oliver had the group distracted and they couldn't concentrate on their needed discussion of 'Galactic Travel from Earth.' He went on to explain how his mother was part of the Education Resources Focus Group; Oliver, several times overheard conversations at home that she had with his father. All the senior residents wanted to open up new ideas and peek the interests for the students to gravitate towards in certain necessary survival arenas. This sounded intriguing to Luna. She started to ask Oliver some more questions, but he casually shrugged his shoulders, and said they better get back to their project. He laughed as he pulled out his tablet with his notes from last night and looked at his group partners and asked in a general question, did they realize how much information they were going to have to review and investigate for their voyage from Earth?

Well, that ended that conversation; and they indeed had a lot they did gather and evaluate for their presentation.

Now with that particular project was over, Luna could think about the people living here and the social structure of the Outpost. One more time, Luna wanted to go to Poppi and ask him about this process. How studies and classes were set up for past generations that were born here, or the original volunteers that came here by travel. She opted not to go to Poppi yet.

Currently, Luna just wanted to observe her friends and family, and the various people she came in contact with at the Botanical Wing, the PBS Research Pods, the Nutrition Supply Distribution center, Life Subsistence center, and of course the Systems Operations Wing. There had to be a correlation. There were serious considerations that must be adhered to such as the Outpost's Honor Contract.

"Prosperity- There Was Always Enough, a Contract of Love" and the Mission Statement that the Original Volunteers 'that words, actions, or activities of negativity, violence or abuse were not permitted in any form.' This would also include the Outpost's population and adhering to healthy genetic markers for sustainability and growth. Luna had asked Poppi about love and attaining a life mate one time, and his reply was she was way too young to delve into that subject. So, Luna went off to the Data Storage Archive and looked at how the original organization of the Galactic Commission had set up the criteria for those who were selected to go on the colonization journeys. Yep, there were notes in the Mission structure for attaining a life mate, Luna saw.

In the early 21st century, many humans were very excited as to taking ventures into space, but these were planned and there was a return trip. As Luna read about these trips and when they would be available to the general population, the humans did seem to have a similar theme. The way Luna read their stories that were chronicalized and accounted for, they wanted to offer some element to humanity. They were also adventurers who wanted to expand their knowledge, and bring the human race forward. And Oh... yes...they wanted to reach for the stars. All the programs for space travel, energy forms for Earth to sustain its self, food, and basic shelter were exponentially growing over the last decades of that century. This was when the Mission Commission was formed.

Utilizing the most impressive of the Earth's progressive minds, it took over 20 years to formulate what type of space travel and colonization they wanted to focus all of their efforts on. The Commission had decided to have three triads of voyagers, with three different destinations. Then everything to the slightest details had to be addressed and focused on. Luna, Oliver, Kai and Sonnet had given their report about this colony in limited form to the class as there was so much data and information available. One day Luna thought as they were reviewing all the information they chose to use for their project, what if... just what if... this colony failed. The next followers could learn and adapt and move forward, from their errors.

By the beginning of the 22nd century DNA genetics was advanced enough that biogenesis could include or exclude prospective volunteers for the voyages. Each vessel of the triad had its purpose. Two of the three vessels were the human volunteers. During travel they would learn everything that was at their disposal about their new habitat. All historical theory data and archives would travel in the 'manned' ships. They would have to learn to create tools and materials for their new living quarters and how to effectively use foods and continue the study of plants in no- or low gravity. They also had to maintain control and stability of the third vessel that was carrying materials and tools for the building of their new home. Recruiting 200 Volunteers of the highest quality of education, creativity, health, and resourcefulness for each planned launch ended up not to be problematic. The Mission ran algorithms to find at least 800 candidates for the three launches. The Commission allowed for a 25% loss of candidates due to the intense uncertainty of the missions during preparations. How many people would in reality, totally give up their families, homes, friends, and earth lives for a 'chance'?

Since this galactic venture was 20 years in the formation, there were engineers and technicians as well as ever progressing artificial intelligence devices that were available and were going on this journey. There were so many tests and counterchecks that had to be made to validate the quality of the people that were 'giving up' everything for this new existence and exploration. The volunteers would be 'gaining' everything also. The Commission had the greatest expectations that the voyages were going to be triumphant at their given destinations. This even went as far as they were going to be able to report back to Earth and communicate with each other as to their destinations and achievements.

This led Luna to what she was pondering today. Were all these people so narrowly selected that that they did not show or exhibit the full range of emotions, one of which was the wisdom of the humans. The one thing that she did know and agree on was the basic premise of the Mission Covenant and Statement. And she had researched that all three of the galactic voyagers had the same Covenants and Statements to live by. (This pleased Luna, as she had researched and read about all the horrible battles, struggles, fights, death, starvation, and misery that Earth had had in its recorded history. She would have loved to know why there was such strife.)

Luna suddenly thought about asking Kai and Oliver if they would like to go do some investigating with her today. She sent each of them a message, asking about joining her. Two pings came back shortly. Both of them wanted to know what she was up to today. They thought that she wanted to go to the Activity Pods Headquarters again for another look at Earth. She told them 'No,' she wanted to go do some interviewing of residents. This peeked their interest and they wanted to know more, but all Luna replied was for them to bring their note tablets with them, and meet her at the Main Concourse Hall by the big Rubber Plant. She giggled at her plan. They were boys... and they had to be with her almost all day for classes, so for her to engage their interest today was a victory.... at least so far. Kai liked to work on drawings and create model rockets. Oliver liked to go to the Observatory and examine the landscape of this planet. He would pull up archived data and had multiple windows open, making it maddening for the on- duty Cosmologists to proceed with their work.

Going back to her living quarters, Luna went to her room and grabbed her personal tablet and jotted down the names of four of the different work sections she wanted to visit today and make inquiries. She didn't feel that she was going out on an interview session that would cause problems with anyone, so she proceeded off to the Concourse. Luna didn't see Mum or Poppi at home. However, they could message her if they wanted to know of her whereabouts, or needed her back at their quarters.

Luna was the first to arrive at the designated Concourse plant area. There was seating there, and sometimes the Sky window was retracted so many of the stars were visible making it a comfortable meeting place for any of the residents. Oliver showed up next wearing a khaki shirt and shorts with his sandals, looking at ease. Luna asked him if he had plans to go to the Observatory today, to which he replied 'no.' He said he was supposed to help his little sister with one of her play projects; so, he was glad to have something else to think about and work on. (He wasn't thrilled playing with his baby sister. He liked challenges!) Kai had on a light blue summer suit with slippers, moseying up to his friends and asked what was going on. Before announcing her proposal for the day, Luna asked Kai did he have any plans or home duties he needed to attend to today. He replied 'No' and said he was just going to read.

This was the opening that Luna wanted. Luna grinned and asked both her friends had they given any further thought as to what Oliver had briefly announced to their group a few weeks ago? The Commission wanted their class to take leads with newly developed projects. Luna went on to describe in her words this was overwriting our current social structure and the Commission wanted to open up occupations and studies to the upcoming academics…us! The Galaxy project was just one of the different projects that we were going to be part of. The Education Board is revamping the teaching structure of the outpost. Think of it! They are observing us. Supporting and adding guidance to focus or lead each of us towards occupations that we could and would excel in. Have you thought about that? They care about our interests, how we assimilate information, and in what direction our aptitudes are taking. Kai and Oliver just stared at Luna one more time. Where did she come up with some of these ideas of hers'? "Guys, today I wanted to go to some of the different divisions and just ask some random questions of the personnel in various departments to verify my intuition." 'This will be a huge opening for us if I am correct.' 'We now have this accepted Social Structure, but they are considering allowing growth through Thought Formation.' 'The Outpost wants us to think.' 'The little snippet of information Oliver shared with us a few weeks ago makes so much sense.' Luna was once again alight with energy and enthusiasm at her discovery. Luna wanted to go racing down the hall now, with or without Oliver and Kai. What were they thinking about? "Look, guys. I have said nothing to no one. We can go and ask some questions very benignly, and see how the Outpost has been built and occupations created or filled in the last three generations, since we have been on 621."

Both of the boys still were looking at Luna and the tale she had come up with this time, in disbelief or amusement, and neither boy could decide which. Luna tried again. "Oliver, your dad is a geologist. You do like the stars and the planets, but would you like to expand your occupation options if possible, like maybe take extra classes or courses and obtain a chemistry-geology doctorate… or add some other study of heavenly bodies? My Mum's occupation is Home Economics. And may I add I think she is very good at it. But from our talks, I know that her great- grandmother came on the voyage from Earth trained in "home survival- foods, shelter, family safety, oh you know!" what will presumably happen as the next generation steps into this assumed occupation. I may want to follow in my Mum's occupation, but I may want to become an engineer, like my Dad, or something else altogether. Kai- you sketch and build wonderful space vehicles. Your dad has built rockets and experiments with alternate fuel sources currently. Is that what you want to do, or would you like to possibly enter another field or expand and compliment what your dad has worked on so diligently?

The light bulbs were coming on. Luna had broken through. Luna didn't even know if either Oliver or Kai had gone to the Data Storage and Archival Studies area to see if there had been computer and analytical update available for them to further their studies to be as competent or surpass their parents in occupations that were chosen by the Commission and themselves. Luna had browsed various occupations in the DSAS, and at the moment, the idea of working with the Education Committee to make more options available and channel 'positive thinking' and 'dreams of the possible' seemed wonderful to her.

Kai and Oliver finally smiled that they understood where Luna was coming from. Kai asked did Luna have any particular work sections she wanted to visit today. Luna replied yes, and they walked down to the salon and stopped for a snack and beverage. Together they agreed on the staff they wanted to ask questions of.

First stop was the Botanical Wing. Luna treasured coming here under any pretense she could come up with. She noted that both the lead Botanist and Horticulturist were working this morning. The three of them walked up to Mr. Rotan, the lead Botanist. He smiled at Luna and asked what type of plants or trees she wanted to inquire about today, winking at the boys with her. Oliver took the lead and replied, 'Sir, we would like to ask some questions of you and your occupation, if that is amenable to you?' The botanist looked puzzled, but was willing to assist the young students with anything to be of service to the Outpost, and help spur on their curiosity about nature, and the basis of their survival.

Kai started with the first question, 'Mr. Rotan, how is it that you became a Botanist?' 'That's easy', he replied 'I was here in the gardens at a very early age following my Pop around and asking a million questions. This was my play area, private sanctuary, and my laboratory.' I never really thought of taking up another career. Pop always said, whatever you do, do it to the best of your ability. So, I studied trees and shrubs. I would ask myself how I could help the Outpost thrive. How could I contribute to making improvements on the vegetative species we have or by studying crossbreeding saplings for stronger or more fruitful plants? She told him she enjoyed the aroma of the dirt and trees so much. Mr. Rotan laughed, and replied, 'I think I have you hooked on nature already.' Luna looked up and thought of another question she wanted to ask, 'Sir how many generations has your family been part of the Botany Department, or the lead Botanists?' This question took Mr. Rotan by surprise again. What was this generation up to? So inquisitive! 'Well, Luna, I'm second generation gardener or Botanist. My grandfather was one of the original volunteers to want to come on this journey. He beamed from every crevice of the wrinkles in his face. 'Every day I give thanks at how lovingly he cared for these plants and trees, and so I have been the chosen caregiver to his legacy.' (Luna thought; this is a new dimension of occupations that she had not thought about. Good thing to ask questions and gather data!) Luna thanked Mr. Rotan, and told him she would be back soon to explore what was new in the wing.

Next they were off to the Bio-Genetic Holographic Pods Headquarters. Walking up the Concourse, Luna was deep in thought. She could see how Mr. Rotan was so connected to the "life" in his department. Kai and Oliver chatted between themselves that they had never thought about the way that Mr. Rotan had looked at his importance and this position in the outpost. They wondered if the other people they were going to question would have similar responses.

It so happened that they were in luck today as Ms. Emagine was in the headquarters checking and monitoring all the Pods. Luna was once again familiar with this staff person. She and Poppi often had brief conversations with her as to what adventures they were going to take that day. This pleased Ms. Emagine so much that the Pods were a useful and educational tool for the Outpost. When she was younger, she too liked to come here and allow her imagination to create a place in the universe where she could travel. Kai once again became vocal and smiled at Ms. Emagine and asked how she acquired a position and occupation of such importance. The engineer took off her glasses and looked even younger than she already appeared. She had a keen knowing how essential the holographic Pods were to the outpost. Oliver, Kai and Luna were observing her comments and it seemed that she almost became one of the Pods in her conversation with them. She bashfully acknowledged that she did not enjoy toys when she was a child; however, her father brought home damaged computer boards for her to "tinker" with for entertainment. It seemed apparent to the Commission and to her family that when the Pod Headquarters was going to need an assistant or a lead replacement, that she would be offered the position first. Ms. Emagine studied very hard in the fields of computer components, microchipping, and lasers, so she could accept and readily understand the Pods, if the opportunity presented itself. Oliver then asked Ms. Emagine a question bashfully, as he wasn't sure if it was appropriate, but he asked anyway... 'Can you tell me which generation are you part of, here at 621?' She smiled proudly and said that she was third generation. Her father had asked her to step into the lead position so she could work with his supporting tutelage, and they could remain a team. Ms. Emagine added that her father was very pleased at her new ideas and the depth of knowledge she had for her occupation.

Luna asked one more question. Did she ever think about changing to a different occupation? Ms. Emagine replied yes, for a short time she considered becoming an engineer at the Systems Operations Department, but when she found out that she would have a very limited amount of work to do with the lasers, she opted out of that occupation. She asked the group if they wanted to use a Pod and do some research or just enjoy and adventure today, to which they all excused themselves and said they had some more data that they were gathering. They thanked her for her time and information, and they turned and headed up the Concourse to their next stop.

Oliver commented that he was glad that Luna wanted to include her dad as one of the persons they interviewed. Poppi was on her list, but she did not want to push the idea of interviewing her dad. When they were talking as they walked up the concourse, Kai and Oliver both made the same reference that the people they were talking to today were of some occupation that was critical to the Outpost's optimum functioning and survival. There were other residents that were on all three lists, such as the Medical Facility Doctor, the life Subsistence director, the lead at the Observatory, Outpost Maintenance and support. But all three decided that Mr. G was their next choice.

Luna didn't think her dad was working today, so she sent him as message asking if he was busy and if he could answer a few questions for Oliver, Kai and her. She quickly got a ping back responding positively, and asked where they wanted to meet. Luna looked at Oliver and Kai in question, not really wanting to go to her living quarters for a chat. Both suggested the salon in the Concourse again for a snack, and the relaxing atmosphere.

The three of them got to the salon first and ordered some manna and crackers and sparkling water. Luna added enough to the order for her Poppi. (She had to remember to keep this interview professional) Mr. G, wearing a loose green wrap with a scarlet sash and sandals to match walked up to the table where they were waiting for him. Kai greeted him with a big smile and thanked him for coming to help with some research they were working on. (Poppi noted that Luna was allowing the guys to take the lead of this venture) When their snacks and beverages were set before them, Oliver chimed in that they were still interested in the Outpost, and information that could not get to with their project they had just finished. Mr. G replied that he would help them with any information he could, but he asked why didn't they go to the DSAC and get their information there. Oliver was ready for him and countered, that they had spent a lot of time the last few weeks at the archives and just wanted to get a 'real' perspective on the information they were tracking today. Mr. G laughed. 'Ok, go ahead, what have you all got on your minds?'

Luna started out, 'Poppi, how come you became a mechanical engineer?' He came back with a simple answer of 'I really liked any math courses and physics available when I was taking classes.' 'My mother was a wiz at making three dimensional diagrams of potential structures or wing additions. My Dad was into computers and how much information could be edited, deleted or copied onto microchips, and he kept writing coding programs making microchips "byte" sizes smaller but increasing the material that each byte could contain.'

Oliver gasped. Gee, that was interesting. He regained himself and asked- 'so you wanted to do the same type of work?' 'Well, no, not really. I wanted the outpost to grow. I wanted us to have room to live on this planet, and have potential. You can only live and be healthy in a very small confined area for so long before dissention and irritability set in. My great-grandfather came from Earth and he said it was the most beautiful spacious place. That was how my interest grew, also how I met your mom Luna. She was into nature... and plants... and food stores...and life. We are both 3rd generation residents. We spent so much time going through the archives and making prototypes of new wings and what they be used for and sustain.' Kai turned to Luna and asked her, did she know this information about how her parents helped support the growth of the Outpost. Luna shook her head 'no,' and was just waiting for what Poppi was going to share next.

Kai then asked the key question, 'Did both of you more or less go into the occupations that your parents and grandparents had when they got to the Outpost?' 'Basically, the answer is yes. Am I happy with my work? Definitely. So is Luna's Mother. But there is so much more all of us need to be doing for this outpost to thrive.' 'The volunteers started this base from 3 recreated vessels making it into a functioning planetary habitat. This habitat with the imagination and creativity of all residents involved has now grown into an evolved 13 'Wing' Outpost with at least 4 designated communal areas for exercise, community, education, and family endeavors.' 'We also have expanded to learning, manipulating and charting our planet we live on as well as the galaxy we live in. I might add, a lot if human determination was and is used, but we also are aided by our computer systems that are integral to our safety and livelihood.' 'Poppi thank you so much for your information. If we need anything else, may we ask for your assistance again?' She went around the table and gave her dad a big hug, she couldn't help herself. She turned to Kai and Oliver and said they needed to keep working at their task for the day. They got up and headed down the Concourse, in a new direction.

Luna was glad that Kai and Oliver were with her, as she was a bit intimidated by their next interviewee. She wanted to speak with the Primary, Mr. Boreas, neither Oliver or Kai objected to this inquiry. Mr. Boreas was in the inter antechamber reviewing some work on several tablets on his desk around him. He looked up and smiled at having visitors to his office, this did not happen very often.

'Sir, we have a few questions for you, if you have some time for us,' Kai inquired. 'Well of course, what can I help you with?' he replied. Luna, started off her survey by asking how did Mr. Boreas move into the position of the "Commission's Principal?" Mr. Boreas was fascinated by the question Luna posed. 'No one has ever asked me such a direct question. It seemed that it was always assumed, that I would transfer into this profession.' Oliver, interested in that response, asked 'What occupation or interest did you have before becoming the Principal?' 'I was following in my father's field of engineering the Outpost's stabilization.' Oliver continued, 'Did you have to take a special curriculum or courses to transfer fields, to occupy this position?' Mr. Boreas was following their' questions, but was wondering what was bringing up such inquiry. (The Principal's position required a person that was intelligent and very quick to capture the whole picture to come to a resolution quickly, on any given issue the Committee had to address. Mr. Boreas possessed this aptitude.) Then a thought came to him, and he wanted to come back, after reflecting a bit with a question to his collective audience. 'Luna since the incident earlier this year, you have seen some of the workings of the Commission, and how we, as a cooperative perform to maintain our Mission credo.' He grinned at her intuitiveness. He then looked towards Oliver and commented about how his mother was working as part of the Education Focus Group. Mr. Boreas then posed his intuitive query to them. 'Are you all investigating the grounds and possibilities of a new educational program that we are considering putting in place to strengthen the students' knowledge base and for the overall betterment of the Outpost?' All three of them looked shocked at how succinctly the "Primary" evaluated their few questions and targeted their direct information and what they were doing. No wonder he was the "Primary"! Luna thought. In actuality, each of them was speechless.

They didn't know if they had done something wrong, or were they so naïve as to just go directly to the Outpost Primary and think they could ask such questions without him burrowing into their intent.

Mr. Boreas was gracious and gentle as he answered his own question. "I do believe you are working on this project. It has not been assigned to the students at all, but I am amazed that you are out here searching for answers that the Education Department (the adults…hum, hum) is also evaluating.' 'Can I give you some insight, and answer any other questions you may have, but I must get back to work.'

Luna, Kai and Oliver all leaned forward in their chairs to get closer to Mr. Boreas and what information he was going to share with them.

'First off I'm impressed with each of you wanting to understand the standard of education and occupation selection for now. I see you want to be a part of the creation of a new paradigm for this generation and those to come. And you each assimilated this endeavor on your own, with the small bits of information that have been passing through the Outpost. This pleases me so much!' 'The Education Research Focus Group wants the Outpost to move into what's called _Thought_ _Formation_ for education within this generation, and away from _Social Structure_, that has been our model since we came to 621. This colony is growing, and we need fresh ideas. All of you did so well with the project and your presentations of the Galaxies and Space Travel. I'm sure you are aware that this whole project was monitored and recorded for future reference for your whole class' creativity and all the information you actually shared and expounded upon. You definitely had my vote for moving towards Thought Formation!

'Now I want to add a bit of information for your collection today. When the Outpost vessels landed, there was a new colonization population of 194 adults, 6 causalities, and 12 actual new "Outpost 1st generation" children. I am of the 2nd generation here on the outpost. A lot of us are 'aging out' but we want to leave this colony in the best and most capable hands.'

'When the vessels landed, there were actually only the three transports that were available for living quarters. The Volunteers were pioneers in every sense of the word! They had to create everything they needed for survival, and lay out plans for the colony to grow. So, look at where we are today!'

'Our population now stands at 257 residents with 48 unclassified children. Doesn't seem like that many reside here, but if you look closely at the outpost, you can see we have grown in our physical living space, so we can survive, create and move forward in the universe.

'Luna, I know you are always researching Earth history and I'm sure you have come across societal and family expectations or codes for occupations and inventions or creativity. I think you have found it was standard for hundreds of generations that children followed in their parents' occupations. Few went outside the family's business to create or build something new.'

'I want each of you to assimilate the information and history you have gathered today. Talk amongst yourselves about what you collected, and learned, but this MUST stay between us. This conversation or any part of it is not open for public discussion as of yet. But I want you to know, the adults are approaching this new curriculum one way and you are gathering and presenting important information from the prospective of young academics living in the deep rooted educational and social system used for generations. If at all possible, when the Education Focus Group meets, I will present this conversation and see if they would like to add you to the new educational program we are designing. I don't know what they will say, or how they will react. So... I need your promise on this matter.' 'Do you have any other questions of me?'

They all responded no, not at this time. But Luna once again asked if they did have any other questions that they could not answer, could she come to Mr. Boreas for assistance. He was ecstatic at what he was witnessing with this class. Mr. Boreas replied to the three of them, 'of course he would be of assistance.' With all this information, they got up and their salutations and headed out to the Concourse. Their brains swimming from all the gathered information about safety, stability, and creativity that they learned concerning the occupations of the Outpost today they each headed towards their own living quarters.

STARS

Luna kicked off her house clogs and climbed up on her bed. She had already put on her Tong pajamas; Mum had customized for her. She pushed the button to open the sky window and heard it quietly glide back to its resting locker. She found Moppet in between her pillow and cover so she puffed and snuggled under the blanket against the pillow with Moppet under her arm.

Luna started to look at the wondrous beauty above her head and automatically started thinking about the Blue Planet. Where was it? This amazing heaven above her was so vast – so eternal. Luna was so sleepy, her thoughts started drifting off. She looked at her favorite star, or was it even a star? She once again went to sleep with the thought "I'll have to find out about my star tomorrow."

The morning 'dawn' lighting was strengthening in Luna's room and she started to rise from her sleep. She then pushed another button to have 'full room' lighting and she once again looked up and out of the sky window and marveled at all the diamonds twinkling above her head. She then pressed the 'close' switch, and the protective covering glided back up its tracks and clicked to a stop at its designed resting position, locking the panel into place.

Luna climbed out of bed and went to her wardrobe to choose what she would wear to classes today. This ought to be an interesting day as the instructor was going to talk about how they got to Outpost 621, the universe, and stars and planets! Luna had no idea how much, or little information was going to be divulged to her and her peer group.

After dressing she went to the dining area to have her morning meal with Mum and Poppi. They were conversing lightly when Luna popped up to the table. Mum had an array of food set out and she was putting together an itemized list of food stuffs she wanted delivered from the Nutrition Supply Distribution Center for meals for the next few days.

Luna filled her plate with a variety of goodies she liked. Today she picked food that was pink and green in color. No one objected so it was her special game with food. After taking a few bites of food, Luna asked Poppi did he know what the instructor was going to give them information about in class today. Luna didn't understand why Poppi didn't teach or lead the classes as he was so smart. Poppi looked earnestly at his little girl, who was always so full of questions and replied in a joking way, with a big smile on his face, that he had no idea what was going to be presented. This was a truthful answer because with each new generation on the Outpost they were creating and pioneering a new society and documenting a new Universal history. Poppi thought to himself the stars, the planets, the galaxies, planet Earth, there was so much new material and data they were adding to their Outpost and utilizing in their daily lives.

Luna was not happy with Poppi's answer to her question. She immediately shot back to him "Why didn't he know?" With this response Mum looked up and the family once again could engage in an interchange of life as they knew it, past, present, and future.

Poppi decided to use this opening for a learning lesson, from the proper source – the classroom, instead of Luna going off to the PBS research pods. His daughter was always trying to be two jumps ahead of everyone and everything she thought about. But Poppi knew this colony was growing and Luna needed background information and the discipline to listen to others and hear their ideas and acknowledge that knowledge they shared if she was going to become the strong intellectual Poppi knew she was going to be. She needed to develop socially and not depend on Poppi for every answer. Poppi even thought he would like to sit in on her instruction today and hear and see what had been added or improved since he took classes at Luna's age. So Poppi – still smiling and being mischievous, answered Luna's proclamation with a challenging comment to Luna that she could not get out of in her usual head strong way. "Luna, I want you to listen to instructor today – and all this week, or whenever there is the topic of 'Stars', and bring back this information, and teach Mum and me about what you have learned." Luna couldn't believe her ears. Poppi wanted her to teach him.

She knew this was the definitive end to this discussion, and she knew she was being challenged by Poppi, so she acknowledged what he had requested of her. She finished her morning meal, she then hopped down from the table, went back to her sleeping room, got her materials for classes, turned off the lights in her room, to the 'rest' position – went back to the kitchen and picked up her snacks for the day – gave each of her parents a hug and kiss and headed out of their quarters down the concourse to the learning classrooms.

Luna kept wondering as to why Poppi had answered her question the way he did, and then as if they were playing a game, he challenged her. What was going on? Why would he do that? Luna trusted Poppi and knew something good or grand would come of this challenge, so she accepted the information he had given her. She went to her classroom and was startled as she entered the room at the various graphics and holograms that were on all four walls and the ceiling too!

She moved out of the doorway to just take it all in – it was like being in the A.I. Pod Headquarters – but she knew that was not possible. Stars and planets, and asteroids, and comets, and galaxies were projected everywhere. Luna could not take it all in.

She looked around the room for her friends, Kai, Sonnet, and Oliver. She searched for their faces for this initial presentation. Each was in their usual seat and everyone in the room just kept staring and pointing at various galactic objects of interest to each of them. There was hushed conversation in the room, but definitely all were intrigued with the stars. Luna stowed her belongings and went to her usual seat and just smiled in amazement when her friends glanced at her and they reciprocated. Today was going to be amazing.

A few minutes later instructor was at the door and when all the students were accounted for, the room went totally black. There was a sudden gasp from everyone in the room as they were taking in the universe and not paying attention to instructor or what he was doing.

After the initial shock of total blackness, the room became hushed and the instructor started the morning with the comment "this is where we live; so large and vast it appears black to us." Instructor then turned on two small lights, one on the dais from which notes and other teaching accessories were laid out. The second light was very small appearing to be a pale blue becoming visible in the corner of the room. Luna's eyes were becoming used to the darkness, instructor walked to the far corner where the pale blue light was and pointed to it. "This is where we came from hundreds of years ago." Luna gasped! Could she actually see Earth from the compound where she lived?

Instructor then hit some switches and turned on different sets of small twinkling lights – being stars, and within the set were globes of different sizes and colors that represented planets. When the students could focus, and assimilate what was being projected, Instructor announced this was the Andromeda Galaxy. Luna was searching for Earth, but could not find it. The "Andromeda" lights were dim, but did not align with where Luna could find Earth. The Instructor then pointed out a small globe amidst this group of stars and planets, with several dark spaces in it, and this is where we live now. This is our home now. This is Outpost 621.

Hands went flying up in the air, full of questions. Instructor quietly said, "Today you will be introduced to the cosmos. Take notes, and write down your inquiries. There is a whole universe we are going to explore."

The stars went black again, and a different set of stars lit up. Luna immediately saw the small blue orb. There were other globes of different sizes and colors mixed in a cloud of solar dust, comets, asteroids, and a larger bright star towards the center. The Instructor announced that this was the Milky Way Galaxy, and again pointed to Earth. "This is from which our volunteered forefathers came from." All of the students were in awe at the presentation, and were looking and writing notes as quickly as possible. Luna knew some of the students had done research of the universe before, but at our age this was so much to take in.

The stars dimmed one more time to darkness, then a third set of stars became apparent at the back of the room. Instructor announced that this was the third closest galaxy to Earth and had been named Canis Major Dwarf. Everyone in the room choked down laughing at a galaxy that had been named after a dog that was a dwarf, only no one dared to comment on this aloud. The only other small light in the room's universe was the small blue orb being the representation of Earth. Luna looked back and forth between the laminations. There was a huge difference. What was coming next?

Instructor next turned off the Cosmos representation that had been created and the students were in the dark again. This time the light button for "classroom bright" was touched, and everyone had to blink and squint to adjust their eyes to what was the room normal to them. The Instructor smiled at the impression that the light presentation had made on the students. He then went to his notes and the holographic work board. He started with "I think we need to go way back in our history and start with Earth."

He then put up some images for ancient Earth locations: The Aztec Ruins; The Pyramids of Giza; The Hanging Gardens of Babylon; The Parthenon and Athena in Athens; and Zhengzhou China/Shang Dynasty Ruins. Instructor commented "All of the wondrous buildings and temples were created long before the cultures of any of the individual civilizations on Earth had this technology. Therefore, the idea, dream, or acknowledgement of space travel had been realized centuries earlier when each of these artifacts was realized. There had been a 'source' that had brought these concepts to Earth, and for some reason their grand ideas were seeds planted and each mutated in their own special way."

"At the time the Commission Planners came together the Earth's population was close to Eleven Billion people. There were many strong progressive thinking people that were behind the project for Earth to take on galactic travel.

Copernicus – Astronomer – published orbit of planets

Albert Einstein – Theoretical physicist – found Worm Holes

Edwin Hubble – Astronomer – He mathematically verified that the Galaxies were three dimensional and that there were hundreds in the Universe

Dr. Robert Goddard of NASA - Theoretical and practical breakthroughs for space travel

Dr. Stephen Hawking – physicist and cosmologist – found Black Holes,

Gene Rodenberry – Published writer who dared to dream of space travel

Sir Richard Branson – a forerunner in privately funded space flights,

There were many contributing time/space continuum researchers that found and verified Time Warps on earth.

These are just to name a few who looked and believed in the stars and the universe."

"Now a brief 'mileage' gauge about what we know at the moment about the Universe we're in, and those around us."

"Earth to its Sun's distance is miniscule to the diameter of the Milky Way, which is 980 thousand light years in diameter. The Milky Way happens to be elliptical in shape and has between 100 to 400 billion stars. The Andromeda Galaxy is where we live now on a planet named Gliese 581d. This galaxy is 2.54 million light years from Earth and is spherical in shape. It has approximately 1 trillion stars and has only qualified 7 planets. We live on one of these planets. The third galaxy we will briefly discuss is Canis Major Dwarf. It is called an Irregular Galaxy as this supposed galaxy has a high percentage of 'Red Giant' stars. It contains an estimated Billion stars, and with information we are currently using estimate this galaxy approximately 25 thousand light years away."

With this the Instructor stopped his lesson and suggested they all take a break.

Luna was overwhelmed, but she wanted to see all the galaxies again. Kai and Oliver came over and asked would she like to join them for snacks. Of course, she would. They went out to the courtyard and found seating and all three had no sooner got their food and beverages out, when all three started talking at once.

Sonnet came over to the table and plopped down, ignoring the other 3 chattering all together. She looked at each of them and raised both arms over her head, and broke out into a loud harmonic lyric that she 'loved the stars and we're all part of them.'

Her friends stopped mid-sentence and looked at her, as Sonnet was usually so quiet. They were all moved and energized.

SPACE TRAVELING
THE STARS

Sometimes class instruction was so boring to Luna, she took the one word or idea and went to seek her own answers. Today was different. Poppi was right. She was glad to be in class today. Instructor had been creative with subject matter at hand of astronomy. Instead of making the universe, space travel, our outpost, all the historical data small and tedious, he had completely brought it into the classroom showing the vastness of the Universe with the hologram graphics making everything come alive! Instructor chose not to compartmentalize each galaxy with use of classroom tools of the student tablets or the classroom holographic work board.

After snacks, with everyone talking and defusing some of their energy, they were all ready to go back to class, and look and listen to what is going to come next. Luna was so excited with this presentation of information, she was already thinking of going to the Data Archives Center to review information she had read about, and cross reference with 'what had she missed?'

With everyone back in class, Instructor was at the dais, ready and awaiting his student's attention. He opened with 'There are different ways we can approach our Stars and Space Travel. We can continue in lecture form, as this morning. Or I know you all have questions, and I can answer those.' A big smile broke out on his face …'or we use them as an assignment to find the answers and then share with the class. We can break into groups and each group can research questions asked in each category, and bring back supporting information and lead the class instruction with what you have learned, and by the end of this project, each of you will have a volume of information you have learned and assimilated on our universe. I will be at hand to assist and support any inquiries that you may come across.' Everyone raised their hands and they were flailing in the air to get Instructor's attention.

'I will step out of the room for all of you to work together and decide how you would like to proceed with this project' The hands came down and determined faces quickly went to their notes they had made; resolute expressions were on each face as the Instructor walked out of the classroom. How could they each, and together, gather all the wondrous facts and impress their peers and Instructor as well? Luna was tickled; here was her second challenge of the day.

Instructor was sauntering up and down the hallway that connected to instruction classrooms, his stride making a rhythmic patter as he went until the enthusiasm coming from his classroom drowned out his steps. He let his students express themselves for a little while until some of the commotion settled down, and then he headed back to his room in anticipation of what choices his class had made.

When he walked in, the whole class had hands in the air waving to get his attention, and all were talking at once.

The Instructor said in a quiet voice "I know you have had some discussion amongst yourselves and have ideas." "Let's address the way you would like to move forward with our studies."

Without even waiting for Instructor's next comment, Oliver voiced a collaborative comment back to the Instructor's opening comment. "Sir, we would like to gather everyone's questions and proposals, then separate them out into three or four areas of Galactic study, and then work in separate groups to research each concept and share with class as a whole." The Instructor's face showed approval as he commented "that is a wonderful way to cover a lot of material and I do believe *all* of you want to participate in this journey of the Universe."

Reaching down under his study area, Instructor pulled out a basket he intended to use. "So, our first step is for you to pass all your notes and questions to me. And please have a single idea on each slip of paper, so we can sort into subjects or concepts."

Everyone went to their notes and quickly and carefully transcribed their questions and ideas onto papers to pass into the Instructor. As he was waiting on the class to finish this step of their newly proposed idea of study, he teasingly asked did the class want to do any 'Instructor lead' lectures about the universe at this time? He already knew they wanted independent research, and he was happy that they were being proactive with the project, without coaxing. Most the class was silent at his question, a few nodded their heads in a side to side in a "no" motion, and there were only a couple of mumbled verbal "no's." When everyone was ready, Instructor started passing the basket around the room, for everyone to put their papers in. The basket came back to him, and he asked the class another question for them to make a collective decision on," Would you like me do breakdown each of the significant suggestions, questions and meanings into groups;

or would you, as a class like to do this? I can see this basket has a lot of ideas in it!"

The Instructor was pleased they were all so excited with this area of study. As part of their continued education on the Galaxies today, the class had chosen to put each of the submissions in the correct category. The instructor rummaged through the slips and could see that this idea had merit as there was a vast variety of questions, explorations and investigations the students wanted to take on. Instructor turned on the Holographic Work board and said, "Let's get started." He wrote across the top of the board five different topics: Galactic Travel from Earth, Andromeda, Milky Way, Canis Major Dwarf, and Space Travelers to Earth. The anticipation was mounting as everyone saw how Instructor was dividing up the areas and groups of study that they had turned in.

Further challenging his students, the Instructor picked up the basket and handed it to the first student sitting on the right side of the room. Taking out one slip of paper, Instructor stated: "I would like each of you to pick out one paper, and read off the request or question." He flipped the tab of paper through his fingers. "Then as a group, I want all of you to decide which category this particular 'slip' belongs in." He then replaced the slip back in the basket. "Got it?" Smiles were on all their faces. Each student awaiting their chance to put a topic on the board, and each of them had their favorite categories, and the Instructor would let them debate the questions if necessary. ('Way to go! What fun!' Luna thought.)

Everyone pulled out a tab of paper and for the most part, there was agreement and equivalent numbers of students for each category. Only one student needed to make a second choice for this project. Everyone seemed happy. Each topic had four students assigned to it, of their own choosing. Instructor then asked the class if they felt that two weeks was enough time to complete their research on their topic.

He then added further instructions that two hours class time each day would be allowed for this project, as well as any out of class time they wished to spend. He further stated that information was available at the Data Archives Center, as well as inquiries were open from personnel at the observatory, information gathered from elder residents could be used. Instructor also said in a modest way, he was totally available for all the students, at any time.

Luna was part of the group 'Galactic Travel from Earth,' along with Oliver, Sonnet, and Kai. She was happy, and it just worked out that way.

Instructor gave two more brief instructions. Each group gathers together independently and makes a rough outline of their subject based on the investigations that the class had posed, from the whole collection of class inquiries. Luna and her group quickly started writing down the ideas that had been brought up from earlier today. Oliver made a master list that consisted of:

Creation of the Commission

Destination- Triad of ships and targets

Social – comprehensive and progressive volunteers

Food- sustainable for journey and at new outpost

Materials and fuel for ship

When each of the groups finished this assignment, the Instructor was pleased with that he reviewed from each group. At this point Instructor dismissed class for the day, and told his students to start their own research for the rest of the afternoon class time. All the class was thrilled with their extra time allowed, and with the project as a whole.

Oliver, Sonnet, Kai, and Luna quickly conversed as to what they were thinking about for starting their project this evening. They all had different ideas, and so they adjourned from the class, and each headed off in their own direction to think about what this project totally entails and to start gathering the basics of information, and ask questions.

Luna was meandering up the concourse toward her living quarters, and her head was full of ideas about Space travel from Earth to where we live now on Outpost 621. She had done some investigation before about this planet, where we live now, and how it related to earth. But this was going to be bigger and fuller and much more interesting. The whole class, all the Outpost volunteers, and all of history were going to participate in this presentation. This presentation wasn't just reading. It would be 'three dimensional.' On the way home, Luna decided that she was going to make notes on all of the items the group was going to make its presentation on. Oliver said, just pick one, but that was so limiting! She had ideas, maybe they were different than the others selected, or her idea went into more detail. Could always circle back and add or drop information. Instructor said that each group would do a presentation after information collection in two weeks, but he did not say how long the presentation was to last. Hummm? Interesting question. Presentation time needed to be clarified for all of the groups.

Luna was almost home, so she let go of the stars and galaxies long enough to have the thought that she was hungry. She wondered what Mum would have for snacks for her today.

When was Poppi going to be home? She had so much she wanted to ask him, and to tell him of their class experience and the assignment given today.

Arriving home, Luna went to her room, turned on the lights. Put her tablet on the study desk, and went back to the kitchen area. Mum was busy fixing something yummy for their evening meal, but she already had a snack of some fruits, vegetables and hummus on the table with some sparkling water for Luna. Fixing a plate for her snacks, Luna addressed Mum and as calmly as she could that she had a great day in class today. Mum looked up at her, and noted that Luna almost sparkled with excitement. Mum wanted to ask why was she home earlier than usual from her formal studies but carefully inquired 'care to share with me?' Luna stuffed food in her mouth so she would not have to answer. She mischievously shook her head 'no'. She partially chewed her food, then swallowed, then replied to Mum "Would it be OK if she shared her day at meal time with both her and Poppi, it was so wonderful." Mum knew that Luna was on track of another exciting activity that was engrossing to her young daughter. Mum smiled and said that was perfectly alright, but she wanted all the details at supper. Almost finishing her snack, Luna grabbed a few extra crackers and headed to her room. Almost dashing to her tablet where she had her original notes, and then the class assignment they had agreed on, and then Luna was looking up information she had already archived on her own tablet about subject matter. Oh, this was going to be fun. Luna got out an auxiliary tablet she used for her own personal notes and research. Turned the unit on and went to a fresh window and started reciting questions and notes she made earlier in class this morning. She then went to the 5 categories of Galaxy study the class was going to do and dictated them into her tablet. Luna then added the theme of her group with the breakdown of the subject areas to her notes.

Creation of the Commission

Destination- Triad of ships and targets

Social – comprehensive and progressive volunteers

Food- sustainable for journey and at new outpost

Materials and fuel for ship

The next list she started working on was the departments or people she wanted to gather information from for their project. Luna knew Oliver would probably be setting up their project in the same manner, which was OK by her. There was a lot of information they were going to cover. Luna wanted to look at 'her stars', and think about how her world had been expanded today. The Sky Window cover slid back into its resting cradle, and she climbed up on her bed, with both her tablets, and started talking to Moppet. Luna had clicked on the microphone of her personal tablet she was making notes with. "Who do you think we should ask for information about our new colony, Moppet?" "I know we'll start with Poppi this evening when he comes home, he always has good ideas." "I think we need to concentrate on the Data Storage & Archival Studies Center, also." "Mum would be glad to help with leading our group in the best directions about food stuffs... oh... that would be present and past!" Luna took a deep breath and looked up at her stars, and she continued with her notes: "I'm sure we could get good information and data from the observatory about how we got here, and where to look in the archives about our ancestors actual travel and arrival on this planet" "I bet there is information that the scientists shared on both subjects that is known in their workplace, that is not generally known around the whole Outpost. But Moppet, if we get some of that secret information, you must help remind me to ask Poppi first if we can share it with our class. OK?" "Oliver will have some great ideas how to collect fun information for our project also, I'm sure." "Moppet, how do you think Oliver will want to break down all this information for our project?" "I know... you want to think about it." "Poppi and Instructor could help us with the other three branches of our investigations." Luna's ears perked up.

The front door shut with a bang after Poppi's entrance of coming home for the evening. Luna sat up, totally alert now, wanting to talk to Poppi about her day. She snapped off her tablet recorder, grabbed Moppet, and ran up the hall of their quarters to greet Poppi. At least four steps in front of him, Luna took a flying leap and landed in his arms. (Poppi loved it when his little girl showed him so much love and enthusiasm) She wrapped her little arms around his neck, gave him a quick kiss, and without taking a breath, started to tell him about her wonderful day in class. Mum was so touched at her family as she looked on, she had to turn and go back to the dining area, to wipe the tears from her eyes. Her thought and prayer was "please allow this whole community to show love, passion, and connection for this Outpost to thrive and survive." Poppi's smile was as big as a rainbow, as he let Luna slide down to the floor. He looked at her solemnly and said, with a wink- "we better go check in with Mum to see when our meal is ready, and you know Mum gets kisses too!"

Walking around the corner to the dining area Poppi, gave his usual hugs and salutations to Mum, and inquired as to dinner time. She replied with a grand sweep of her arm and hand that it awaited him. Luna always laughed at them play acting like that. But today it was special as she knew they both wanted to hear about her day in class. Poppi took Luna's hand and they went to do a quick wash up then return to the table for their evening meal. Luna knew there was a family protocol, but she was busting her cheeks she wanted to talk so much.

Luna went back to her room and picked up both tablets and brought them to dinner. She knew this wasn't normally allowed at meal time, but there was information she wanted to share, and she would ask permission if she could share what was on her tablets before just opening them and making a distraction at dinner. When they finally sat down at the table, and they all had their portions of food on plates before them, Poppi finally asked Luna how was class today? "Poppi, Mum, I saw three Galaxies today! Have you seen the three Galaxies that are the closest to us? I saw the planet Earth in the Milky Way! Do you know where that's at?" Mum and Poppi were trying not to chuckle out loud at Luna's gusto in her opening sentences. They both knew there was a lot more where this was coming from.

Luna shared her day with both her parents, and they were amazed at her retention of information so far; she hardly referred to her tablets, even though she asked permission to bring them to dinner. She revealed how the Instructor had set up the study of the Galaxies and the Outpost volunteers travel to this planet for the class with all its grandeur to her. She disclosed her dismay that from this planet where we live now, that you cannot see Earth, her Blue planet, as they did not align. Luna kept her excited pace up with sharing all that she was mesmerized with today, and how the Instructor have given the whole class free reign for research, investigation and explorations of this major part of their history. She shared that her friends Kai, Oliver, and Sonnet were her group partners. At this point Poppi and Mum started making comments about the project and asking questions. Luna picked up one of her tablets and turned to Poppi and asked him if he would be one of her resources. Before he could answer, Luna shyly looked at Mum and asked the same question. Both parents laughed at the situation and whole heartedly agreed they would help her and her group in any way they could. The three sat at the dinner table a long time after the meal was finished chatting, full of anticipation of what these young academics were going to come up with. This was one of the inspirations that the Outpost perpetually offered. This was a young colony and with the influx of youthful energy and growing inquisitiveness, the Outpost could and would stay on its Mission Covenant. Finally, Luna asked to be excused as she was tired. She went back to her room and dressed for sleep, picked up Moppet and climbed into her warm soft bed. She wondered "what is Oliver and the others going to bring to class tomorrow for our project?"

THE INVENTION OF HOME

Luna had been doing studies about the Outpost history and how they had progressed over the last hundred years, but today it seemed as if she was not really aware of how this Outpost came to be, as she was living in it today. She gave thought to all the different wings and departments, and all of this had come about with a fairly constant population of about 200 residents, mirroring the original volunteers. How was this possible? Luna thought about asking Poppi and Mum, or even Grandpapa Sebastian, but decided she wanted to do some research herself first. So, she set off to the Data Storage and Archival Studies wing with her own thoughts and only her tablet to make notes with. She knew she had to be back at their home in time for the evening meal, so she just sent Mum a message of where she was going because she wanted to do some research.

When she got to the Data Archive Center she signed in and had given some thought as to what was going to be her 'Search' criteria. She had opted for 'Mission Voyagers' Landing.' She knew from documented history that there were three ships that landed on Gliese 581d one hundred and two years ago.

When Luna put in her search information, data started popping up. There were various documented articles from different departments. She first noted that the three ships were stocked, loaded and carried materials and people in a very strategic manner. Ship number one carried the voyagers, and minimal staples and machinery for the trip. Ship number two carried the rest of the volunteers and all food stores and necessary seeds, plants and animals for the colonization. Ship number three carried all the computers, materials and building supplies for the creation of their new Outpost. It was important that the guidance systems were programmed in sync for the three ships to make this uncharted voyage, and no really knew if it was going to succeed. To date Luna knew that there not any communication from planet Earth or the other two teams of voyagers that left Earth at the same time with different destinations after they went through the Worm holes.

The three ships landed unharmed and the volunteers were glad to be at their destination on ground again with a gravitational pull to it. They were especially aware of the different speeds they traveled at during certain intervals of the trip. The volunteers had practiced their space flight stressors, but the constant uncertainty of direction had left all their bodies with tension. Upon landing, everyone knew their assigned jobs and stations they were to be working at.

Immediate attention was given to the third ship with all the building supplies and computers. They had to unload rovers and drones to make room to access other necessities and access the computer systems to get them online so they could start their assembly processes for the mandatory build out of the Outpost. Everything seems a jumble for the first few weeks on the planet, in their very confined quarters. The information here was informative, but dry in its content.

What about the people? That was her first question she put into her tablet as she realized that there was going to be a good bit of information available about how the Voyagers prepared for this trip. How had they physically, emotionally, socially, and spiritually held up?

This was her home; she wanted to know how it was built. She went back to the data journal she started with. The reading was fascinating. Before leaving Earth, the Volunteers had practiced loading and storing goods and equipment and how to easily access it once in a different gravitational setting, as well as disassembling and reassembling parts and components to start the core of their outpost. This was done with the use of the drones, rovers, grabbing devices and their own know how and adaption to this new environment.

They first must find water, or be able to purify and recycle the water. This planet had shown results with a high capacity to be able to complete this task. The second task was for the geologists to take samples and test the composition of rocks, dust and minerals that the outpost truly had to use now. The hypotheses quantities of materials they thought were available from their acquired data on earth were equivocal and not valid in their current situation after evaluating these items, hands on. There were qualified engineers that quickly started disassembling the third ship and part of the second ship to make working stations where analysis and life support could be set up. The first ship mainly stayed intact for housing- sleeping quarters, recreation, and food preparation. This journal referred to another journal as to volunteer assignments, and duties, a daily cycle for each volunteer of 11 hours of job obligations or review of newly acquired data studies, 8 hours for rest and relaxation and 5 hours for eating and personal grooming. There were three shifts distributed to all of the volunteers, and this meant the 2/3 of the population was up and constructing or enhancing their Outpost and

1/3 was resting, so they could keep strong and focused on their responsibilities. The Botanists and gardeners set to their tasks within weeks. The plant cultivators set to work on expanding and feeding the large crew a wider variety of healthy meals and work on what could be grown quickly, with positive results with the "growing houses" they were setting up, with the assistance of the dietitians.

Within the first 6 months the community had settled into this new lifestyle with little opposition. They all were well trained and knew this was their major legacy to new colonization, and human life going forward. The whole Outpost depended on each and every one of them.

Luna had read enough to know that she had not accessed some critical data journals or reports as to the human condition and equipment and food stores, so she decided she would stop her research this afternoon, and go see Grandpapa Sebastian on her way to their home quarters. She was sure he could help direct her in where to find the missing records that she was interested in. Probably just not putting in the correct search words, since this was older archived information, not accessed much in recent years. Luna felt she had made some interesting finds today, and she was eager to start drawing pictures of what she imagined these ships and the original infancy of the Outpost looked like. She was happy to go and speak with Grandpapa Sebastian again, so she sent him a message asking if she could meet him at his engineering command in the Observatory and ask him some questions about the beginnings of the Outpost history. She sent Mum another message that she was stopping to visit Grandpapa, and then would be home in time for the evening meal.

As she was walking towards the Observatory, she got a response from Grandpapa Sebastian that he would meet her at the door and he'd be happy to help her with her questions. When she turned the corner and saw him there, he had a big smile on his face anticipating her arrival, and what was his granddaughter up to now? He opened the door, and simultaneously held his arms open to give Luna a big hug. She cuddled into his strong upper chest and reciprocated a hug, sliding down after they had crossed the security of the observatory entrance. Once again they headed towards the lounge area for them to have a chat. 'What are you looking into now, Miss Luna? What Can I help you with?' Grandpapa Sebastian asked as he arranged two chairs for them to have an intimate conversation. Luna knew how valuable Grandpapa's work time was, so she pulled out her tablet, glancing at her notes, and looked up at him, diving right into her direct inquiries as how to locate the information she wanted to read about. 'Grandpapa Sebastian, I want to know how we built the Outpost. How did we make this our home? In the allotted time that we have been on this planet, how did we become so advanced?'

Grandpapa Sebastian was once again surprised at the insightful subject matter that Luna was investigating. Grandpapa settled back into his chair and looked into Luna's big blue questioning eyes. 'This is a broad subject that you are asking me about, Luna. What area of growth, expansion or history do you want to know about?' Luna smiled and quickly replied 'Everything!' Grandpapa Sebastian laughed. 'That's a tall order!'

'Well young lady let's start with how the volunteers documented the history of their voyage. Since they had limited access to communications while they were traveling, they chose four historical scribes to work in different journals that are now housed in the Data Archives Center. The first being was the distance traveled and anomalies observed. The second journal was the daily function of equipment. The third journal was the human mindset into such an extraordinary voyage. The fourth was an inventory catalog. Have you located these journals yet?' Luna was wide eyed with this much information being available and replied to Grandpapa, 'No, I have no idea where they are at in the center; but I do know where the mission statement is located and I refer to the Archive's digital copy all the time,' she said with a smile. Grandpapa smiled back and said, 'That's very good.' Luna went on to say that today she used the archive's data and pulled up information on the three ships landing on Gliese 581d and their first few months of initial assembling and research of the planet.

Luna turned up her nose and told Grandpapa that this was very interesting historical undertakings and achievement, yet it was really dry since there wasn't human commentary or thought included. Luna lit up and asked Grandpapa Sebastian, 'Where would she find the four journals he was referring to and was she authorized at her age to handle and review them?' Luna got a serious look on her face with that question and asked, 'Grandpapa, how long do you think it had been since anyone has even looked at these journals?' He looked back at her and replied, 'Luna, I am not sure because most of this history of these journals was relayed to me by my Grandfather since he was an original volunteer. I think you will need to ask one of the archive's docents where these precious journals are kept and your ability to review them or if the data from those journals have been transferred to a digital format that you can review.' Grandpapa Sebastian was elated to turn over this treasured information to Luna to satisfy her quest for enlightenment about the Outpost.

Luna was twitching in her seat. She was so happy that she now had information to go back and search for... her intended subject matter. Grandpapa so readily directed her where to find information. Luna looked up to her Grandpapa Sebastian with tears in her eyes and told him she wished she could hear these stories first hand from her family that had lived through this. 'I think I have enough information to go back to the archives and look for the journals and information and start my own vision of how the outpost was created.' She looked up at him and asked, 'would you like to see a drawing that I started today with the information that I did find?' He looked up with a big smile on his face and said, 'Of Course!' Luna quickly pulled out her tablet, flipped to the page where she started her draft of the Outpost compound, and handed it over to Grandpapa Sebastian.

He was so amazed at what she captured and visualized with the information that she did find today, he had tears in his eyes. She was such an asset to the Outpost, he thought. Where was his granddaughter going to end up? Luna saw his reaction, slid off of her chair and told him that she needed to get home for the evening meal. She gave him a hug and thanked him. She had enough direction that she could search in a new direction for the journals that he had advised her about.

Luna took off, out of the observatory, almost running to get to her quarters and share with Mum and Poppi what her project was for this week. She calmed down by the time she got home, going in to wash up for the evening meal. The front door finally opened, Poppi made his entrance and Luna jumped into his arms with all the excitement she wanted to share about the day. Neither Poppi nor Mum could get a sentence in, because Luna was telling her story so colorfully. Their daughter had finally calmed down and wore herself out by desert. By then, Mum suggested she take a bath and go to bed. Luna readily agreed. She hugged Mum and Poppi and set off to find Moppet and go to sleep.

The next morning, Luna woke up with anticipation of being able to get to the Archives and start looking for the journals, but she had to do her normal daily routine first... breakfast, school and lunch. That didn't feel like much fun today. She wanted to explore. She made her appearance with Moppet in hand and munched on her breakfast. Mum already knew the answer to her question, but asked what Luna was going to do after school today. This set her off and she shared with Mum that she was going to the Archives to learn how the Outpost was built. She then brightened up and asked Mum did she want to see her initial drawing of the frontier Outpost? Mum was astonished, replying, 'You're already doing an illustration of our establishment?' Luna grabbed Moppet, went to her room, put Moppet to bed, got her tablet and school books, and went back to the dining area, handing Mum her tablet with her drawing displayed. Mum asked her, 'Where did you get this concept from?' 'I'll have to tell you later. I have to get to class.'

Out the front door she went, down the concourse to her classes hoping the day would go quickly.

It seemed as if classes would never end for Luna today. She was totally lost in thought of what she would discover in the Journals that lay in wait of her attention at the Data Archives Center.

Finally, Instructor dismissed the class and she was free to go to the Data Center. 'Luna, wait a moment, please, I would like to speak to you,' the Instructor addressed her as she started for the door. Luna's shoulders dropped. What did she need to do now? Why was she singled out again? She turned and walked over to the Instructor's lectern in response to his request. She looked up at him inquisitively awaiting his request. His face relaxed some as he asked her the question of where her thoughts had been all day, as she certainly wasn't attentive in class, as usual. 'Sir, I'm sorry I was not giving my full attention to my studies today, but I have a special project I am investigating. I want to know about the invention of our home, here on this planet.' 'Oh really?' the Instructor replied not having any idea of what Luna was researching this time. 'Sir, I have started reviewing data in the Archival Center about how the Outpost was started. I spoke with my Grandpapa Sebastian yesterday and he gave me some more ideas of where to look for the information I want.' 'You do know that next year we will be addressing that very topic of study, The History of our Outpost,' Instructor countered. 'I did not know that, Sir. If there is anything you do not want me to divulge from my research right now, I will gladly keep the information for my own personal interests. I do not want to interfere with your teaching curriculum.' 'Luna, do you feel you need to make a special individual investigation of our Outpost history for your information alone?'

'Well Sir, I just want to examine data for my own personal interests, and see where it leads me.' She took a breath and continued. 'I became intrigued at all the tiny bits of information I found in just a few hours yesterday. I would like to continue, if you have no objection?' Luna became suddenly leery that she was doing something that she was not supposed to be looking into. The Instructor leaned back on his chair, and smiled, 'I have no issue with what you chose to discover or investigate on your own time, but… you must keep this project out of the classroom right now. You must focus on your current studies. I'm delighted to see that you still do investigations to understand and gather information, even when out of our structured class setting. If there is anything that I can be of assistance with, let me know, and we will see if we can work through the issue together.' Luna gave Instructor a big smile and was asking for a dismissal, 'Thank you Sir, I will be much more attentive and will ask if I need assistance about our Home.' With that she turned and left the room heading straight for the Data Storage & Archival Studies Wing.

When she arrived at the center she sought out Mr. Tomohiro, the lead Docent. She was sure she would need to be making her requests directly to the Senior Engineer for the information she wanted to examine. The Docent came out from a back hallway, walking up to Luna as if she was the most important person of the community. When he stopped before her, he asked how he could be of service. Luna had never needed or met this man before. He seemed genuinely happy to be of assistance to her. He was only a few centimeters taller than she was, so Luna felt totally comfortable at this point to ask for the very special historical journal records, as they casually stood at the information desk. Mr. Tomohiro was taking in every word of the request that Luna was making and sizing up the relevance of this young girl's interest in the journals. She went on to say she had been in the Archives yesterday and found some information, but it was not getting to the root of what she was looking for. She also relayed that she had spoken to her Grandpapa Sebastian and he was the one that suggested that the original journals may hold the insight she was looking for. This peeked Mr. Tomohiro's interest as this was Sebastian Grandiose Vite's granddaughter and very rarely had anyone in recent years come to the Archives requesting to review the Outpost's earliest journals.

He had made a decision as he was listening to Luna. He asked if she would please follow him. They trekked up a few hallways making a turn right and left along the way to a special see-through enclosed room that was locked. Mr. Tomohiro was unlocking the door telling Luna this was where original documents were kept in a climate controlled, dust free environment, for their upmost safety. He asked that Luna leave her personal belongings outside the room. Luna understood this was part of protocol; it didn't have to do with her age or any other possible aspect. He put on a pair of gloves as they walked between a few aisles of books, prints and paintings. He stopped in front of another glassed-in bookcase with four shelves in it. Pulling himself up to his full height, in the most dignified and professional manner he pointed to the journals that Luna was looking for.

'If you would like to view these journals, I will be glad to assist you, however for historical artifact safety, I am the only one allowed to handle these books. Although, please note, in addition, that everything has been digitized and is available for your reading and research pleasure. I will take you to that area later so you can continue your exploration.

Luna was amazed at the prized dignity and responsibility that Mr. Tomohiro gave to his position and the historical data that he was guardian over. She humbly asked could she just see the books in their original version. Mr. Tomohiro was hoping she would make such a request. He opened the case and brought down four journals and took them to a small table for the both of them to sit down and review.

Luna's heart swelled and a big smile broke out on her face as Mr. Tomohiro opened the first journal. This white book was older and tattered, showing a lot of use and handling. The book's aged cover had an apparent webbing pattern, creating an almost translucent pearl effect. Upon opening the book, he went to the first section that was the log of all 200 of the volunteers. Their ages and occupations were in separate columns. The docent looked up to Luna and told her that this book was comprised before they left earth and had the complete registry of everything that was accountable for their survival. He just showed her a list of the volunteers; he then flipped to the next section that was the log of all food stuffs which was divided into two categories. One was for food and water during flight. The second was for seeds, plants and animals needed for food upon arrival on the new planet.

Luna raised her hand and wanted to view the list that the page was open to regarding food stuffs and how it was accounted for. Once she had taken in the information that was available on that page to her, she was ready to go to the next section. Luna told the docent 'Thank You' which was their signal to move on to the next section.

Mr. Tomohiro flipped to the next section which was clothing and housing supplies, recorded in the same manner as the food items. This satisfied Luna's interest and she asked if there were any other sections in this journal? He nodded 'yes' and flipped to the next section which was the machinery, tools, electronics, building supplies, and computers that were on board. Luna looked at this section with interest and asked if the docent could show her a couple of other pages. When she was finished looking at these, she was amazed at the detail of each of the items that were needed and documented. The docent flipped more pages to reach the last section of this journal; there were only about pages four left. 'This was next to the last section of this journal.' He readjusted himself in his chair, inquiring of Luna, 'Do you have any idea what is in the last section of this journal?' Luna's eyes grew large as she had no idea what he was referring to, and shook her head no. On the first page was one of the first copies of the Mission Statement written out. He went further and turned a few more pages. At the top of the new page was The Commission's mandatory pledge that each of the volunteer's made for the voyage, taking the vow to uphold the Statement, surrendering their earth surnames for the betterment of mankind. Underneath the statement was a listing of signatures of every volunteer. Luna was stunned by what she was seeing and reading. She looked at the docent and exclaimed, 'Really?' Mr. Tomohiro nodded a solemn 'Yes.' 'Our ancestor's made the ultimate sacrifice for this journey.' Luna, responded, still stunned, 'Wow, yes they really did!' With that he reverently closed the white journal.

Mr. Tomohiro was happy that Luna understood the importance of the documents she was viewing with him. He asked, 'Are you ready to move on to the next Journal?' She smiled and scooted her chair closer to the docent's as he put the white journal on the table and pickled up the next one, which was red. None of the books were labeled, and

Luna had no idea of what this Journal would relay. She asked inquisitively, 'Why are there different colored journals?' Mr. Tomohiro smiled so broadly his teeth showed. 'You are a clever observer, young one! Each journal color is an important identifier as to who was responsible for that log, and each color had Eastern Japanese significance. The white was the purity and honesty of the voyage, the red represented energy and ambition, the blue was the universe and travels, and the last color, was the all-important green. This symbolizes our population and outpost growth and renewal. I was going to point this out in a later journal, but you already are adept at how everything on this mission had a place and purpose.'

Opening the red book, this one was broken down into categories also, but was not a ledger, it was a journal. This book represented tedious notes on paraphernalia of all kinds. Separate departments of different types of equipment, next was a date, and then a ledger entry of what was new, unexpected of the equipment, or what was malfunctioning and what was needed to correct the issue. This went on for page after page. Luna understood the significance of such detailed information to be able to refer to at any needed time, in their current time or in our present time period. Luna was very impressed by what she was seeing, and being allowed to experience. She tugged lightly on Mr. Tomohiro's sleeve, signaling she was ready to move on to the next Journal.

This was the blue one, travel and the universe. Mr. Tomohiro opened is book to the first page was dated and signed in as date of launch from Earth. They had left earth through an Energy Vortex that had propelled them further than expected; the flight plan was staying on the expected course. Trajectory of launch was successful.

This journal had a straight forward date and entry for each significant incident that the Volunteers felt was worthy of making notes about. There were lots of notes and comments from the astrophysicists' and engineers on the pages Luna was taking note of. Then the docent stopped on a page that the book had been opened to many times and Luna looked at what Mr. Tomohiro was pointing to. It was a date and subject was "Time." They had passed through a worm hole, and the voyagers were not sure how long they had been in it as their capacity to tell time was lost. None of their time pieces were accurate any longer. With this new dilemma, they had to call an emergency meeting of the Mission Flight Committee to create a new way to measure time. Time is infinite, but it is necessary to measure and be able to base calculations on. This must be adjusted and ratified as quickly as possible.

Luna was just staring at the words on the page; she had never given any thought to the idea that the Outpost was not using Earth "time." Every venture she went on in the hologram, she was in some unknown time-space continuum. It was a new creation that was invented for their voyage and from that day she read about in the journal, forward. 'Pretty incredible, isn't it?' Mr. Tomohiro asked Luna. She looked up at him, with all sincerity, and said 'that was one thing I had never given any thought to.'

The next entry was about two days later when it was documented that there had been no communication that had come through of the other two groups of Voyagers, since they had entered the Worm Hole. It was noted that more data on subject would follow as 621 would start tracking this information void, to see if communication would be reestablished.

'Are you ready to go to the last journal, or do you have any other questions?' 'I think I'm ready. You said you were going to show me where these books have been transcribed into a digital format and stored, correct?' 'Yes, young lady! These manuscripts are only part of your tour today.'

He put down the blue book, and picked up the last one; the green one. Opening this journal, Luna noted that this journal also started on the day that they left earth. Date and time entered. Followed by the six assigned Mission Flight Committee Principals: Primary Manifest- (White) Levi Pranay, Equipment Log- (Red) Asher Dalton, Travel Journal- (Blue) Gatlin Altair, Human & Population Condition- (Green) Luljeta Sage, followed by two alternates- one being Aaden- Occupation: Theologies and Philosophies, and Alva- Occupation: Master Engineer of Robotics and Computer Coding; who happened to be Grandpapa's grandfather. This was the most important information on this day.

Luna followed that Luljeta had continued each day with the daily routine and minor conflicts that needed addressing as they came up. Mr. Tomohiro pointed out that immediately behind the Flight Committee that there was a list that allowed for expansion, of the Voyagers that had started pairing off, or coupling, or held ceremony for their union. This was a very important part of the Outpost's survival, and it had been discussed and reviewed before leaving Earth. Further into the journal were a few special community notations of how the whole crew immediately broke up and started working their appointed positions, in actuality, or by sketches or notes of what they would attempt first. There were the notes on how they would care and house the animals they brought with them. Starting seed beds for the fruits, vegetables, trees and shrubs that needed immediate attention. There was all kinds of notes and comments that Luljeta had made for there to be the historical record of the makings struggles and successes of the Outpost Community in its infancy.

Luna was taking in everything that Mr. Tomohiro was displaying for her review. He looked to her and asked was she pleased with this visit so far? Luna exclaimed an excited 'Yes!' 'Are you ready to go to the digital archives? I can escort you to these journals where you would have complete access and be able to read everything available. If you have any further questions, I will be glad to assist you,' he replied with a broad smile once again. 'I am indebted to you for your time and assistance, Mr. Tomohiro.' Luna was eager to find out where the digital copies were so she could explore on her own as to what each page would reveal in each of the Journals.

Closing the last book, he picked all four of them up, after standing, then with a care and lightness of touch, he returned the books to their sacred safety of the enclosed case. Luna followed him, and watched the delicate procedure of securing his most important annals of the Archival Center. They started walking to the outer door, where Luna had left her school supplies and tablet. When they got to that point Luna asked could if she could take a few minutes to make some notes for herself as to what she had just witnessed, and items she wanted to make sure she looked up later in the different format. Mr. Tomohiro bowed slightly at the waist to her and said he'd be honored.

Outside the door, Luna rummaged in her school backpack to retrieve her tablet. Once finding it, she leaned against the wall and slid down to the floor to sit while she pulled up the pages she wanted to use to input the information she had gained today, and the subject matter she wanted to further explore and expand on. She was deft and quick at completing her entries. Looking up she said she was ready to go to the digital center for the rest of her excursion today. Luna stuffed everything back into her school sack, stood up, and followed Mr. Tomohiro once again to another part of the Archives.

They walked side by side, up the hallways through the stacks and computer stations towards a different part of the archives data center that Luna had little familiarity with. Mr. Tomohiro, being inquisitive asked, 'Miss Luna do you come her often?' She was thrilled at his question, and beamed back at him, 'yes, Sir, every chance I get. I'm trying to understand where we live, how we got here, and why are we on this planet. I'm learning a lot. I come and find recorded information, then go to the Holographic Pods and create an adventure to learn about earth and the stars, and anything else that Grandpapa or my Poppi help me think up.'

Mr. Tomohiro was very impressed at this young girl's pursuits, with her family's help and guidance, she took information that was two- dimensional data, and created a three- dimensional interactive environment where she could exercise all her senses to ingratiate her learning experience. He did not know of any other resident that challenged themselves or even attempted to expand their inquiries to this superior level.

They had reached the section of the Archives that was somewhat secluded with five work stations that posted date and subject titles in twenty- year increments, at each station. Mr. Tomohiro said, 'I'm sure you will find more than enough information here to satisfy your needs today.' Luna squinted up one eye and looked back at him. Was he doubting or questioning her? She decided to let the comment go for the moment. She had plenty to work with here. 'Sir, thank you so much for your help and guidance today. I will relay to Grandpapa Sebastian and Poppi how much assistance you have been, and offering to help me in my pursuit of this independent project I have for myself.' 'Miss Luna it has been a pleasure, and I hope to see you soon.' He bowed slightly again to her, and abruptly turned and walked back into another area of the Archives to attend to his normal responsibilities.

Luna checked her time, and realized she really couldn't do much in depth work today, but she would stay long enough to review the catalogs and time frames on each of the work stations. Pulling out her tablet, she set to her task. There was so much information here she had to focus. What was her decided theme that she wanted to explore, that she wanted actual information about. It was the "Invention of Home."

She quickly realized that she had accessed information yesterday that was in the white and red journals she had seen today, only summarized. She knew that she needed to get home soon as Mum would be wondering what she was up to, and she didn't want to be late…. And she knew she had homework she had to do for class tomorrow as Instructor was already on her about her inattentiveness in class today. She could not let either her parents or Instructor down. It was time to head back to her living quarters. Luna was so pleased with the information she accessed today, and knew how to utilize it to her advantage for Creation of her Outpost Home. She put her belongings once again in her backpack, and hurried out of the Data Archives Center, skipping with joy as she traversed the concourse on her way to her family's quarters.

By the time she entered her home, Poppi had already arrived and Mum was setting the table for the evening meal. The food was being kept warm, awaiting Luna's arrival. 'I'm sorry I'm late in returning home. I was at the Archives on a tour with Mr. Tomohiro about the Journals that were kept about our history of traveling to this planet and how we colonized the Outpost.' Luna went around the table, dropping her backpack at the hall entrance, proceeding on to Mum and Poppi to give each of them a big hug and kiss. 'May I go wash up for the evening meal? I'll be right back and tell you everything!' 'Yes, that will be fine.' Poppi answered. Luna quickly reversed her path, grabbed her school supplies and dashed down the hall to put her things away, and wash for their meal.

Mum had filled their plates with vegetable omelets, each had a small dish of mixed fruits, plus she had put tumblers of water on the table for refreshment with their food. Luna had to take a deep breath to calm herself; she wanted to be as mature as possible, having her conversation with Mum and Poppi. Luna figured she had once again to start by addressing the not-so-good stuff; getting it out of the way. This was her attention in class today that Instructor questioned her about, and then his seeming displeasure that she was researching the travel to Gliese 581d and how the Outpost was established and had kept growing ever since. He had emphatically relayed to Luna that the Outpost's history and formation was part of the curriculum for next year's studies. Luna went on to explain to her parents, that she did not feel she was being rude or stubborn in her current research, and that Instructor did finally relent to her project. His main request of her though was for her to keep the information to herself and out of the classroom for now. She looked intently at her parents' expressions to see if she could read if they were upset with her, or had she really done something inappropriate. Both of them chuckled, relaxed and asked what she needed to do to make up for today's class work. Luna stoically replied she did have homework to attend to after her meal and before she went to bed for the evening.

Poppi said, 'Good, you must pay attention in class. If you don't, you may miss an important nugget of information you will need in the future. Besides, if you don't pay attention, this leads to further disruption in the classroom, and causes the Instructor frustration.' That was all that was said on the subject. Mum then asked about the sketch of the Outpost that Luna had presented to her this morning. 'Oh, Mum, that is from information I looked up yesterday. I couldn't find any drawings or photographs, so that was my own interpretation. What did you think of it?' 'Luna it was very imaginative! Katavon, do you know if there are any blueprints or photos that are available to look at during the initial construction of the Outpost?'

Katavon looked over to his wife, in multifaceted thoughts. Luna had not shown him her sketch of the Outpost, and usually she initiated any of her projects with him first. Poppi did not know what they were talking about. His next thought was that he was sure there photos existed of the original space ships that arrived here, and that there was photographic documentation of the planet as they found it. There must be records of the setting of the foundation and the initial building of the outpost. His thoughts progressed to Luna, probably also wanting to see and conceptualize what the outpost looked like today. Poppi nodded and smiled back to his family, 'I do believe we can locate photographs of Gliese 581d and the Outpost in various settlement and construction phases.' Poppi smiled at Luna and told her he liked her new research project. His thoughts went further in that he had seen various departments or wings being depicted, but he now realized that Luna had no idea of what the outside of our structure looked like. Luna was once again excited with all the different phases and information that this project entailed, but she realized much of her day she had been totally submersed in her project; so, finishing her meal, she asked if she could be excused and go concentrate on her homework that she would need for class tomorrow.

In her room, Luna pressed the button to open the sky window so she could see the stars, and imagine Earth. She picked up Moppet, then sat down at her desk, opening her tablets for her to study and process the data that she needed to get caught up on for tomorrow. She was very tired from all the new materials and data that she had been introduced to today.

After a quick bath, with Moppet under her arm, she headed to the salon to give her nightly kisses and hugs to Mum and Poppi. They returned her loving gesture, and she toddled off to bed. Luna was asleep before she totally had Moppet and herself snuggly under the covers.

Lux and Katavon were getting ready for bed and Katavon opened the conversation with his partner about Luna's new research project. 'What do you know about the project that Blossom is working on now?' Lux looked up to her husband and replied with a sensitive questioning appeal in her eyes, 'I only have a brief idea of her investigation of the Outpost origins. She really surprised me with the primitive sketch she showed me. Luna not showing you the sketch first definitely confirmed to me how determined she is on this project.' 'I agree. But I have been thinking and I think we ought to make this a real family project. We'll see of Grandpapa would like to help with this project also. What do you think?' 'I think that is a wonderful idea, Katavon!' 'Let me discuss this idea with my father tomorrow, and in the morning give our approval for Luna to continue on her exploring and investigation.' Climbing into bed, Lux smiled brightly, then grabbing her husband giving him a big kiss and pulling him into bed with her. 'I think we can all work together, and encourage Luna. All of us learning and sharing our heritage.' With this tricky situation having a form of support and creativity, they settled into a comfortable intertwined slumber for the night.

In the morning Poppi made sure he left for work after the family had breakfast together. Luna came out in her indigo jammies, with Moppet for breakfast. Mum and Poppi were already dressed and ready for their day's activities. Mum had already set the morning meal out of each of them consisting of a hot cereal with fresh berries on top, a dish of yogurt and nuts mixed together, two tumblers, one of fresh juice, the other sparkling water. Luna was elated that Poppi was having their morning meal all together. She went around the table and gave each of her parents a hug and kiss. She even offered up Moppet to get a kiss from both of her parents, and they complied, she then hopped up on her chair at her place at the table.

Poppi picked up a spoon to dig into his breakfast foods before him. He looked up at Luna and asked, 'When can I see your sketch of the Outpost?' 'Oh... Poppi! I haven't shown you my picture yet!' Luna had a look of horror on her face and she quickly jumped down and ran to her room to get her tablet. (She didn't even think or stop to ask could she be excused) Running back to the dining area, she nestled up close to Poppi, and scanned over to the page that had the primitive drawing she had sketched of the Outpost, handing it over to him when it popped up.

'This is very interesting. Where did you get the concept as to the appearance of your design of the Outpost?' he asked. 'I have been hunting for information about the first Voyagers and how the Outpost was created and how is it our "home." Luna answered, continuing with, 'I went to the Archives and found information first, and geez, there was a lot of it a few days ago. I realized there was a whole lot of data that I came across, and was not sure where to turn. So, I went to Grandpapa Sebastian and asked him where I should look and I followed his instructions yesterday. ...AND..I found even more information because I was introduced to the four Journals where all information and data was first recorded and they started before the Mission left Earth. If I have permission; I would like to go to the Archives today and read what was in the journals as all of the information had been put into a digital format for safety and easy use by anyone that inquires about the Mission origins and the beginning of our Outpost home.'

'That sounds like a good way to spend the day, Luna; but do not forget to eat and get some exercise.' Poppi replied with a wink. 'Oh! I won't. I'm trying to figure out this planet and our Outpost settlement by myself. But if I need help, I will ask. Geez! There are a lot of records and data.' 'Don't get over tired, you're reviewing over a hundred years of information, Blossom. If your plans change, Let Mum and me know what you are up to next, OK?' 'Of course, Poppi. Am I excused now so I can go to the archives?' 'Yes, and Luna, that was a very good sketch of the Outpost.' Poppi affirmed.

Luna took back her tablet from Poppi, and headed out the front door, heading off to the Archives.

Katavon looked over to Lux and said that he would talk to his "Papa" today about Luna's project. He gave Lux a kiss on the forehead and picked up his case he took with him to his work station, then he was out the door also. Taking a few steps away from their quarters, Katavon turned and returned to their home, and popped in the door, startling Lux; nevertheless, he continued with his question, 'Have you ever seen or read about the four journals?' She replied 'No, I haven't.' Katavon smiled and said, 'I think, once again, we all have some learning and discovery to do.' With that he blew a kiss to Lux across the room and made his second exit.

Katavon went to his work station and checked everything that was in his daily charge. He then made the decision that he would send "Papa" a message in a few hours to talk to him about Luna's project, and his idea that they make it a family event. That's what Luna was searching for was family and home, so let's do it!

Luna arrived at the Data Archives Center and went straight to the section of the area she had left yesterday afternoon. Now she could delve into the materials that were her focus. She went to the first, earliest dated work station and turned the computer on. Pulling up the catalogs that were available, she followed Mr. Tomohiro's lead and went to the White log first. She studied the preliminary six Volunteers entrusted, which were fundamentally the first Mission Council members. These people were needed of course, on such a long voyage to make sure that directives were followed and problems that may have developed were addressed and satisfied in a constructive manner. Each of these people was intriguing to her, and she wished there was more information as to their backgrounds and education. She had not found any details about the 200 Volunteers, except they passed what was considered the upmost stringent educational, personality and biogenetic testing.

She then started browsing through the inventory, making notes for things she couldn't answer or that she required some help with. There was so much detail to what was listed in the log, and this was all written in cursive, at the beginning. Luna slowly read through the list of the 200 Volunteers for the voyage. At her age and Outpost exposure she was not sure of how coupling, partners or marriages were certified and performed. Maybe Mum could help her with this question, or for that matter how did she and Poppi become a couple and have a ceremony. She took her time and connected families where she could; she noted the differences in cultures and theological and philological beliefs.

Taking her time, she reviewed the supplies that were taken on board for the trip and the second quantity of supplies that the Volunteers would strictly use when they arrived at Gliese 581d. It was fascinating, and the Volunteers must have adhered to the protocol that was outlined for there to be success and their Outpost to grow and thrive. There didn't seem to be enough of anything to make this project work, to what she was accustomed to today, but they did survive and there was enough. There was community and they shared and they knew their responsibilities. After a few hours at looking at the White log information, Luna switched to the Blue book directories which held their space travel and what had occurred in their long voyage. She knew that it was lore passed down that the community worked together and practiced Yoga and meditation and did creative writings for them to go into this unknown planet and environment, and keep their minds fresh and focused as to what they had signed up for on this uncharted, extremely alien mission. But their one connecting base foundation and connection was for the "2nd chance at humanity." The volunteers could see the way that communities, politics, food sources, empathy, and human safety were falling rapidly apart in the fleeting decades that the Mission was putting together the three experimental voyages. Luna was so sad, disheartened, and scared when she read about how their ships had lost contact with earth and the other two groups of voyagers. This meant they were in the universe at this time alone. That meant, with and without saying they had to depend totally on each other. Once again, there was the flavor that the two hundred volunteers had to cloister together to uphold their pledge to their Mission Commitment. Within all the professions and needed individuals, with their special skills and creativity to make this excursion, after the Worm hole, they had to reevaluate their commitment to life and continuation of humans. Partnership, coupling, "marriage" of these people and in vitro fertilization moved to the top of the survival list. Luna, once again would have to ask Mum if she had more information about this, or did she need to talk to one of the Medical team at the medical Repository and Wellness center. Population maintenance was urgent; at the beginning expansion was optional.

Luna wanted to take more time in the logs about the observances and anomalies while on their voyage, but right now, she had to focus on "Home."

Katavon noticed that about three hours had passed since his reporting to his position in engineering. He decided to send a message to "Papa" and ask if they could meet in the Concourse Salon for a light luncheon or snack and talk about Luna. He was fairly sure that "Papa" wasn't on duty today. A message came back rather quickly, saying he would be delighted to chat with his son about the undertakings his specially gifted granddaughter was interested in. He added that she was the most enchanting and challenging child.

They agreed to meet at the Salon in 30 minutes. "Papa" came attired in a brown print caftan, and Katavon was in his blue working uniform. They found a table to sit down for a quiet conversation. "Papa" was overjoyed to be called back into his family's activities, to be of service. Katavon was very pleased to just be spending time with his "Papa" again, also. Everyone had duties, and their time was always committed. (This was still standard Modus Operandi at the Outpost, with its limited population)

The Salon Attendant came and took their food order of a vegetable plate with Hummus, manna, and sparkling water. She said she would return shortly. Katavon got straight to the point, 'I understand that Luna came to you the other day to inquire about the landing of the Voyager ships and the initial colonization of the Outpost.' 'She most certainly did, and I was impressed that she has been doing small bits of Mission research individually, and she wanted to attempt this project on her own also. That is why she didn't come to you first about her project. She amazed me with her insights and knowledge she has already.' 'I was honored that she came to me to ask questions, but I only pointed her to the Archives to get information that is available and start her from the beginning.'

"Papa," I would like for you, me and Lux to help Luna create the "Home" she is looking for. I know you told me stories that were relayed to you by your Great grandpapa. Luna is very enlightened and sensitive. I would like to gather actual photos of the Outpost being built, and how we went about excavating the terrain for us to start building the foundation of our Outpost. You and I can access engineering records and photos of work being done for the build out of our Station. And I think Lux can help her with the finer points of how families have developed over the last hundred years, for her understanding. "Papa" I think you and I know that we're are in the most stable and routine of age, at this time. But we all know how fragile this situation is. I think Luna is attempting to figure this out for herself, and she sees things that entail the welfare of the whole community, she doesn't do anything that has self-gratification in it. She really lives by the Mission Statement. Were you aware of that?' "Papa" cleared his throat as the food was set on the table; he asked if she could also bring them some goat cheese to add to their sustenance. She nodded and scurried off for a second trip. He reached for some tasty morsels to put on his plate and start snacking on. Katavon followed suit with the food; and "Papa" went on saying he had heard from Mr. Boreas that Luna had been to the Leadership Commission Chambers several times this year about an upset in her class, but she maintained a mature demeanor and was knowledgeable about what was happening, and she had approached the

Council with very solid positive suggestions to the issue at hand. Katavon was somewhat taken aback that "Papa" had not spoken to or inquired about his granddaughter during this whole fiasco; although he did seem to be in the know of what was happening and how it was being handled. Luna was a champion in Grandpapa's eyes!

Continuing their luncheon, "Papa" asked, 'How do you want to assist Luna without overtaking her project?' Katavon had been thinking last night and this morning about how to approach this set of circumstances, without Luna knowing that her family was putting in place assistance for her project. 'I think each one of us is going to have a particular area of details, facts and hopefully pictures and diagrams to assist her with when she had questions. Luna is absolutely known to have questions, or want more information about anything she was researching.' "Papa" burst out laughing at that comment. Katavon looked at him questioningly, what was so funny? "Papa" quickly answered, 'When she came to me asking for information about the flight and the initial colonization, I asked what information she needed, and her response to me was "Everything!" I understand the immensity of this project, and I agree that we can be of great assistance to her, without taking the joy of her undertaking away from her.' "Papa" looked at his son and asked, 'Have you spoke to Lux about participating in this data gathering mission?' 'Only briefly last night, and she was in agreement with it.' "Papa" I'm sure you and I can get pictures, diagrams and logs to the buildings foundations and appearance. I'm going to ask Lux to help Luna with the more domestic aspects of creating 'Home,' families, food and the expansion of all of our wonderful venues that we have developed over the years.' 'In the meantime, Luna will be busy doing her own research and will be busy with her classes so we can retrieve data, and put this all together for her, when it's needed. And I feel it's important to my daughter that this is a family project.' 'Katavon, I can't agree with you more! Let's do it!' Their meal finished, they got up and "Papa" went around and hugged his son, at the show of love and support for his daughter, as well as being asked to be active within the family unit again. Katavon smiled, thanked his "Papa", and headed back to work. "Papa" decided to go to the Observatory, and start looking for recorded data that was held in this wing about their landing and the landscape of the planet they were landing on, and where they were going to start the foundation for their Outpost. He was happy to have a project himself.

After reviewing the information that was recorded digitally in the White Log and Blue Journal, Luna decided she was going to take a rest and process what she had written down as questions for her to follow-up on, and she needed a snack. So, she headed back to her quarters.

CREATIVE THINKING VS. ARTIFICIAL INTELLIGENCE

Luna was roaming around the family quarters and was not quite sure what she wanted to do today. Then she started noticing everything in their home. She became quite intrigued as she noticed all the different gadgets and equipment that was automated in some way assisting in their lives and private living space. Like a detective, Luna started going from room to room, making a mental note to herself of all the things that were doing duties for their home, where none of the family members had to activate the undertakings.

Luna told her Mum that she was going out exploring, to which Mum answered, 'OK, Blossom,' knowing that Luna would be back soon with a lot of questions, as always. Luna started walking up the hallway, and already added three items to her list. This was like a treasure hunt! Luna knew she could not remember all the items she was encountering, so she ran back to their quarters, and into her room, and got her tablet to make notes with. Told Mum good-bye for the second time, then went outside the door to their quarters and started making her notes of all the things that worked without people assisting the gadgets. She walked around five of the hallways and to the Concourse Salon. She sat down, got a snack with a beverage and started studying her list. She had never noticed these things before. They were everywhere, and they were doing all kinds of "work" chores. How was this possible? Luna wanted to go to the Data Storage & Archival

Studies Center and start to figure out this puzzle, but she needed to talk to Poppi first. Poppi could help her understand all these apparatus they were living with. She knew today that he would be at his work in the Systems Operations Center. She pulled out her communication device and started to send Poppi a message. She then thought, 'Oh, here are two more, my tablet and my messaging system!' She did need Poppi's assistance. After sending her message, she started walking towards Poppi's work place, as she told him she would meet him at the entrance.

Poppi was always happy to see his little girl, but what was wrong that she needed to interrupt his research, and why it couldn't wait til he got home, and they would discuss her inquiry when they were having their evening meal. Poppi walked outside 'the Operations' doors and Luna was already waiting for him. She started chattering faster than he could understand as she kept referring to a list and pointing to her tablet. Then Poppi caught on to what Luna was talking so excitedly about. She had discovered the heart and life of the Outpost. Poppi smiled broadly one more time at how intuitive and probing his daughter was. When Luna spilled all of her inquiry out to Poppi, and she could tell he understood her interest from the look on his face, she fell silent awaiting his response. Poppi knew everything; he would help her understand this unique place where they lived. Poppi took a closer look at the collection on her tablet.

'Luna, I think that this would be a good time for you to get some assistance from your Grandpapa Sebastian. I'm sure he would like to spend time with you and help you learn how the Outpost has grown.' Luna had not thought of Grandpapa, as he was always so busy with his position of maintaining operations on the Outpost, but Luna knew he was as smart a Poppi, maybe even more so! Luna beamed at the idea. 'Is that possible? Can I go speak with Grandpapa Sebastian?' 'Blossom, most certainly! I will let him know you are on your way and the secrets of the Outpost you want to talk with him about. Do you know the way to the Observatory?' Luna nodded in affirmation, and told Poppi thank you. She also apologized that she interrupted his work. She was so excited; she forgot it was his work shift.

Luna had never been to the Observatory to visit with Grandpapa Sebastian. She must have stumbled on to something exceptional for her to get direct passage to see the Outpost Commanding Engineer! When she got to the Observatory doors Grandpapa was waiting for her, she felt special once again. He reached out, taking her in his strong arms and gave her a big hug. Luna became a bit bashful at the moment, but quickly overcame her shyness as Grandpapa inquired about what she wanted to know. He took her hand and said quietly, as if a secret, they would go into the Solarium. Grandpapa Sebastian said they had the covers to the sky windows opened and they would close the door to the work area of the observatory, and have a beautiful view of the colors of the landscape and horizon. They could then talk about whatever Luna needed to talk about in the special surroundings and comfortable chairs of this private room.

They sat down in the big soft comfortable chairs, and Luna pushed herself back in the seat, so she could sit up straight and be as formable as possible for her inquiries with her Grandpapa. Luna noticed that when Grandpapa sat down in the chair it almost looked as if it was too small for him, but he still looked relaxed when he crossed his feet together at his ankles. Then he asked, 'My dear Luna, how can I help you, or answer questions for you today?' With that permission, Luna went off with her excited chattering, much the same way she had with Poppi, only Grandpapa was not used to how quick Luna was, so he put up his hand in a gentle movement, and said, 'One thing at a time, young lady.' With this Luna realized she needed to speak in her adult articulate voice, she did not want to seem as if she was whimsically chattering about nothing. She was sure what she noticed today was important, so she needed to relay her information she found clearly to her Grandpapa.

'Grandpapa Sebastian, this morning I noticed many gadgets around the outpost that I never paid attention to before. I didn't have much to do this morning as Poppi was working and Mum was doing her tasks around our quarters. I didn't feel like calling on my friends to do some activity, so I was just wondering around. Then I started noticing all the activity going on in our home, which was not aided by instruction or direction from us. The vacuum was cleaning the floors, the dishes were being cleaned by the dishwasher, our clothes were being cleaned and dried by another machine and the lighting in our quarters grew bright and dimmed as we moved around to the various rooms. I never thought about any of this before, Grandpapa. Can you explain it to me?'

Grandpapa Sebastian had the same big smile and twinkling eyes that Poppi had, and he was thinking as how to answer Luna. This was an excellent question. Grandpapa asked, 'Do you want hear the short version or the longer version of the story as how these machines came to be?' Luna happily responded to her Grandpapa, 'Do you have time to tell me the story? I love stories about the Outpost.' Grandpapa usually didn't have much available time to spend with his granddaughter, but today, he made the exception, and wanted to spend time with her, and see how she was progressing. 'I will be honored to tell you the longer story of all of our marvelous equipment and advances. Do you want to pull your chair closer to mine and we can have a nice afternoon chat, and if we want to, go exploring visiting these inventions?'

Luna bounced off her chair, and pulled it closer to Grandpapa. While she was moving her chair, Grandpapa sent off two messages promptly so their conversation could begin. One was to Lux, Luna's mother to let her know where Luna was going to be for the afternoon. The second was to an assistant out in the observatory to bring some refreshments for them to snack on while they were together. Luna climbed back up in her chair and resituated herself in the chair, as poised as she was before, ready to take everything in that Grandpapa shared with her.

'Luna have you done your history studies yet as to the landing and how the first colonization of the Outpost that was started?' 'Only very briefly, Grandpapa. I usually go to the Data Storage Archival Studies Center and research anything I don't understand. Or when I want to know more about what was briefly introduced during class or an experiment.' 'Excellent! my child.' he replied. Grandpapa Sebastian had been keeping reports of how his granddaughter was progressing with her studies and her adaptation to the Outpost since she saw very small. Today happened to be the first day he could spend with her and investigate her inquisitiveness and intelligence for himself. Usually he got to see her only at holiday and social gatherings, but she was a delight in action even with those small amounts of interaction.

'Have you done any historical reviewing of when groups of peoples migrated on earth due to certain circumstances, such as war, drought, persecution, or religion?' Luna answered in the affirmative and said she knew that a combination of those, plus a growing earth population, as well as the "idea of adventure" was behind the Commission. This was a grand voyage that they wanted to pursue. 'Good for you, that you are investigating how special we are, and not taking this Colony for granted. I'm very proud of you Luna!' Grandpapa announced.

'Well, I will start with the three voyaging ships' landing.' 'All of the volunteers were so grateful they had successfully landed their ships. Much the same way other humans over the millennia were glad they had reached their appointed destinations.' 'These travelers had lost contact with Earth and the other two sets of Commissioned voyagers after they had gone through their first Worm Hole, in fact they all were the first travelers to attempt to go through the rigorous flight plans that was created by the commission to get to other planets. Please remember Luna, I am relaying this story the way my Grandpapa told it to me when I was about your age.' Grandpapa Sebastian sighed; the colony had been through so many struggles and challenges. The ones his Grandpapa relayed to him and the ones he had lived through in his lifetime. 'How familiar are you with the beginning and growth and education of the humans on earth for at least 4000 years?' Wow! Grandpapa, that's a long time!' Luna exclaimed. 'I want to make two distinct parallels that fold into each other Luna, and I think that you can keep up with my story and the Outpost history if I use the parallels.' Grandpapa looked quizzically at Luna and asked her jokingly, 'do you know what parallels are?' She smiled back and reacted quickly in the best way she could to describe the word. She put her two index fingers up in the air, right beside each other, bunching the rest of her little fingers into a ball in each hand. 'Grandpapa this is an example of parallel lines.' 'That is a good example. I like that.' Grandpapa Sebastian replied, because he expected her to know this word's definition.

'The Volunteers had now landed on a planet surface, with very little knowledge of what to do or how to live here. They had brought with them any and all the data that was available for them about Planet Gliese 581d before they left earth. Only they didn't know how accurate it was, or if they were going to really be able to create a sustainable colony here. I'm going to assimilate this story as best I can as to the creation and progression of our journey to that of early man on earth. I think of this first period much as the 'cavemen era' of many millennia ago. There existed some type of humans that were on earth with no tools or skills to exist or live with. They had already found and utilized water and knew it was a necessity for life; they were nomads and roamed the areas they lived. They had no comforts or protection from the environment around them. Three things that they are credited for, that allowed their existence to survive and thrive was they created housing, usually a cave, or hole in the ground. The next was they created fire to keep warm with. And they learned that with something round like a stone or stick, they could move their meager belongings much easier than by using their own strength pushing or pulling that object. However, each of these discoveries were created, used and controlled by man himself. He used his own creativity or intelligence. Here starts the first parallel.

When our ancestors arrived here, they had all the newest equipment, materials, computers, food supplies, with many years of stored history and data to assist the voyagers in their quest to colonize this planet. They also had a Mission Statement to help guide and ease some of the strains and burdens that are put on the humans in trying to survive. When the vessels safely landed, they all gave thanks to 'the Creator', and asked for further assistance and guidance in this very strange land. They were much like the caveman in that they needed to construct a water system for the whole colony to use, meaning viability for plants, animals and humans to thrive with. They needed to test this planet's air, and produce and refine the air that the whole invading colony needed. They needed shelter; they needed to test the soils available to them so they could start reproducing much needed food. The voyagers felt that they were graced in that *they were giving humanity a second chance.* They had planned for two decades for this venture; they knew how to work together on projects. They knew how to encourage new thoughts; however strange they may seem at first. This created a harmonious community that could work swiftly and move forward without strife; that the caveman and mankind as a whole endured for many eons that followed.'

'Our ancestors knew they first had to disassemble, access the robotics and rovers they had brought with them, small as they were, and then reassemble the vessels into a formation of living, working, and computer quarters for their first home on this planet. They had to set up and get all of their computers on-line as quickly as possible, smaller simple computers and the mega computers that could process terabytes and zettabytes of information. Shared utility, functional and living space was a necessity. Sounds rather disgusting, doesn't it?' Luna turned up her nose; her first thought was she wouldn't like to have to live with a bunch of boys all around her. She just nodded yes to Grandpapa. He continued on with his parallel images of the early humans and how they communicated by drawing pictures in stone walls or carved into stone statues. Hundreds of years later, they were finally able to make pencils and paper. Do you know that pencils are made of four simple elements- wood, graphite, clay and wax? The first 'paper' was made of animal hides and then woven reeds, or weeds, I like to say. And it took these humans hundreds of years to figure out how to create these simple items.' Luna laughed at Grandpapa's humor.

'My Grandparents came here with computers that they could use to communicate with, store data they were gathering and make decisions about air, soil, water, or the place for the permanent Outpost was to be located. My Grandfather told me never take anything for granted as our ecosystem is so fragile and interdependent. I'm going to call the volunteer voyagers 'the settlers' from now on in our story. Is that OK with you Luna?' Luna chuckled again at the way her grandpapa was really making this a living adventure for her. Luna's comeback at his question was a resounding 'Yes!' as she was enjoying his story and the time with her grandparent so much. Now Grandpapa Sebastian took both of Luna's hands and had her index fingers poking straight up and said 'this hand is earth human from about 4000 b.c. to 2200 a.d. And this hand is our time period from 2200 a.d. to our current time, which is hard to tell as we don't really have a calendar or orbiting Sun or other measure of time that we can use.'

So, Grandpapa took Luna's right hand with finger pointing upward and moved it to about a chest high position. He then moved on to Luna's left hand and dropped her hand down to below her knee with the finger pointing upward. Then he stated for his demonstration that the left hand was the caveman peoples, and the right hand was the Outpost settlers. Grandpapa swept his hand through the space between Luna's two small hands and said, 'This is a few thousand years apart in earth time. A lot of good and bad history has passed through here, useful inventions designed, all done by man himself, or man aided the invention, so they could function.' Grandpapa stopped moving his hand that was representing the movement of time, very close to the bottom of Luna's right finger. 'This is where the industrial revolution appeared. Machines started working and doing simple tasks with engines providing energy for the equipment to work. Oil, gasoline and wood were fuel energy sources. Our humans kept inventing. They showed remarkable technological growth from the early 1800's until the time our ancestors left earth.' Grandpapa took both of Luna's hands, not moving their position, and made the statement, 'See how long it took 'the caveman humans' to use their minds and technology to get to where we are today?' 'There were a lot of educated people in this time period. Colleges, universities and entrepreneurs came from every corner of Earth to work on projects to advance humanity. The Commission is just about at the pinnacle of this time period.'

'Would you like to stop for a snack while we continue?' "Yes, please. Some snacks would be nice, I'm hungry.' She replied. 'Can we continue while we eat?'

Grandpapa asked with love in his eyes, 'Luna do you see that we were and all are one?' Luna nodded her head 'yes' because she could understand the comparative illustration that Grandpapa was making for her. 'Of course, we can.' He acknowledged; he was so proud of Luna's deep comprehension.

'Luna, I use this parallel demonstration because we have so many more advantages than the caveman had. Yet we are in a much more precarious situation because we are on a different planet, and as settlers, we have to work hard to create, build, stabilize and maintain an environment we can live in. Volunteers that wanted to make this voyage started with advanced testing performed by computer algorithms of the types of persons needed. The computer made recommendations of cultures, gender, talents, education, creativity, and personalities. This took a lot of time, as there was an excellent pool of applicants that applied. Then it took a lot of time, preparation, and education as to what they needed to learn and what was going to be their new normal once they arrived. They had duel duty, Luna, to be on a space mission for an extended period, and then they were going to colonize a new planet. That was the Mission's objective, for there to be four uniting communities, each independent, and each knowing they were part of the much larger universe.'

Luna was picking at her fruit and crackers but listening intently to Grandpapa Sebastian. 'Our settlers, when they got here, worked hard to build solid structures for our Outpost. How did they do this? With the aid of computers, we had artificial intelligence at our finger tips. We had to analyze, maintain, and upgrade our computer systems every step of the way. In the last 100 years our Engineers and Information

Technology (IT) departments have made prototypes of everything we need or can use. Did we have materials we could use, repurpose, or completely have to break down to a molecular level and recreate items? What would work, what was too complicated at the time, do we have the materials readily available or can we manufacture them? We have been successful so far on this Mission.'

'Luna, can you see that it's like our positions in the universe have been reversed with the cave man. We have had to recreate everything. Some items were simple modifications of equipment or appliances used on earth. A lot of the engineering, imagination, and materials manufactured were needed to construct the wonderful expansive Outpost we have today.' 'I must emphasize that we need and use all the collective Creative Mental Thought we have available to us as the settlers. That is part of our basic Mission Statement, to be positive, to try new objectives, to recognize and respect all people and for us to work together to build a better civilization we are experiencing at Outpost 621. The Outpost also uses anything we can in the way of Artificial Intelligence to do daily or mundane chores, as you noticed this morning. We use this Artificial Intelligence also in many of the Outpost's monitoring systems, as AI's can pick-up, identify and even correct problems before a human engineer may even notice it. A.I.'s are an incredibility important part of our Outpost. Our talented settlers, alone, could not run, function, or even possibly survive without them. We need the high level of human creative thought as well as artificial intelligence for the monitoring, watching and 'at task' creating. We use both techniques, evolving us to expand into an ongoing more normalized human colony.'

Grandpapa Sebastian smiled, and asked 'have I explained the differences and complimentary interactions of how these two mechanisms are integral on the Outpost, my dear Luna?'

'Oh, Grandpapa Sebastian, I am so grateful for your time and explanation. I was going to go to the Data Storage & Archival Studies Center today, however I'm so glad I came to Poppi and you first to explain some of the basics to me. I'm sure if I start researching earth and the Outpost history now, it will be so much more rewarding. And I give you an *A plus* today! Your story was so special and told from the heart of our family, not just dictated notes.' Luna bound out of her chair and jumped into the arms of her Grandpapa and gave him a big hug and kiss (which she did not get to do very often).

Grandpapa Sebastian was surprised at her emotional expression of appreciation, and he could not help himself from saying, 'Luna, come back and see me any time you wish.'

'Oh, thank you so much Grandpapa Sebastian, it has been wonderful!'

"THIS DROP OF BLOOD"

After a week off from studies, Luna was not happy at going back to classes. She had been in the Exercise Pod with her friends, Kai, Oliver, and Sonnet in the mornings. They were engaged in various activities of running, skating, scavenger hunts, rock climbing or playing "Chase the sphere" in teams and against each other. They would break for their mid-day meal and rest for about an hour, using the time to come up with an adventure they wanted to take in the Activity Holographic Pods. They came up with visiting the African Jungle, which was more frightening than they had expected. They went to the Swiss Alps to see and play in snow. They went to a 16th Century Castle on Earth, where they played at being knights and fair princess'. The gardens and forests they created there were breathe taking. The four of them were miserable when it was time they had to leave this place. They next decided to go to the Grand Canyon in the United Stated and thought they could go repelling down the cliffs, until they arrived at the Canyon and saw how truly deep it was. They went to the Great Coral Reef in Australia, and thought they could play underwater, not realizing how deep it was. When they got there, they reasoned that scuba gear was a definite necessary, so they just played along the beach coast. The last day of using the Holographic Pods they decided to use one of Kai's rockets and go out into the stars. That became very problematic as they didn't have a functional rocket or a plotted map of where they were really going. First, Sonnet got scared, and then Oliver suggested they should try an adventure with less intense design and mapping. Luna was game to keep exploring, because she knew the allotted period in the Pod would timeout; however, she was much more familiar with the Pod activities than her friends were so they came out of the Pod and changed their option, and decided to go spelunking in the Caves of Sagada in the Philippines. They had such a fun filled week; classes seemed so lifeless today.

Dressed and with her class supplies and food for the day, she set off with every intention of changing her attitude about her lessons starting this week. Luna was one of the first to enter the classroom today. Everyone must feel the way I am about coming back to classes, Luna thought. She put her food and supplies in her compartment of the storage closet, and with her tablet in hand, went to her seat to await the arrival of the rest of the class and the Instructor. Turning on her tablet she went to the syllabus to see the intended topic of study they were going to be approaching this week. This week was blank. 'Oh' Luna thought, 'was this going to be another one of the project weeks?' This idea excited her, and she began to imagine what subject their study may be about? She was aroused from her daydream by the Instructor entering the room, and the other classmates filing in, stowing their extra materials and going to their seats.

The Instructor greeted everyone, and asked how they spent their time away from classes last week. He honestly wanted to know how his students spent their free time. He made some notes for future reference as almost everyone in the class offered up some report as to their activities. He noted that they freely included if their adventures were in group, accompanied by a parent, or on their own investigation. After Instructor listened intently to the class' escapades, he light heartedly told them that he went to the pool and swam and lounged for the week. Jokingly he said he needed a rest. He had their attention and had lightened the mood, because he knew this next topic they were going to broach was a bit solemn and intense.

Instructor pivoted and turned on the holographic work board. He took a marker and drew a simple picture of what looked like a very old- fashioned light bulb. Then he pointed to it and said this is going to be our study this week. All the students were curious as to what this bulbous shape had to do with their lessons. He went on to share, that since this was not his area of expertise, and he had invited several guest lecturers to our class so everyone could get the maximum challenge and knowledge on this topic. Luna was really puzzled by this introduction because she had queried a 'non-existent' topic for this week, now there was this strange shaped object that was part of the week's topic. "Humm, perplexing?"

Instructor went on to tell the class that they were doing a special biology class study as it pertained to the Outpost with 'this drop of blood,' as he once again pointed to the strange picture. Instructor was keeping the suspense going by using a simple generic hand drawing instead of an actual retrieved three-dimensional picture of a drop of blood to introduce the topic. Luna, listening intently, was sure by now that this was going to somehow be another one of the "new curriculum' projects. The students within her age group had only been exposed to Biology, in the study of nature, trees and plants, so far. Luna kept thinking and processing information, so far, trying to out- guess Instructor, as he kept speaking. Instructor asked the class to keep their tablets out so they could take notes and be prepared to ask questions at the appropriate time later today, or later in the week; as more information was given to them. Instructor didn't have to make that request to Luna a second time. She was ready to jump on this new area of biological study that was about humans, that was going to be presented.

'Our first Speaker and assistant with this project today is Dr. Dignita. As most of you know, he is the lead Physician at the Medical Repository, Health and Wellness lounge. And if some of you are healthy enough and coordinated enough to not need the services of this fine doctor, I'm sure you will be pleased with his acquaintance by the end of his chat with us today. May I introduce a fellow resident and fine colleague that takes care of all of us on the outpost?'

Dr. Dignita strolled into the classroom in a nonchalant way that would put anyone at ease that a 'doctor' was coming to visit them. He carried a medical bag with him, slung over his shoulder that Luna was sure had mysterious equipment and devices that he was going to reveal today as his part of the lecture went along. Luna couldn't help but wrinkle up her nose at the thought of a doctor and blood in the same topic. She silently scolded herself, and put a big engaging smile on her face as to what Dr. Dignita was going to have them start with today. He reached in his medical bag and started pulling out objects that none of the students had ever seen before. He started his talk as he was setting up his demonstration with the basic principles of how important the examination of a drop of blood was for human health and welfare. The simple items he had brought with him were a few glass slides, a small plastic bottle with a pointed spray nozzle containing water, even smaller square glass slide covers that looked very fragile and a few sealed lancets. He then brought out a small microscope and set it by the assembled items on the table in front of the room, where he was speaking from. Instructor had gone somewhere and came back with two additional microscopes that he set on tables on either side of the room, so as their lesson progressed, there would be three observation stations so each pupil could observe and understand exactly what Dr. Dignita was talking about. Donning laboratory examination gloves, the doctor then picked up a glass slide in one hand, and a lancet in the other; explaining what he intended on showing them today. 'In a healthy drop of blood, each of us has the following components: red and white cells, the nucleus, and the mitochondria.' The doctor was keeping his blood description brief and generic as all his pupils were total novices. Here the doctor stopped and told his students that hygiene with sterile conditions were of the upmost importance, so could they all excuse themselves for a few minutes and go wash their hands and arms up to their elbows. He added in a jocular manner that they were going in to surgery. No one in the class seemed to mind his surgery comment. Everyone made a break for the door, or the sink that was in the class room to wash up, so they could continue with their lesson. 'Now I need three donors of one drop of blood, each. Do I have any volunteers?' Hands shot up in the air to assist Dr. Dignita. 'Will you all divide the class in three groups around the microscopes?' Without hesitation the pupils scattered towards the three microscopes. 'Now let us begin. Please be patient, as collecting a blood smear is of the upmost delicacy and importance. If you rush, the whole process can be destroyed, and sometimes in an actual lab, you will not be able to recreate or gather enough of a sample to finish testing required. I will start here, and go to each group to prepare a slide.' He held the glass slide up for all the students to see. "Please have a test subject ready for me to collect a donation of one drop of blood." He looked at his group standing immediately around him, and almost everyone was volunteering their fingers to be quantified as the specimen donor. Dr. Dignita was very skilled at working with his medical apparatus, so he gently took the hand of one of the pupils, singled out the index finger, breaking open the lancet at the same time, and with a swift direct prick, hit his target and had a small drop of blood appear. He turned the finger over and allowed the blood to drop to fall on the glass slide. He then added a tiny drop of water, and quickly placed the slide cover over the sample. The children all squealed in amazement and asking 'did it hurt' to the donor. The doctor was on to his next group, and almost finished preparing the second slide by then. Dr. Dignita finished circling the room and was at the third station and stopped for a second to comment to please leave the finished slides where they were until he or the Instructor could place them correctly under the microscope lens. The doctor had everyone's complete attention as to what their exercise was. Luna could not help herself. So, she maneuvered herself into position to be the third donor. She wanted to know what it felt like to be 'a donor.'

Both adults swiftly and accurately placed the slides under the microscopes lenses' and adjusted the viewing power.

Dr. Dignita stayed at the station where he was at and commented that he was extremely pleased at the interest and concentration each of the students were showing him with this topic. By this time, Instructor had set up the second slide and had it focused for the next step of their lesson. Instructor stated 'Please have your tablets ready as I want each of you to make a sketch of what you are seeing through the microscope lens. Allow each of your fellow students' time to view the slide also. You can take turns until each of you have a finished product that you feel is representative of the drop of blood.

It took the class about 20 minutes to complete looking and studying the real drop of blood and making their sketches. Luna was enjoying this new course of learning. She did not think this morning that she would be having so much fun in her class studies.

Instructor called for the class' attention and said it was time for a break; they would reassemble to continue in 10 minutes. All the students headed to the storage locker and retrieved their snacks, and headed out of the room so they could talk about this morning's instruction. When they got to the luncheon tables, Kai, Sonnet, Oliver, and two other students all sat with Luna. 'Did it hurt to be stuck by a needle?' 'No,' she replied. 'I was surprised he had already taken the drop!' 'How do you think your drawing of the blood drop turned out?' Luna knew that Kai and Sonnet's sketches would be great. They could interpret anything quickly and make an accurate diagram of what they saw. They continued to chat while they quickly ate their snacks and then hurried back to the classroom.

Dr. Dignita and the instructor had cleared away the medical equipment and secured the bio-hazard samples while they were out of the room. With everyone back seated in class, Dr. Dignita opened this part of his lecture with his holographic diagram of the human body with all the blood vessels and arteries exposed. He articulated a brief summary of the how blood was the transport system for the entire body's movement of nutrient intake as well as waste disposal. A person's health or illness was reveled when this tiny isolated blood drop specimen was studied.

At this point Instructor stepped in to join Dr. Dignita. The two of them had devised an assignment using their diagrams that they had made, wanting each of the students to examine the blood droplets. They flipped the picture to a blood drop that was on the work board. The doctor pointed to various small shapes with distinctive colors to each part, calling special attention to their explicate assignment of the components of the blood. Each student should recall what had been explained and labeled from the lab exercise today. They could also examine any data they chose to learn additional information about. Find out how and why each element and its contents are in our human blood, and how the body uses each particular system. Then how this particular molecule relays information magnified by examination, to the doctor. The finishing note was what did this drop of blood mean to the doctor as a whole, looking at all of the components in this one complete drop. Luna was impressed with her homework assignment and already knew she would go to the Data Archive Center to retrieve much more comprehensive information about human blood than we touched upon today in class.

After the mid-day meal was taken and the students came back into the room, there was another studious person standing at the front of the room speaking with Instructor. He was amused that all his pupils today were returning early from their breaks and seemed to be enjoying this new topic of study. He halted his chatting with the female standing beside of him. She was petite, tawny skin tone with a bobbed haircut. She was dressed in a long off-white flowing lab coat over a light brown, a high collar, fitted blouse with matching slacks. Instructor started his introduction of Dr. Inga Sohan, a Genetic Mitochondrial Specialist that worked in both- the Life Subsistence and Medical Repository departments. 'I'm sure Dr. Sohan could recognize each of you by your DNA profile that is a daily part of her occupation, so meeting each of you 'in person' is a new experience for her also.' Instructor was attempting to indoctrinate these new intricate personnel and their fields of study of the Outpost to these young pupils. He was quite sure she could take over and fully have their attention quickly with her knowledge and the special studies and research she did for the Outpost. Luna was quite pleased with herself that she was familiar with the Outpost and the various departments she had visited and been exposed to. Luna knew that most of her fellow students had not had taken advantage of the opportunities that they had available to them.

Dr. Sohan grinned back at Instructor, at his complement and the understanding as to what her position entailed. She spoke with a soft but authoritative voice. 'I would say that Instructor is probably correct. I am pleased to be here today and to be a part of this project. I spend my days working in between the two wings that are intensified monitoring of the survival of this Outpost. I enjoy my work immensely. (Luna knew exactly what instruments and equipment that she must use every day. How thrilling!) Everything I do is on a microscopic cell level.' To ease into her topic, she went on to ask if everyone would identify themselves by their first and last names.' She did this as a type of test to see if Instructor's intuition was correct about her knowledge.

'Instructor introduced me to you, so I would enjoy the reciprocal pleasure.' Each of the students had not done such an exercise in many years. (They felt rather silly doing this drill.) Most of the pupils were in an age grouping and stayed together until they reached the maturation where they would start special studies for their occupations. These were agreed upon by the student, parents, the specialized department, and the Commission leaders.

Dr. Sohan smiled once everyone had spoken, and said she did recognize names, and now had happy faces to accompany data she worked on.

'My position entails that I review DNA profiles of each of the residents, and all of us have DNA- which is short for Deoxyribonucleic acid. And I'm sure it is more than you ever wanted to know today.' 'Mitochondria cells house the DNA sequences.' She started making strange markings of little lines in different colors on the work board. 'There has been intense discussion from the beginning to the end of the 21st Century as to the origin of DNA, and it could be as old as 25 million years.' Then she drew another time line picture for the century, on the board. 'DNA contains four organic building blocks: G, A, C, and T, constant to all humans. This was actually discovered in the mid- 19th Century. In the later part of the 20th Century, with the invention of the micro-computers, it was discovered the repetitive patterns of DNA elements in humans, and this further developed into following innumerable algorithms that there were no repeating human DNA genomes.' The study of DNA grew exponentially for decades to follow. The study of human DNA genetics was born, and geneticists, biologists, researchers and more scientific fields opened up and created positive uses for humanity.' Dr. Sohan drew a few more time lines on the board, representing the data she was relaying for the first time to the students.

'Genetics played an important part in the selection of the volunteers that were to take on the Outposts commissions.' Dr. Sohan continued with, 'It was of the upmost importance for the selection of a cross population of people with such diversity among them that wherever their travels would send them they could cohabit and create a stable colonization on a new planet.' 'I take pride in that my direct ancestors were chosen, and I am on their path for the continuation of this Mission. We are into the fourth generation of this Outpost, and the monitoring and data collection we continue to get will hopefully keep this Colony strong and healthy. In my studies I find that we are all so different, but we are exactly the same! It is amazing!'

'I do know this has been a totally new and informative day for all of you. So, I will turn you back over to your instructor, and please follow up on what you feel comfortable with in your studies this week, of WHO WE ARE. If there are any questions, as a group we will find answers. Thank you so much for you having me here today.' Luna's head was spinning. Thank goodness she stopped talking, Luna thought.

Instructor walked back to the holographic work board where the four letters were posted that Dr. Sohan had talked about. Behind each letter was a strange word. Luna turned on her tablet again and wrote down the letters and the accompanying words. Instructor was curious to see how this lesson was going to work itself out. He announced that class was dismissed for the day so they could work on their homework assignment. He added that there would be one more guest speaker tomorrow after they had reviewed and discussed their homework assignments.

Luna wanted a snack and to talk to Poppi. She was not sure if she needed to go to the Data Archives Center for any further information until she discussed her class today with Poppi. She commented to Oliver, Sonnet, and Kai that she would talk to them later. She started home, then turned back to her friends, and asked what did they think of the class and their subject matter today? Oliver and Kai thought the day was very interesting, so they were ready to go do their homework and dig deeper and find out more about the blood. Sonnet took a different approach, she picked up on we were all the same. What a lovely picture that played in her head. She decided she would do her diagram homework, but then she wanted to use colors and sketch the people she interacts with every day. She had visions of what each one represented to her, and how she could now depict their individually. All of us are beacons, or silhouettes that are layered, and interwoven. Luna was fascinated the way Sonnet interpreted things or people around her. She was excited to see what she would present in class tomorrow as to what DNA represented to her.

Luna got home, went to the dining area to find out when Poppi was coming home, and Mum said 'after a while.' She asked how her first day back to class was. Luna told Mum it was a special new biology project, and they had guest speakers to help with the lectures, and they did an interactive lab that was fun, but everyone was left with homework, her voice trailing off to a whisper. Mum cut up a fresh apple for her, and put it out with some cheese and popcorn. Mum was sure Luna would feel much more herself after her snack. It must have been intensive for her to have such a response, Mum thought. After eating, Luna went to her room, turned on her tablets and sat in a chair with Moppet and started learning about the neat stuff that was stuffed into a drop of blood. Her spirits were rising. She had finished her homework when she heard Poppi come home. She ran to give him a hug, and she announced that she found out today that we were all the same! Poppi had no idea what Luna was talking about. But if he gave her enough time to catch her breath, and for them to get ready for the evening meal, she would deliver a full account of her days activities.

After their meal, Luna asked to go to her room, as she was tired. Mum and Poppi looked at each other because Luna would never say she was tired. Poppi picked up his little girl, and as he carried her to her room he comforted her in saying she had a very demanding day, so rest was a good idea, and he was glad she thought of it. She loved her Poppi… and Mum. Tucked in with Moppet and her favorite pillow, it didn't take but a minute or two til she was asleep. She didn't even look at her *'stars'* tonight.

Next morning Luna was up with the light starting to brighten her room. She prepared and dressed for classes. She kissed Moppet and told her that she couldn't go to school with her today, but she would tell her all about her studies this evening, and even let her help with her homework. Luna zoomed down the hall to the dining area and popped up on her chair. She ate with urgency; she didn't want to miss anything today. Mum was fixing something over at the food preparation counter, but Luna was deep in thought as to what was their lessons going to be like today. Luna kissed Mum, went back to get her tablet and picked up her food snacks for the day and out the door she went, heading to classes. Poppi, happened still to be home, and asked what was with Luna. Mum just replied, 'she's like that some days.' Poppi had a touch of hurt in his heart as he realized his little girl was growing up, and he missed so many little things that occurred daily that were special and unique. Katavon (Poppi) looked up at Lux (his life mate) with a smile and realized what a wonderful family unit he had.

Instructor wasn't surprised when all of his class was awaiting his arrival. Their supplies were out and homework ready to discuss. To keep the subject stimulating, and as non-threatening as possible Instructor had each of the students, one at a time, go to the work board and pick out one of the objects that was integral to the blood drop. They would then call on another classmate to give the facts that student had gathered about what the student at the work board had pointed out. If there was any other information a third student had, that had not been shared yet, it was then shared by the third student, and the fourth, and even higher if some of the classmates had really gone digging for information about a red blood cell, a white blood cell, plasma, and platelets. Instructor was surprised at how much information all the students had located and shared in class with each other, the nucleus, mitochondria, functions of each cell, formation in body, cell life expectancy and make up of each of the blood drops functions. Two students' even ventured special reports as to there are four blood types that can be identified by special tests from a drop of blood. They then sheepishly looked at Instructor as if they possibly were giving out information that was going to be part of today's lesson. Instructor was very proud of them, and could not wait until later when he shared their assignment results with Dr. Dignita.

Spending a few hours on this assignment with intensifying excitement and inquisitiveness, Luna sensed that the Instructor felt a bit of a killjoy when he announced that they could take a break. Today for some reason, no one seemed to be in a hurry to leave their discussion, or the room. Well, Luna decided, she wanted some food! Finally, everyone broke up their discussions and filed out of the room for a brief break.

When the novices returned, seated and ready for their next part of this week's topic, Instructor could see the intense focus that was on him in anticipation of what was coming next. He could not keep them waiting any longer. 'I have asked Dr. Mackenzie Otago to be our speaker today about historical DNA genomes.' She was tall, fair skinned, dark hair -pulled back in a knot, with quick comprehending green eyes. The Doctor was dressed in dark green pant suit with a light wool lapel.

She smiled, blushing somewhat, at being out of her element, and speaking before young intellectuals. 'I will put you in the good doctor's hands,' the instructor said as he quietly backed away from the front of the classroom, allowing all attention to be on Dr. Otago, and the helpful information she was about to deliver.

'I would like to thank the Commission and Instructor for the opportunity of introducing the scope of work I do for the outpost, and how it came to be.' 'I happen to have a Doctorate in Genetic Studies, which is not like Dr. Dignita which is a physician. My work is in the scientific and exploration arena; where as Dr. Dignita works and cares directly for people.' Dr. Otago walked across the room changing the subject.

'As I am sure you are aware, there was no paper or papyrus available for thousands of years on earth. There were hieroglyphs etched into stone for communication and small stones used for mathematical endeavors. History and events were relayed by stories being passed down through the ages.

Walking back to the center of the room, she continued 'Then DNA studies took a huge change as a 1500-year-old ancient Bible was found in excavated debris in the European country of Turkey in the early 21st century. The artifact was then sent to paleontologists and archeologists in North African and Europe universities of ancient studies.'

'The best they could understand from this ancient writing that was bound and had survived for centuries until it was uncovered. It was written in the ancient native language of Jesus! Aramaic, a long-lost forgotten language. It had become redundant through the years due to the arriving populations of Iraqis, Syrians, Turks, and Iranians, most of which were Kurd Jews and there was no need of an additional language to learn.'

'This scientific discovery was just that of an artifact for years. Then a few colleges in Europe and North America were experimenting with computer algorithms that the new microcomputers could now decode, and information that could be compared or translated. They stumbled onto the fact that the Aramaic Bible had the exact words, phrases and quoted sections of the Bible. Linguists and Philosophists verified this pairing of genomes and languages. This made enormous genetic news, because the Aramaic language was written in a code with the same four letters that are in our human DNA coding. The different arrangements of the letters had a matching similarity to our current computer code language. The letters they found exclusively were, G, A, C and T. I don't think those letters have been explained to you as of yet. They are as follows,' and Dr Otago turned and pointed to the work board. 'The four chemical bases are: adenine (A), guanine (G), cytosine (C), and thymine (T). With Computer use and dedicated complimenting sciences there had been over 6 billon sequences tested and the counting continued accentuating each human's exclusivity. Same common identifiers, but making each person's DNA completely unique

'When genetics started to become so popular and cost effective in the early 21st century, once again, random human genetics were studied from all over the earth, and it was found that all of us are related. It was traced genetically backward from every country on earth that we all came from only two ancestors, one male and one female from the mid- section of Africa.' That is a whole other topic of genetics about populating the earth and how the communities moved and migrated, and for what reasons. You can find some of this information in the Data Archives Center.'

'The science grew, and when the Commission was formed for this voyage, they felt it was necessary for there to be personnel with the group that could understand and intercept this viable coding information. If there was incoming data that we received, or there was a way to transmit to others in the universe, what they had deemed as the Universal language code. They hoped that we could communicate, and we were advanced enough to communicate.'

'For the time being, I review all the incoming space 'noise, and at different intervals I set up messages to go travel out to other galaxies or planets in hope that we can be heard. I also run tests on the DNA of random plants and peoples to see if I am finding any anomalies with the specimens I test against the time we have been away from planet Earth where this precious language information was imbedded in humans.'

'I do think that Instructor wants the class to do a few experiments with DNA genomes in the Holographic labs of our current and the ancient DNA strands.' Luna was excited at once. This was going to be in another area of scientific instruction that not everyone had access to. 'I will be available to assist you and help set you up for running your sequences. And I certainly thank you for this opportunity to share how wonderfully connected we really all are.'

Instructor walked back to the front of the class and turned and put out his hand and took Dr. Otago's, he then personally thanked the doctor for all the enlightening information she shared with the class. Dr. Otago took a step back and turned and left the room.

Instructor then beamed at his class. 'I want you to remember that you are the first group of non-classified students to be introduced to history and sciences at this accelerated level. I am so proud of all of you! I certainly hope you enjoyed the lessons and demonstrations the last few days as it appears to me you did.' Since we're nearing mid-week, I am relieving all of you from formalized class structure for the rest of the week. 'You're not home free!' he smiled. 'The rest of the week, you are doing independent study of what we have discussed yesterday and today; blood, genomes, DNA, and the history or discovery of any or all of the above.'

I would like for you to do as you did with your assignment last night. Research, review, gather pertinent data and be able to make a presentation to me the first of next week. Once again, you can use any resources you choose, and I'm sure any of the speakers would be glad to work with you and of course, please have the courtesy of going in groups if more than one of you have specific questions of information in their fields. The Archive Data Center will be a great resource and of use to you.'

'I only have one request. I would like your assignments to be full of facts that you have learned and understand. It would not be helpful for you to do this project and fill in with statistics that are above your point of understanding at this time. That is not the task. We have opened the doors to new studies, and so far you have been incredibly astute and creative in gathering the next level of information. I want you to continue on, and let's see how this goes with the rest of this assignment. Also, I want to point out, if one area of the lectures interested you more than the others, you can put your focus on that subject. But please review and make commentary on the other two areas.'

'Class dismissed.'

There was a loud buzzing of the novices all talking about this new assignment and area of study they were embarking on. Even though class was over, they all had ideas and wanted to share them with their fellow students. Luna was part of the group and chatted a bit with Kai, Sonnet and Oliver, but she wanted to ask Poppi some serious questions about these projects, this week. So, she gathered her belongings and thought about going to Poppi's work area, then decided she would wait til he got home to ask him questions. At home she greeted Mum then went to her room and just sat quietly thinking for a while with Moppet in her arms. Once again, she absorbed a lot today, and was tired, but she still needed to talk to Poppi.

ARTS, SCIENCE, PHILOSOPHY, AND MUSIC

Sonnet came dancing into the room on her toes, arms spread wide, embracing the air and light energy. Whirling and twirling to take everything in, she filled all her senses. Luna looked up noticing these elaborate movements. Sonnet looked like a butterfly, or a flower gently swaying in the breeze that Luna had seen in the archives, as part of a holographic adventure. Luna was somewhat mesmerized by what she was seeing. She finally asked, "Sonnet, where did you learn such movements? You are so delicate and beautiful!" Sonnet stopped her dance in front of Luna's desk, thanking her and asked if she ever danced or experienced fluid movement before? Luna answered "No," and was a bit taken aback about this in-depth question that encompassed body movement along with thought and body language. Luna was intrigued with what she was observing as beautiful art. She had never seen Sonnet exhibit such an elaborate creative form of art and beauty before.

'Have you taken dance classes?' Luna asked, in total innocence. 'Yes and No' Sonnet answered doing a pirouette. 'I have spent a good many hours in the 'Mind, Spirit, Body Exercise Wing' over the years. My Parents are instructors, facilitators and guides of the many disciplines that are offered. Since I was very young, I started learning various forms of dance.'

'Oh,' Luna responded, surprised at the exceptional talent that Sonnet exhibited. 'How much time have you spent in the MBS Exercise Wing?' Sonnet asked.

'Not much. I have spent a lot of time with my parents in their fields of work. I usually only go there when we have an actual activity of entrainment in a group setting.' Luna thought for a minute or two, as Sonnet began to move and sway again, she was wondering if she would be interrupting if she continued talking to her, since she seemed to be more focused on her dance.

She decided to take a chance, and asked 'Can anyone go to classes, or seminars, or just observe the different contributions that this group has to offer all of the residents?' Sonnet made graceful balanced skips across the room and stopped in front of Luna again. 'Of course! Arts Education is open and inspiring to the whole colony! Why don't you come with me after classes and see for yourself?' Sonnet smiled softly at Luna. And… Luna noted to herself that her smile was even more open and feminine than it usually was. 'I would love to come with you, I haven't considered any of the many activities at the Arts Wing before, and it's time I checked it out. Thank you for the invitation. May I sit here and watch your dance until class starts. You are so talented, Sonnet!'

Sonnet took a deep Plie`, replying 'thank you, we have a date!' and did a Grande Jete` away from Luna and continued in her own realm of happiness.

The class studies went by quickly, and it was soon time to adjourn for the day. After Instructor finished his lesson they were working on, he readily released his students with commentary to go explore their interests and gather further information of their choosing. This was usual for him, signaling they were adjourned. Once again Luna was ready to go off on a new adventure of learning and experiencing her existence. Sonnet came quickly over to her desk and asked did she still want to accompany her to the MBS Exercise Area? Luna replied yes, but she must send her Mum a message of where she was going, and that she would be home in time for the evening meal. Sonnet nodded 'Of course, I'll be waiting for you in the hall.' Message sent, Luna caught up with Sonnet and they started their trek to the MBS Exercise Area. They were both quiet, in their own thoughts for a little while. Luna thinking that this was the first time Sonnet had offered or initiated and outing or excursion. Her thoughts went deeper... all of us have special abilities and qualities that comprise a wonderful, living thriving Outpost. She has experienced this with her family, instructors, and the Mission Council, but this was a first from one of her peers.

Luna's attention was brought back to the present when Sonnet started speaking. 'Luna, I have been overwhelmed with dismay at what you have had to go through this year. I so wanted to help you or let you know that I am truly your friend and comrade. I look to you as a sister. I know you had support from the whole colony, but I don't think anyone knew how to help your heart and spirit heal. Your parents and the Council have been amazing.' Sonnet cleared her throat, as she was being overpowered by the emotions she had been holding in for months about her best friend Luna.

Sonnet took Luna's small hand in her petite, delicate one, squeezing it tight. 'I am so delighted to share with you a new part of the Outpost that is so important for all of our wellbeing. This is my gift to you and I know that this edification will strengthen the beautiful lady I already know you are.' With this, the tears streamed down Sonnet's cheeks, and for the first time Luna really felt the pain she had been carrying. Luna realized she wasn't alone; that the whole colony wanted to comfort and support her in some way. Sonnet figured out one way to help her heart and mind to heal. Luna, breaking out in a big smile, squeezing Sonnet's hand in return. 'Please share this amazing place that you know about. I'm ready to absorb all of it!' So, they picked up their pace heading as quickly as possible to the MBS Exercise Area.

As Sonnet and Luna neared the MBS large double doors; the doors had a new enticing theme that Luna was suddenly aware of. Sonnet had already embraced this energy that was beckoning them to enter. Luna now noticed that the portal framing seemed soft, wispy, and glimmered. The sturdy doors were illuminated with varying pastel colors.

How had she not noticed the contrast to this area before, she asked herself. They came here often to go to the play/exercise area. Was she once again not paying attention to another wonderful creation of the Outpost? Sonnet saw the distressed look on Luna's face and urged her to come and let her be Luna's personal guide to the wonders of this area. Luna relaxed and followed Sonnet into the MBS Area. Once going through the doors, Sonnet took a few steps and stopped. Luna, so engrossed in her surroundings, almost walked right over top of Sonnet. How has she not noticed any of this before? Sonnet brightened, doing a twirl on the spot wanting Luna to note the colors on the entry walls of the wing. There was a pale green panel to the left with a small electronic monitor for calculating those attending such classes as Yoga, Tai Chi, and Qugong, with beginning, intermediate and advanced offerings. On the opposite wall was multiple panels of light blue, a monitor was attached here also for data entry as to which of the varying types of dance and free movement the students chose. These too had different levels of difficulty that students could move through. Freestyle, Contemporary, Ballet, Acrobatic, Bollywood, Belly Dancing and others, which Luna did not know anything about. There were also couples' dances that ranged from Waltz, Salsa, Argentine Tango, Cha Cha, Paso Doble and many others, again that Luna knew nothing about. Sonnet excitedly told Luna that she was in a ballet class and she was going to be part of a recital they were having for the dance classes soon, so she had to practice her movements. Sonnet backed up at few more steps to the second panel, on the left that was beige in color with a monitor attached for martial arts classes of Aikido, Kung Fu, Capoeira, and Tae kwon do. A third monitoring orange panel, followed on the left, closest to the hall that went to the exercise area where there were games played in team or multiples, again registering participants. This was where Luna always went, they climbed, swung in the various swings, and played ball games.

Luna looked up and happened to see the last class selection on the green panel that offered "Goat Yoga." She busted out laughing. Sonnet leaned in closer to her and asked what was so funny? Luna asked, 'Really? Yoga with a goat?' Sonnet replied, 'Oh, yes. It is quite popular. I am not yet coordinated enough to do yoga with a goat, but that is a goal of mine.' She replied smiling broadly. 'It is one of the times where residents can interact with the animals here at the Outpost. It is very soothing and the class conveys our oneness with all life. Come let me show you the different areas for activities.' Before they started off on the tour, Luna noticed a large panel with varying class or study options that was on a magenta panel. It really stood out, and caught her interest. This panel had offerings that was subdivided by art, science, music, and philosophy. Of course, these classes were also monitored for class size, and personal instruction or study. This captivated Luna, as she thought everything was in the Data Archived Center. She contemplated on this notion, following Sonnet deeper into the BMS Exercise Wing.

Sonnet stopped short again, turning around seeing Luna peering into the entry hall that was right beside magenta notification and sign-in panel that accessed the large dance studio and her mother's adjacent office area.

She asked, 'Would you like to meet my mother? My Father may be around here also, but I'm not sure.' Luna was surprised by Sonnet's graciousness today. It was very becoming of the sweet companion that Luna enjoyed spending time with on many days. 'Thank you, I would like to meet your parents, I also want to thank you for showing me all the wonderful events, entertainment and learning suggestions this Wing has for our health and welfare.

Sonnet seemed to be at home here, and showed Luna all the various venues for the many activities that were offered to the Outpost residents. All areas were clean, smart, and inviting. Sonnet made sure that Luna was apprised of the equipment areas, and lockers for wardrobe changing between activities. Sonnet went on to say there was no limit as to how many activities a resident was limited to, only that they must keep in good standing with what was their job or educational requirements for the Outpost. They went through a second internal set of doors that led to other departments within this wing. The main hall split off into four subdivisions. Luna looked up at the identifying signs, in three different languages, over the doors to each distinct area sector of activities. Sonnet pushed open the first door to the left, a solid door, soundproofing the area of music. Once again Sonnet was excited and went to the wall where catalogues and collections held all types of music. Sonnet bubbled in joy as she asked have you ever seen so much music collected? Luna replied that she had done some exploring of music and variation in the Data Archives Center. Sonnet pushed some buttons and skipped across the room and plopped into the big overstuffed chair and waited til the music became audible. There was a strange set of sounds, but definitely in a rhythmic pattern that Luna was clueing into. She kept listening. It became relaxing, but it wasn't any tune or musical pattern she was familiar with. After about 10 minutes, Luna's curiosity got the best of her, and she asked Sonnet, what were they listening to? Sonnet almost twinkled in her enthusiasm, as she replied that they were listening to 'Space.' 'Did you know that 'space has a rhythm all its own, and all we have to do is to quiet ourselves to be able to hear and partake of it!?' Luna was amazed, and sat quietly and listened for a little while longer.

Then Sonnet shot up and ran her hand down the wall at all the categories' and individual pieces of music. There were all types. Music for dancing, music that made you happy, music that was intense and told a story. She smiled brightly, and said, follow me. They went down a hall to another anteroom, where there were various musical instruments. Sonnet pointed out that all of these had been created here on the Outpost in the last 100 years, as there was not space for them on the voyage. They were created by the original volunteers, and they were crafted the best they could with loving hands by the blueprints they had at their disposal. There is a wide assortment of instruments here, and they are honored and cared for with reverence. Luna looked around the room, and realized that she was looking at instruments that she had only seen in the holographic chamber before, and she wanted to go and touch and hear them, but Sonnet quickly pulled her hand away, and said we will play music another day. You still have more to see!

Leaving this area, they went to the next one, and it was Art. Luna was wondering why there was a department in the MBS wing for Art? What Sonnet showed her was again, catalogs of works that had been done by residents of the Outpost over the last 100 years. Paintings, Sculptures, and Etchings were their own personal renditions of great works of art that had been left on Earth. There were stations set up for the creative and adventurous visitor to do hands on drawings or painting. Other stations were set up for working in other formats for sculptures. Art formed from unique materials that were created within the strict parameters of Gliese 581d. It was a chronical of our history of the past, present, and moving into the future. There was so much representation here, all in one place, for a student or principal to study. Luna was beginning to see the purpose of this collection. Luna could now come here and see and explore things that she only pulled up in the holographic pods before. She didn't have a time limit, and she could do comparisons. Luna's heart was becoming lighter and more fulfilled. Almost the same expression that Sonnet was exhibiting. Luna chuckled to herself, and smiled at Sonnet.

Sonnet grabbed Luna's hand and they went to the next area of the MBS Exercise area. 'This is for Science.' Sonnet said quietly as the door closed behind them. "Mostly this room is now used for young children, before they start classes. Also, when an instructor wants to investigate an area of sciences that his students may not be too familiar with. Right now, we are doing experiments and project designs in class, but at one time this was a bustling area of information, and confirmation of where the ideas certain principals or residents wanted to go, without disturbing the whole Outpost. I like to come in here and play or teach little children, and you know what? Most the time I still learn something further myself that is important and applicable to our lives today." Luna looked around the room at the area for biology: flowers, human needs, dirt & water…etc. Then to the other wall was computers, a full bank of mainframes, that could analyze data and do computations independent of the data center upstairs. There was an area of stones and dust particles that had been gathered and studied and opinions made over the years about Gliese 581d. What was usable, what was not, and what had future potential. There was an area set up for studying the stars and our galaxy, and the galaxy that we came from. This was done with projected photos, and was more two than three dimensional. Luna could tell that this was a work room that had sufficed for many years, but the colony had advanced past most of this equipment at this point. Luna giggled to Sonnet that this area really needed an update. Sonnet, being perfectly serious, asked 'Are you offering?' 'I don't think so.' was Luna's reply to her.

They went out the door and Sonnet tugged open the last door to the Wing. This was the Philosophy area. It had a larger area in the center of the room, sparse on furniture, and had four smaller open concept rooms, also without furniture. The platform here was for community and sharing of thoughts and ideas, without structured leadership. All were equal representatives of the Outpost, and all could share their ideas without being upstaged or being made to feel subservient. This really impressed Luna. She asked, 'Can anyone come to the discussions held here?'

Sonnet, replied yes, but a lot of time the topics were hard to digest since adults were the main participants. 'I don't come here very often at all, but I love the music and dance, and attend the exercise areas regularly. You could come check it out if you would like at any time.'

Sonnet and Luna left the far areas of activity pods and headed back up the hall towards the main exercise areas and the sign in panels, at the main doors. Sonnet took a quick left and dotted off into a small hallway, Luna followed, not knowing where they were headed this time. It turned out to be Sonnet's Mother's office area. Her Mother was sitting at a desk, working on an activity on her computer. She closed the lid and looked up as Sonnet started speaking to her, introducing Luna as her classmate, and told her mother that she had just given Luna a tour of the facility. "This is my mother; Annalise." Sonnet turned to Luna and announced, smiling broadly.

Annalise smiled at Luna and welcomed her to the BMS Wing, and inquired if she had ever been here before. Luna replied that she came here often with her classmates and friends to do activities in the exercise area, but she had not realized the facility had all the different projects and educational pursuits for the residents. She went on to say that "I am a bit overwhelmed and excited at the ability to be creative and immersed in activities that I have only known about and used in the holographic pods until now." Annalise came around her desk and stood right in front of Luna and asked her would she like to come her on a regular basis and start taking a class or two? "Oh, that would be wonderful!" Luna replied. "But I have to discuss this with my parents and ask for their suggestions and permission." Annalise was intrigued by Luna's formality and respect she was acknowledging to all the adults involved. "Well, I am here, and if your parents have any questions or inquiries as to what would be a good fit of classes for you to attend, I'm always ready to assist in any way possible. We want everyone to have a good time, to learn, experience, and want to grow further in any of their endeavors." Luna beamed at the invitation, responding she couldn't wait to tell her parents about her visit here today and ask if she could indeed attend some classes. "Thank you both for your time and showing me this fun filled, wonderful part of the Outpost."

"I do think I had better be heading home now, I'm sure my Mum has our evening meal about ready, and I shouldn't be late." Luna turned to leave, looking over her shoulder, she smiled broadly, and did her own version of a hop and skip out of the office of the MBS wing.

Luna couldn't wait to get home and tell Mum and Poppi about the MBS Wing and all they had to offer for recreational and educational opportunities within this area. She wanted to ask permission to attend one of the activities also. Luna now was very curious as to what her parents may suggest for her to participate in.

When Luna got back to her quarters, she rushed in and went to give Mum a kiss and hug, and she asked if Poppi was home yet? Mum answered that he wasn't home yet, but would be here at any time, and their evening meal would be ready by the time Poppi got home. "Mum, I've got something I want to talk to you and Poppi about while we eat. I went to the MBS Exercise Wing today and it was amazing! I'm going to go change and wash up for our meal, then I'll tell you both everything!" Mum replied, "that sounds wonderful, I'd like to hear about the activities there"

Luna skipped down the hall to her room and grabbed Moppet, and swung her around, as if the doll was her dancing partner. Luna told Moppet about her adventure today, and promised that she would share everything she learned at the MBS Wing with her. Luna changed into her blue tunic and matching shorts, then ran to the lavatory to wash her face and hands for the evening meal. She suddenly heard the front door of their quarters close, so Luna ran up the hall to greet Poppi and jumped in his arms to give him a big hug and kiss. She slid down his side, landing both feet on the floor, and chattering to him as quick as she could that she some something wonderful to share with him at the evening meal. Poppi happily agreed to await the news she wanted to share, as he sauntered into the food prep area to give Lux a good evening kiss.

As they sat down for their evening meal, Mum had prepared a large salad with nuts and toasted manna chips on top, with a dressing of herbs with a goat milk base. For dessert she had made them a parfit of mixed fruits that was frozen then whipped into a delectable soft slush. When they all had started with their meal, Luna's enthusiasm came bubbling out as she explained her visit to the BMS Exercise Wing. Poppi and Mum were watching and following her every word, because they had to keep up with where their child was going with this escapade she was expounding about this evening. She explained that she had missed how large and varied the activities were in the wing, and she had not seen almost the whole center as she had just been going there for games and exercises with her classmates. But… there was dancing; and music; and art; and eastern Chinese martial arts and exercise. There also were areas for study of science; and philosophy; and of course, the exercise and game halls. "Poppi, Mum, I met Sonnet's mother today and she invited me to come and take a class or two if I wanted to. What do you think? Could I have permission to take a couple of classes?"

Poppi and Mum looked at each other and then at Luna. Mum started with "Do you think you would have time to take extra classes with all your interests and hobbies that you now have?"

"Oh, Mum, I think they would work in together wonderfully with my interests. What caught my attention was the Music area, with all of its information, instruments, and recorded types of music available. I have been intrigued with the small glimpses of music that I have been coming across and want to learn more. The second class or area of study is philosophy. I looked up the definition of that study which is classical and contemporary philosophical writings, the nature of truth and knowledge, mind and body, freedom and determinism, right and wrong, and the existence of God. I think that would be a good source of information to help me keep track with your learnings about our credo, and the Mission Statement. What do you think? Luz and Katavon, once again, after absorbing every word their daughter shared with them, looked deeply into each other's eyes. They both surrendered to each other with a slight nod of their heads, and Mum turned to Luna and said "Let me speak with Annaliese about your ideas of classes, and get details and times. If you would like to pursue these areas of arts and thought, we will support you, as long as we all are working together for this project."

"Oh! Mum! Poppi! Thank you so much. I think I had better get to bed now, and dream of wonderful things to come!" Luna replied, climbing down from her stool, and rounding the table to give both parents a good night kiss, and was then off to her room.

THE CHRISTMAS TREE

Luna was so glad it wasn't a formal studies day. She had the idea to go to the Botanical Wing today and Kai and Sonnet decided to join her.

After breakfast, she asked Mum if her friends and she could go to the Botanical Wing. It's amazing how much free time each of the Outpost inhabitants had, since so much of their livers were assisted by A.I. devices.

Out of curiosity, Luna went to the Data Storage and Archival Studies Building a few years ago and pulled up "human daily survival" for 12th through 21st centuries. How did these humans live? How did they survive all the environmental, and physical, issues they had to deal with? This intrigued Luna enough to go to the Activity Headquarters Pods and retrieve different eras, planets, cultures, seasons (oh – that was a good one!), languages, and people. She always went on these adventures alone – as she was learning about how Outpost 621 came to be.

Each piece of travel brought her new insights from the past and the major struggles and adventures that especially humans on her Blue Planet had to overcome. Other planets she visited from various galaxies were for more advanced that the Blue Planet – and it was never said or documented but her assumption was the Blue Planet was an Outpost at some ancient time period – especially as she visited the Pod explorations and noted technology skills advances and losses.

Luna headed off to the Botanical Wing – by passing the Life Substance department today. She wanted to be with her friends and she quickly knew how she could lose their attention. By asking questions or challenging them on any topic – She wasn't really challenging them – She was just looking for answers. At this point the superintendent leadership had decided that the fourth generation of youth would be given an open opportunity to pursue any interest they chose – from a very early age. Of course, parents had guidelines and certain instructions as to various phenomena in a vast array of fields and forms that the young ones must be exposed to. The organized daily instruction – would engage or present some example to make sure parents were implementing their given responsibilities.

Luna often wondered if her peers were as active or as curious as she was, but given the amounts of free time she had, she strived to believe they were as ambitious as she was. To her, their behaviors and actions didn't show it, and she let it go. She was not on the Outpost Occupations Identification Board, wasn't her decision to identify their attributes or abilities.

Arriving at the Botanical Wing, Kai and Sonnet were there waiting by the huge wooden doors. The doors were intriguing to Luna as they had carved marks- that could have been a different language or hieroglyphs or just an artist's special rendering, but they were beautiful and it had taken years to accrue the wood necessary to create the functioning necessities. These doors were a special textured dimensional portal to tease and entice and all to enter and behold beauty and wonder. The Outpost was being urged on for discovery by the mid to 21st Century. Things were happening on the Blue Planet that went two different ways – one of a new place of habitation for expansion, the second was habitation for survival.

There was an exciting jump forward in the early 21st century when a plant – that was first thought to belong to the Blue Planet's solar system Pluto – was debunked by astronomers then reevaluated when the New Horizon's Probe did a fly-by and established that Pluto was a planet, from the Kuiper Belt – and of utmost importance the planet had mountains, valleys, snow, and chemical elements of nitrogen, carbon monoxide and methane. All of which the Blue Planet had in different chemical structures – which would support life as they know it on earth.

This was why plants and especially trees were so important to the outpost. Poppi explained to her: These plants, shrubs, trees, grasses were what sustained the outpost. Poppi made it simple: The trees had to be nurtured with artificial light – as we have no sunlight for photosynthesis. The trees had the most specialized and trained Botanists' and Horticulturalists to ensure that the trees react in a normal function of absorbing carbon dioxide and sulfur dioxide from the air and releasing a fresh supply of usable oxygen for the humans and the Outpost's essentials.

With, Kai and Sonnet in tow, Luna headed towards the large forest area where there were gardened hard woods and soft woods such as pines living together in harmony with grasses making a plush inviting park area. Luna liked the word "PARK". To her it meant: Stop, stay, enjoy. No need to rush.

Sometimes all three of them would attempt to see how many species of plants and trees they could identify before becoming bored or tired. It was amazing how many were thriving on the Outpost.

Today they meandered around in the soft woods trees. There was a delightful aroma that was eluding from the trees. The mixture of the scents made Luna feel refreshed and full of energy. They kept wondering around and collecting species data and identifying each ones' uniqueness. Then they entered a part of the parkland that had a small sign, almost obscured by the grasses under and around the nearest one. It read "Christmas Trees". Luna froze – what were these – she had not seen this sign before. She asked Sonnet and Kai about the small sign – and they didn't know anything about them. Luna was piqued with curiosity as to what was a Douglas Fir, Pine tree, Christmas tree. Gee – this was getting complicated. She set off by herself – telling Kai and Sonnet she was going to find someone to explain this tree to her.

Kai and Sonnet resigned themselves to "there she goes again", and decided to go find a different activity to do after having some food. Both agreed they were hungry from their morning exploring.

Luna figured her best and most efficient was to get her question answered was to go back to the Life Substance Department to locate someone that worked there and identified the trees and could clarify this type of Pine. What was it?

Soon enough, Luna found a Botanist and excused herself at interrupting his work, but she had a question about type of tree she had found out in the pine park. As soon as he turned around, when she had delivered her question – he smiled broadly and told her they were special, to be honored, and magic. Now she was frustrated. Why would he allude to such a definition for a tree? He seemed happy enough, and that was all he was going to share with her.

OK, so with determination, she decisively set off for the Data Storage Archives Center. Luna could not imprint her finger quick enough, so she could start her research of "Christmas Tree." She put in known description from plaque in park. She added the words the Botanist had relayed to her. Instantly her HD-LED screen brought up a picture of something she had never seen before. It was beautiful. It certainly didn't look like the tree in the park. She could tell there was a pine tree in there, but it was covered with all kinds of things, and they were shiny and sparkling. Luna was intrigued further and researched Christmas tree from archive data.

Oh, my goodness! These trees had been around for centuries all over the world – honored by all the Blue Planet. What had happened? Why didn't the Outpost have Christmas Trees? With this much information, and many more questions, Luna decided she had better go to talk to Mum and get some help and guidance.

Bursting into the galley at their living quarters – Luna finds Mum going over food stuffs to be ordered for delicious and nutritious family meals and snacks. Having a variety of fresh vegetables, fruits nuts and some meats – Mum always made sure there was wonderful faire to be had. Actual food assembly was now completely done by A.I.'s, but Mum skillfully monitored to make sure dishes were prepared to her family's liking. She rummaged through culinary blogs and food data chronicles always checking and experimenting with available herbs and spices.

Luna ran up to the granite bar – placing her tiny hands on the edge to keep her balance she was so excited – awaiting Mum to recognize and address her. Looking up Mum could see her child's eyes wide with exhilaration. What was Luna up to now Mum thought? Mum had to be the balance in Luna's young life. Answer questions of importance and at the same time stimulate further query and research.

"And how was the Botanical Wing today?" Mum gently elicited. "Mum, I found Christmas Trees! I don't know about them, but I did step in at the DASC to get some information. They are beautiful; they make your heart open-up. Why don't we have Christmas Trees?" Oh, Boy – This child never ceases to amaze me! "Mum? Mum, please?"

'Oh, Blossom" Mum started "sit down and I will share what I know – then we may have to do some extra research." Mum drew Luna into the time where the first commissioned volunteers prepared for travel and arrival at Outpost 621. They knew their focus was on building and creating sustainable housing, living, and prospering with minimal materials to work with. The whole unit was so elated that they had sources of water, soil, oxygen and gravity they could use, manipulate and maximize at their Outpost. Mum stopped and asked Luna about her research the Blue Planet in the 17th and 18th century and what the indigenous peoples had to work with. Tools, food, and lives necessities were sparse.

Registering her prior investigations – Luna's face and spirits fell. Mum knew she held Luna's attention and had her attention. Mum continued with - the same was true when the commissioned arrived here. They did not have much. They had to work hard and use their skills, be inventive, and utilize resources. They were fortunate enough that so much history, artifacts, articles and tangible items were brought or at least able to be accessed by the archives that the communities could move forward quickly. Luna twitched in her seat and blurted out "What about the Christmas Tree?" Mum was patient in laying the foundation of the struggles that the Outpost had faced over the last Centuries. "My dear Blossom – something as precious as a Christmas Tree was not an item of survival – but it has never been forgotten." "Oh" – Luna thought remembering the definition the Botanist had brightly shared with her earlier in the day.

Mum changed the mood and tone requesting that Luna have some luncheon. She needed nourishment and know her daughter would be off on this new project just as soon as she had enough answers to satisfy her immediate urgency – so food was a necessary intervention. Mum fixed a small plate of vegetables, fruits, nuts, some cheese and several pieces of flat bread for Luna to nibble on as this facet of her background was brought to life for her daughter. A stable environment of housing, water, food, expansion were at the greatest import. Mum emphasized the DASB was one of the first Buildings fully finished and was created with extra protection against possible damage. This was where the Christmas tree was kept and still is until it's time to be revealed and carried further into the universe.

Mum took a deep breath then and started to describe the hundreds of types of soft wood trees that were the beginning of Christmas trees over the centuries. First, pine sprigs were brought into homes. They represented life. They were green. *"Forever"* green – representing ongoing life. Giving hope to all to progress through the harsh cold winters and terrible destructive storms. The fragrance of the evergreens was intoxicating and up lifting. The peoples in time started sharing gifts with the tree. They would put treasured gifts on the tree, of food or shiny objects, or a commemorative item of some importance that had happened that brought joy to the household.

In many parts of the Blue Planet there were many days that held much darkness, much as we have here on the Outpost, so they started putting candles or artificial lighting on their trees so the house and tree would be light and warm and inviting for a much longer period. Seeds, saplings, and cuttings were all brought to the Outpost centuries ago. Mum turned and faced Luna – and remarked – Did she know that the identifying marker for the Douglas Fur – Christmas tree was a recent addition to the softwood forest? It had only been identified as a species before. Mum smiled at Luna – maybe now was the time for Christmas trees. Luna got all excited again. Mum had to interject a reality of the Outpost though – Luna could never force or impose anything she knew or discovered on other inhabitants due to their backgrounds or studies and areas of interest.

After eating – Luna's mind was abuzz with the idea of Christmas trees, and she asked Mum if she could continue her day out by going to the Data Archives Study Wing. She positively wanted to know more. Mum always grateful Luna wanted to learn and know more about any subject or item she came across and was happy to dismiss her to investigate the Christmas trees more deeply. Luna thought a minute about seeing if her friends wanted to join her. However, quickly realized that was her surprise and adventure. She did not want to stop and explain or answer questions to anyone right now. Luna almost ran to the DASB and quickly printed herself to gain entry to the archives. Where would she look for Christmas trees? They were obviously stored away in some special place, because she hadn't come across them before.

Mum had insinuated the trees were world-wide and common place with all communities on the Blue Planet for centuries or even millennium.

So, Luna picked the Blue Planet and put in Christmas tree. She then identified some grand cities within various areas of the Blue Planet.

First, # 1 USA – New York – Rockefeller Center – 29 meters tall. 50 million lights – a Balsam Fir.

#2 Sweden – Skeppsbron –Amongst the information was the tallest Christmas tree- 38 meters with a 4-meter star at top – Luna stared at the colored picture in amazement.

She kept entering locations and looking at the information being given back to her.

#3 Brazil – Rio de Jaerino – Tree- 85 meters tall that floats, and has fireworks illuminating it.

#4 Russia, Moscow – Kremlin Square – a 120-year-old tree, 30 meters tall – decorated in native vintage light and figures.

Luna looked at the last tree she programed into the data archive.

#5 Australia, Sydney – The Queen Victoria Building tribute tree, weighing 6.5 tonnes with 65,000 lights and 82,000 crystals.

Luna stopped here and pondered. The tree in the softwood park was young – she would guess. What was wrong with it? She would guess the tree in the park was almost 5 1/2 meters…what a huge discrepancy!

The pictures she saw and the information of the Christmas trees was overwhelming to her, but something was incongruent. Luna had made notes and bookmarked data so she could come back to it again. This was turning into quite the puzzle. She was getting tired, so she shut everything down and headed back home. She needed to sleep on this.

That night all she could dream of was Christmas trees. They were so big – did something go wrong with the storage and transfer of the seedlings to the Outpost? Was everything so big on the Blue Planet? The next morning Luna had an idea – Poppi had taught her – use the Activity Investigation of the Bio-Genetics – DPB Holograms in the Pods.

"Morning Poppi, morning Mum - I'm going to the Activity Pods – for research, be back later." Mum stopped her for a few moments – eat first – Luna grabbed some fruit and nuts and put them in her pockets. He parents just smiled – What was she up to – the girl shows such creativity and potential.

Luna checked in with her finger print reading – was glad her hand wasn't sticky from eating, then pulled out her tablet with the Christmas tree notes.

Today she was assigned Pod 24. Going to the panels – she started pushing buttons on the first set of data of the Christmas tree she looked up. She applied all information and when she got to the 5th panel – she pushed the button – "Observe". She wanted to be objective and access what she was seeing. The adventure was on – she went through the doors and came into the center of a huge city with the most outstanding dominate of Christmas trees. Luna looked and studied the tree and the human's reaction to it. They all seemed to relax, become peaceful and happy. They were enjoying beauty. For the moment, this was all the information that Luna needed. Five more trees to go, so, she exited the Pod, went back to the panels and reset the buttons destination for the next tree. Upon entering Sweden, the tree was much more beautiful than the picture had captured. Luna's eyes filled with tears at the grandeur and beauty...but she was here to learn and research. Once again she noted all she could about the tree itself but the human responses to the tree were amazing – the humans responded the same way as when she visited the first tree. Only this time she noted she was pulled into the peace and beauty also – and she had marked this activity as 'an observer" on the 5th panel, but she had tears of joy and love – How could this be? Luna had so much more to find out – so she departed from the 2nd Christmas tree lab experience.

She went out of the Pod and reset the Panels for the next two Christmas trees. Each one she saw made her heart grow happier and lighter, she actually wanted to engage with the peoples around the trees. Happiness, enthusiasm, love, amazement, reverence, humility was all coming through this holographic experience and she was still only identified as an observer meaning: she wasn't real – they were. But it was all flowing into her. Luna did her best to stay objective and take sufficient notes of each Christmas tree and surroundings. She walked out of the Pod – ready to reset the data for her last tree.

#6 Location: Outpost 621, time current – location softwoods park – Douglas Fir - `8 meters tall – Soil, ambient tempter light – current – Odors indigenous to park. All 4 panels set – but she couldn't push the button to make her an observer this time – she had to participate with her own tree. So, she pressed buttons for appropriate attire and gear to be in the softwoods Outpost park. She walked forward – looking and anticipating her own 1st Christmas tree – She touched her pockets to make sure she still had her notes from the other trees with her. Touching the door, she entered what seemed to be a dream, because of its exactness in replication of the park. She wondered back through the trees to the softwoods and found the Douglas Fir Christmas Tree. Here her excitement grew because she could touch this tree.

Touching was not allowed in the botanical wing due to possible contamination of the rare specimens they were cultivating. She had on a botanist uniform – complete with pruners, trowel, a claw and ruler in one pocket. Another kit had a scalpel, forceps and slide plates, if needed to take samples. She walked up to this huge representative of a Pine tree, her Christmas tree – and she was free to look, touch, smell and analyze here in the Pod. She started making notes, asking questions of herself – were there male and female trees? Was this tree always green? Were the green "poky" prickly things really leaves, like maples, birch, and oaks? She did confirm with herself that these grew all over the earth, they needed, soil, air and water; and they easily propagated.

Upon closer examination – the spiny leaves had a waxy coating – research. The leaves were attached at the stalk with some form of special fiber woven around them in bundles. Luna noted on 2 bundles she cut off and dissected were either 3 or 5 "leaf" clusters – but with the weaving so tight, when she loosened the leaves by cutting a cross-section – you could see the intertwined was a perfect circle to allow growth, feeding, and rest. She had learned this was true with other hard woods.

At the end of the stalk was a star-like yellow cluster of leaders that were the inception of the next year's new growth. The pine cones must be valuable as we always had pine nuts to eat ….note…must research.

But here Luna was at a loss – how did this become a Christmas tree? She went back to the path and closely observed the tree – She stood and waited for what, she wasn't sure but she was awaiting some sort of answer. Then Luna noticed spider webs across many of the branches, glistening white from the morning watering and new day's light touching the water on the strands – randomly stretching from various branches, seeming in an iridescent pattern, but at random. Then the yellow star like collectives on each of the branch tips became more intense with color as the light got brighter in the park, peaking out as Christmas bulbs adding color and dimension. The morning light awoke the robins, wrens, and doves living in the tree singing from their special nests that decorations they had made their homes, safe, secure and protected, continuing life and love. A few squirrels now came bouncing in for a visit and snacks setting the tree into vibrancy and motion. A few pine cones still hung on to the branches as the highlighted quests finishing the full display of the Christmas tree.

This finished this part of Luna's investigation. But she had the nagging huge missing piece she didn't understand in the middle between the delightful magnificent worldly Christmas trees and the Outpost fledgling.

The Botanist and Mum had used special words and images – she was attempting to recall. Both had deep knowing smiles on their faces as they answered her. Magic, honored and special. Mum used words following "the tree was precious", never to be forgotten, it gives of life and love, it was intoxicating and uplifting. What was this concept?

Sitting outside in the concourse – Luna was trying to assimilate all she had learned about a Christmas tree. Then she thought – She had the beginning and an end of grandeur. What was in the middle? For this evening she went back to the MRC to do another search. This time she used choice planet period eras and plugged in Christmas tree. She started

263

having data appear with history, antidotes, struggles, pictures and community surrounding and protecting the Christmas tree. Stories started with a branch or small evergreen brought into the house – then progressed to adorning with precious or scarce items in hopes of bringing abundance.

This has been done world round. The next addition is addition of foods of fruits and sweets to share with the powers that be. Candy canes, apples, popcorn to identify a few. Then the peoples in all classes had more money and creativity – they put candles on their trees then electric lights – that were clear, colored, flashed and danced or could appear and disappear. Bulbs and ornaments were treasures from the heart – of continuing life. First home, first car, first baby, a diploma, tiny hands in clay, a necklace of strings and pasta, anything and everything made each tree "the most perfect one." There's never an ugly Christmas tree – it owns our hearts and lives.

Final stop for today was back to PBSD Research Pods. At Pod 16, she programmed in each set of data she had separated and identified in a chronological time sequence – for her Christmas trees. Only observing – but clearly noting the reverence and grandeur each new installment she was building was more formidable than the last. She changed lighting, indoors and out, types of adornments and her heart melted. She wanted a Christmas tree – She must share with Poppi and Mum. But she knew she already had one she could cherish and share that everyone could be made aware of at the Botanical Softwood Park.

OUTPOST 621 RESIDENTS FUTURE EXPANSION

Luna awoke, stretched and decided to push the button to open her sky window so she could admire and take in the stars this morning before starting her day. Another day of classes, and the Instructor already gave a hint that the students were going to have a new project to work on. Luna looked at her stars and wondered what the project was going to be, hopefully more research about the galaxy and her stars.

She hugged Moppet, knowing she must get up, dressed and ready for her new day. She could hear Mum in the food preparation area fixing the morning meal and snacks for her family. As soon as she was groomed and dressed to her satisfaction, Luna headed to the dining area and hopped up on her stool, after greeting Mom and Poppi with a hug and a kiss. Poppi noticed that Luna was somewhat more reserved than usual this morning, so he asked was there anything she wanted to talk about. She looked up to Poppi and said that her class was going to have a new project to work on, and she was perplexed because that was the only information the Instructor gave them yesterday. Luna's face brightened and she replied to her parents that she would have more information this evening. At least she hoped so, she didn't like situations where she only had part of the story or information.

After eating, she went to her room and picked up her tablets and supplies she needed for her studies, then went back through to the dining area and hugged and gave each of her parents a kiss for the day. Now she was feeling more optimistic and inquisitive as what was going to happen today. Luna smiled back brightly as she went out the door and headed towards her classroom, she was always up to a good challenge.

She ambled along the hallway hoping to meet up with either Oliver, Kai, or Sonnet. But none of them appeared this morning so she continued towards the educational wing. Luna was wondering what her friends were thinking about the new assignment that the Instructor was going to give them today, only she hadn't had the chance to inquire of their thoughts. We had had so many new projects this year; what was next?

Luna slipped into the classroom, and readied herself for the day. Everyone was present and the day progressed along as usual. She was getting a bit fidgety after their recess and noon meal break. When was the Instructor going to give the class information about their next project? A short while later, he made reference to the time that has been spent here on the Outpost, naming several milestones the Volunteers and their families had been challenged with and overcame. Luna started listening very intently. This was his lead into their new project, she just knew it!

Instructor then went back to his podium, tall and formable. He started speaking in a tone that demanded the attention of his students. Soft and inviting, pitches of highs and lows in his voice, and every student was hanging on his every word at this point. Then it came out, "We have been given a special project by the Commission, as fourth generation residents, to address the Outpost stable growth, and our aspirations heading into the future."

"You can use any information in the Data Archives Center to assist you, and please feel free to use your own visions and imagination as to what you see the Outpost and our residents growing and expanding into." "I'm sure that you will find this a rewarding as well as challenging project. You will all work independent of each other, and when the projects are finished, I am expecting you each to give a presentation to the class as to your findings and ideas. I am giving the class four weeks to work on this project, because of the magnitude, and scope of areas to be inspected and possible proposals for changes. We will start oral reports four weeks from today."

Well, there it was... the new project. Luna let it churn in her thoughts for a few minutes, but it kept growing in her creative visions. This was no small delegation at all, yet the Instructor had delivered this huge project to all of his neophytes in three sentences! Luna finally settled her thinking down enough to get out her tablet and take notes on exactly what Instructor was expecting each of his pupils to produce.

"Class is dismissed for today, so you can each work on your own ideas of this assignment. I would like to review your first outline of areas you would like covered within three days, and we can adjust accordingly. I'm looking forward to some stellar work for each of you, as you always exceed my expectations," instructor closed the day with a happy satisfied look on his face.

Luna gathered her materials from class and headed straight for Oliver, Kai, and Sonnet, before they left the room. "What do you think of this project?" she asked in candidness, to the others, with a subdued look on her face. Oliver and Kai, replying to Luna with comments of "this sounds like a wonderful project," had expressions of excitement on their faces. They knew they could now fully create relative proposals to what has been their hobbies of Gliese geology and rocket propulsion and designs. What an opportunity!

Sonnet was more subdued, so Luna inquired as to what was her thoughts on this new project. Sonnet replied that she didn't know how she could advance the Outpost and the residents. Luna giggled at her modesty and underestimated abilities. Luna came back at her quickly with a question and a challenge, "what about all you know and contribute to the Outpost with the Arts? You make all of us think and create outside of our normal circumstances. Sonnet, you bring life, and color, and further dimensions to all of us. Isn't that a starting place?" "Oh, I hadn't thought of that. I will think on that theme tonight." Now Sonnet was smiling and turned to head towards her home. Oliver turned and asked Luna what was she thinking about for her project? Luna's face lit up and she told Oliver quite defiantly, "Expansion!" Oliver shook his head, and said "I shouldn't have asked." Luna laughed at his reply, as she had learned not to take his commentary to deep. She knew when she made certain statements that it only made her classmates dig deeper and work harder to excel for themselves. The three students now filed out of the classroom and headed to their next appointed designations. "Talk with you all tomorrow." Luna said, back over her shoulder as she headed off to talk with Grandpapa Sebastian for a few minutes. On her way, she sent Grandpapa a message and asked was he available for her to visit for a little while about a new class project? She promptly got a "chirp" back on her tablet, he would be happy to visit with her, so please come by his office.

Luna was met at the door of the Observatory, and they walked hand in hand up to his office. Grandpapa had already positioned two chairs facing each other for them to have a discussion. Luna climbed up into her seat, and made herself comfortable, as Grandpapa settled into his solid office chair. "And what have you on your mind today, my dear Grandchild?" he asked smiling broadly at Luna's animation as she spoke with him.

He listened carefully, and nodded at her ideas of the new project that was presented to her class. His face deepened into a reservation, as her commentary went along, at all comments and suggestions she was inundating him with, and wanted to present in her assignment. "That is a very large undertaking that you have in mind, my dear child, but I will say that it is all noteworthy and needs to be addressed soon. Didn't your Instructor want you to do an outline of your proposed project topic?" "Yes, sir." Luna replied. "Then why don't you make up your outline and present it to him, and see how he would like for you to proceed. He will have more information about the viewpoints and subjects your classmates have to offer, so then there will be the widest range of information that can then be presented to the Commission." He softened, and smiled, "Make your outlined list, and present it to the Instructor. Accept his observations with a positive attitude, and follow his lead, for now."

Luna got a bit distressed by Grandpapa's comments to her about what she had thought was a brilliant program. "Please don't worry my child, this is a lesson for you to learn about leadership, and being part of our all-important Outpost team. You have outstanding abilities, in addition to keen instincts; and I see you starting to mature into them.

Take your time and listen. That is a very important tool!" He stretched out his large arms for her to come close to him. She hopped to the floor, maneuvering over to his chair and he folded her into a tight hug. Then gave her a light kiss on her forehead. Luna relaxed as he said, 'my young granddaughter, you have a wonderful grasp of what the Outpost can grow into, and where we go. Allow the Outpost to come to you, to be a beloved leader!" Luna could feel the wisdom of love that Grandpapa was giving her, and knew that he, as well as her own Poppi had these special skills well in hand. "Oh, thank you for your assistance and guidance. I will do my own work on this project now, as requested, and polish and expand on what is requested of me right now. I need to get home for our evening meal, and tell Mum and Poppi about this new project. I will keep you updated as to my progression with this, if you like?" Grandpapa beamed that Luna offered an invitation to observe her progress. "I would like that very much, Luna. Now, get along on home, you have a lot to do this evening. The Outpost, and your family are depending on you," he said with a wink in his eye.

Luna scurried through the halls to the family quarters, entering and allowing the door to close with a slight bang, which startled Mum. She quickly spun around and seeing it was Luna, asked what was going on? "I just came from talking with Grandpapa Sebastian about my new class project that is going to take a month to gather information for and put together an oral presentation for the class. He was most helpful to me," she said in high spirits. "When should Poppi be home?" she further inquired. Mum was taking in the cheerful attitude that Luna was displaying, replying, "Any time now." "I had better go get cleaned up for the evening, and I can share all the news about the project with you and Poppi over our meal." Luna noticed that the table was set, and everything was ready for when Poppi arrived. She hurried off to her room, and first thing grabbed Moppet and hugged her doll. "Oh, Moppet, we have a big undertaking that we're going to do for us and for everyone on the Outpost. She ran to the other bathing room to wash up, then came back and put on a clean jumper that had brown stripes, and her evening slippers. At that time, she heard Poppi coming in the front door, so she ran up the hall to jump up into his arms and give him a kiss, and told him" Have I got news for you!" Poppi started laughing, as Luna always seemed to have some sort of information or news for her parents. "Let me get ready for our meal, and I'll meet you in the dining area." "OK, I'll be waiting." They parted, Luna turned and headed to the dining area, where their evening meal awaited them, and Poppi went up the hall to his room to take a quick bath and put on fresh clothes. Everything seemed to happen like clockwork, and soon all three were seated at the table with their meal before them. Mum had made a toasted cheese filled piece of Manna for each of them, a vegetable salad with citrus dressing in a small carafe on the side. She had also made a rice pudding with berries on top for dessert, and of course, lots of sparkling water.

As they started to eat, Luna launched into her project that Instructor had given each of them today in class. Luna decided to relay her ideas on her presentation the exact same way that she had done to Grandpapa. She hadn't told her parents as to her whereabouts today after class, so they probably presumed that she had gone to the Data Archives Center, as she most frequently did. She instinctually wanted to know what her parents thought of her concepts and subject matter she wanted to address in this project. She explained that all presentations were going to go to the Outpost Commission for review. She chattered along, both her parents enthralled at her ideas in certain subjects, and her creativity of the overview of the whole Outpost.

"That sounds like a vast inventory and lot of information to address for one presentation, Luna. You did say that the Instructor wanted to review your initial ideas and outline within three days before you started information gathering, correct?" Poppi asked as diplomatically as he could. He knew his daughter well, and when she had her mind set on something she wasn't easily detoured, but she was very sensitive that a satisfactory outcome prevails. "Oh, yes Poppi. I guess so he can monitor that all of us are not collaborating and going to turn in the same report, or varying parts of the same subject. (Luna chuckles at the idea.)

Poppi went on to ask Luna had she made her outline or list yet as to all the working parts of this Outpost? Her reply was to the negative. Mum was very intrigued by the way that Katavon could always cox and reigned-in his daughter's fantastic awareness. In a very relaxed tone, Poppi asked Luna, "why didn't you take some time this evening and start making your own list and outline as to what you want to address in your presentation?" "Oh, Poppi! I was going to start on my list this evening after our meal. I have a million concepts running around in my head!" (Again, she giggles.) "Well, if you're finished with your meal, your excused, and go get started. I want to see what you have in mind for our future!" Luna hopped down from the table, ran around the table kissing Poppi, then over to Mum, kissing and thanking her for their food. Leaving the room, Luna stated that Moppet was guarding the tablets so they could get started on writing down her ideas and potential improvements tonight.

She ran to her room, put on her pajamas with the gold stars embroidered on them. Hopping up on her bed, she opened her sky-window, then picked up her tablet in one hand and stuffed Moppet under her arm. She started making the list, peaking at the stars to help keep focused, or put her to sleep, whichever came first.

Lux turned to her husband after Luna had left the room, and asked how do you do that? "You know what she's intently got on her mind, but you so delicately pulled her back where she can see what she wants to do is not attainable in this one project." "My job as a parent; and to help teach our upcoming leaders, is how to make appropriate decisions, that will matter and come to fruition. Not create havoc! She will figure a lot of this out herself within a couple of days. You wait and see." He winked back to his wife. "Let's get these dishes put in the washer, and go relax. I think there is going to be an exciting month coming up." Lux smiled back at her husband, "I agree."

Luna started writing, and kept on putting down her ideas about the various departments and people on the Outpost until her long dark lashes came to rest on her cheeks. She fell into a deep slumber, under her "Stars" with a smile on her face, Moppet cuddled close to her, as she snuggled even further under her warm bed covers.

She awoke refreshed, before it was time to get up and ready for classes. Luna chose just to lie in her bed for a few minutes and think about her presentation, and ALL of her ideas. Poppi was right; Grandpapa Sebastian was right. She had to decide where she could possibly share her strengths with the Outpost. What mattered the most to her? She continued staring at the stars, and then put her small finger on the button for the sky window to close for today.

She got up and bathed. Everything about her from her long dark hair, her flashing keen blue eyes, and radiant skin, glowed this morning, as she finished her ensemble with a fresh tunic that was a soft turquoise color, flared chalk colored kakis, and her darker blue clogs.

When she got to the dining area Poppi was sipping on his Maya Nut Coffee, and Mum had set a mug out for Luna to have a cup of Cacoa with her morning meal. They all were having a veggie omelette, small oat cakes, and fresh mixed fruits, and sparkling water. It felt like a holiday, anyhow Luna enjoyed her refreshed feeling, and special morning meal.

Poppi finally asked how was Luna's list coming along. She brightly looked up at her father and replied in a serious tone that there was a lot of information she had to consider. Both her parents laughed out loud at her comment, but Poppi quickly composed himself and asked was she going to rewrite everything that she had been reading and studying about that was already in the Data Archives Center? "No, Poppi. I just had not thought that my concepts were so vast, and how much information is already available, and doesn't need fixing or amending. The original Commission was so intelligent with the information they sent with our ancestors. I will keep working on my list today, and then start sorting it out properly so I can address the information my instincts want to address in this project." Poppi smiled at his daughter and could tell she was already queued into the monumental concepts she really wanted to address. "After classes are dismissed today, may I go to the Data Archives Center and review the information I want to address?" Mum spoke up, "of course Luna. But please be home for the evening meal, or if you get tired. Remember this is a month-long project." "Yes, Mum." She went to her room and picked up her tablets and stuffed them into a tote that Mum had made for her, and headed back out through their quarters. She kissed each of her parents, and told them she loved them, as she gave each a big hug. Then she sprang out the front door and was off for her adventures for the day.

Luna got to the classroom, and found that Instructor had put some notes on the holographic board for all of the pupils to consider, and she was amazed that some of her fellow students had already come to class, she presumed to work on their assignments. They were probably as excited as she was for this ambitious presentation, from their point of view; to be reviewed and considered by the Commission. Luna though a few minutes. This really was quite a compliment and discovery expedition the Commission was bestowing on her class as they were not yet to be put into a classified organizational vocation for two more years. They were still learning and studying about their home, the Outpost.

The Instructor came in at the appointed time and referred to the notes on the board, to be used or considered in their presentations. But the class must still address normal studies for part of the day, then they would be released to go do research and gather data for their projects.

The morning seemed to fly by as there was a condensed version on each of their subjects that they challenged today. Luna was highly aware today of the significance of their 2nd and 3rd Dimensional Comprehension, Languages, Vocabulary and Spelling, Geology, Astrophysics, Math, as well as Body

Health- Anatomy and Physiology. This was just this year's curriculum. Next year more subjects would be added and others expanded. Luna attacked each topic with a keen new interest. How would any or each of these help her on her quest of putting together her selected topic presentation?

The time came, and class was dismissed for their midday meal, a bit of relaxation, then they were allowed to work on their assignments in any form they saw fit. Instructor reminded the class that he wanted to review their outlines and intended growth possibilities within the next two days.

Sonnet came over and asked Luna if she wanted to join Oliver, Kai, and her for their meal. Luna smiled in approval, and was glad for the invitation to be included. "Give me a minute to gather up my belongings, and I will join you. Where would you like to go and eat and relax?" Luna asked. "Oliver suggested the Concourse Salon," Sonnet replied. "Sounds great!" Luna answered. Thinking that as soon as they were finished with meal time, they each could easily go to anywhere on the Outpost they wanted, to delve into their independent studies. She was all packed up, and quickly caught up with Sonnet and they walked along the corridor to the main Concourse to the Salon. Kai and Oliver were already there and had a table, and had ordered something special to add to their luncheon food stuffs they had brought to class, for all of them to share. They each discussed briefly what topic they were going to choose for their presentation, but being adolescents, they each held information back, afraid that their project concept would be stolen from them. Luna made a mental note about this attitude, and she was just as reserved as the others about sharing her ideas.

The day definitely was going quickly, and Luna was excited and in an anticipatory mood to go to the Data Archives Center to collect more information for her list, and to see how the topics she wanted to explore could be developed or were too expansive for her use at this time. But, as Grandpapa Sebastian told her, to keep the original list! She smiled at his comment today. Luna finally excused herself from the group and heads off to the Data Archives Center. Once entering through the doors, she felt as if she could breathe, and take everything in. She knew her answers were here. She just had to seek them out.

Luna sat down at a table and pulled out her tablets. The first tablet had her list she had started last night of ideas for her presentation. The second had information about the subjects that the class had studied today. She sat there pondering her dilemma, and Mr. Tomohiro walked up to offer greetings and asked if he could be of any assistance. Luna beamed that the docent had shown up. His relaxed presence always helped her to focus and feel empowered. Maybe it was because he was the keeper of all the Outpost's knowledge. He could sense that Luna was not in her usual mood of doing some research, something deeper was troubling her. He sat there patiently quiet, waiting for his young resident to share whatever her deep secret was, so then they could look for the answers she needed.

The spell was finally broken, and Luna started sharing with Mr. Tomohiro that each student had special independent projects that the Commission had requested of what our class thought of our Outpost's past accomplishments and where we, the fourth generation, want to assist in growth for the future. "My goodness, this is an immense undertaking!

No wonder you are perplexed. And this is an independent study project for each student? Two parts? Our past and our future? He lowered his head in silence, to which confused Luna further.

When Mr. Tomohiro scrutinized the novice that was in front of him, he started speaking slowly, with focused clarity, his eyes twinkled in delight, "Luna, you can choose any topic, subject, place or people that are on our Outpost. You come to the Archives routinely to learn about life on Earth, life of the Voyagers and our Ancestors. These were not assignments, it is your higher knowing pulling you in this direction as what matters most to you, and to all of us."

"I am pleased that you have been assigned such an expansive critique and proposal. How long do have to compile, organize and ready your project for presentation?" Luna spoke in a low steady voice, "One month, Sir." "Luna, you are a very special and skilled neophyte." Mr. Tomohiro enthusiastically stated. "If anyone can do this undertaking with outstanding results, I know you can." Luna looked up to Mr. Tomohiro with her big blue eyes, trying to take in everything that he was saying to her. "Young one, think of the journals, think of what is really in your heart. I know you can master this undertaking if you are true to yourself and the Outpost."

Luna looked questioning at the docent, but he put a finger to her lips to silence her. "This is your bliss! I have already spoken. It is time for you to follow your passion. I can help with research, but I can say no more. You, Miss Luna can do this!" Mr. Tomohiro looked down, with a calm pleased knowing at Luna, as he stood up.

As he walked away, Luna once again looked at her list. It was massive, it was extensive, it was more than she needed now, she realized.

She went back to her notes on the four journals and decided to go do further research on them. She went to the catalog and pulled each of them us, and reviewed what each contained, and what nuggets she may have missed in her first review of this important data. She added notes to tablet, under the already created heading of the journals. She continued for a few hours, and realized she was getting tired, so she decided to go back to her quarters, get a snack, then take a nap. She knew she had a lot of work to do for the next month, so don't try to do it all today.

Luna worked diligently all through the next day so she would have a list as thorough as she felt she needed. She knew what she was going to have as her presentation topic. So, she was being as careful as possible to include all the areas of the Outpost that could be impacted. She was satisfied, tomorrow morning she would present her initial outline and selected topics to Instructor for his review and approval to start working on the next steps.

Upon waking the next morning, she followed her normal routine in readying herself for classes, checked her tablets one more time, and went out to greet her parents and have her morning meal. Poppi asked her if she was satisfied with her topic selection, and had an organized outline to present to Instructor for his evaluation. She smiled and nodded her head in an affirmative motion. She was ready. After finishing her meal, she went to her room to pick up her bag with the tablets and other class items she needed for the day, and headed back through their quarters and stopped for a moment kissing her parents, then she headed out the door towards her classroom.

The Instructor was already at his work desk, so Luna took the opportunity to ask word he like to review her presentation outline now? He looked up at her, and said she could leave it on his desk, as he had two other students outlines ahead of her to evaluate, then he would be glad to go over hers. She took out her work tablet and put it on his desk, and thanked him, then went to her seat to get ready for today's usual studies. An hour or so later, Instructor asked Luna to come up to his work desk. She was ready to see if he would accept her idea for the class assignment. As she walked up to talk with him, and get his input, she took a deep breath, to relax.

He looked up from her tablet, and smiled at her. "Luna, I think you have a unique and important topic for your project. Do you think you can give a fair and full accounting of what your intentions are, for the Outpost to move forward?" "Oh, yes, sir! Did you read through my outline of what I wish to cover?" Luna replied. "Yes, I did." He acknowledged, "but I don't want a sentence answer, I want to know how this can be approached, and implemented. And I do want to emphasize that this is your project, the Commission and I want your ideas." She smiled again, responding that she clearly understood her task. Instructor handed her tablet back, and declared to her that she was on her way. Congratulations.

Luna worked hard gathering the information she wanted to use in her thesis. YES! That was what she wanted to call her project; a thesis. She formalized her outline into three parts; past, present, and future. She wasn't sure of correct procedure for such a document, but she researched that protocol also. Luna was ready to launch her undertaking.

The day had come and she was ready to give her talk to the class. She had asked Instructor if her parents could be in attendance and hear her finished presentation, as this was the first time she had ever done a project unassisted. He did not object to her request. When it was time for her to deliver her assignment, she went to the front of the classroom, and prepared herself.

She cleared her throat, and announced that the title to her project was "Outpost 621, the Resident's Expansion."

The intention is to cover Outpost 621's success and future potential due to its dedication and allegiance to the Mission Statement. The fantastic journey into the unknown was taken by three groups of Volunteers, all Voyagers, that pledged commitment for themselves and their descendants.

This project was started by an elite group of men and women on Earth in the mid- Twentieth Century, where great minds from many areas came together to examine Earth's forecasting and global organization. To their conclusion, existence on this planet was going to implode on itself. With this information collected, they set out to charter a global event of potential astrological travel with new planet colonization, that had never been considered before. According to records in our Archives, this project probably, in reality, took almost 80 to 90 years in planning and refining. Once they found the planet that humans could inhabit, Gliese 581 d, the whole team focused on a documented 20 years for a proposed launch. Volunteers were tested and interviewed for this adventure. There were a wide variety of highly educated and skilled peoples available for their project since space flight had been opened to the private sector of people in the last part of the 20th Century. There were many advances in aerospace parts durability and reliability that also aided the substantiation of extended space flight and habitation on other planet environments made in the first part of the 21st Century.

There was a quote that resonated with the whole group by George Santayana, born in Spain, about their goals and Mission, "Those who do not remember the past are condemned to repeat it." There were so many topics, physical items, historical data, skills needed, computers, life support necessities, educational and languages to take with them. How was this all going to be managed? With much consternation and debate the Commission as they now called themselves, decided on three different sets of three ships each, that would set out to inhabit chosen planets, in the far distances of the Milky Way and the Andromeda Galaxies. We live in the Andromeda Galaxy. All three sets of ships launched to their chosen flight plans at the same time. After traveling through Worm and Black Holes, communication with the other two sets of ships was lost to us. We hope they landed and succeeded in their colonization as well as we have so far. What each group of ships took with them was 4 carefully crafted Journals with specific information in each of them.

Luna went on to report that the original copies of these Journals were in the Data Archives Center kept in an air and light protected sealed case for historical importance. There was a set available for study and review that had been digitalized for all residents. These Four Journals are originals that left Earth and are the foundation of our Outpost. They consisted of:

The 1st Journal, the White one: the first section starting with the log of all 200 of the volunteers, organized in separate columns were their ages and occupations. There were different sections to this book that comprised of foodstuff, for flight and colonization, another section for housing and clothing, and the last pages of this Journal were the voyage Preamble, the Mission Statement, and Covenant, with all voyagers' signatures.

The next, 2nd Journal was Red; and its significance represented tedious notes on paraphernalia of all kinds. First was a date, then separate departments of different types of equipment, next a ledger entry of what was new, or unexpected of the equipment. Followed by what was malfunctioning and what was needed to correct the issue. This went on for page after page.

The 3rd Journal was Blue, and this log chronicled, travel and the universe. The first page was dated and signed in as date of launch from Earth. They had left earth through an Energy Vortex that had propelled them further than expected; the flight plan was staying on the expected course. Trajectory of launch was successful. This journal had a straight forward date and entry for each significant incident that the Volunteers felt was worthy of making notes about. There were lots of notes and comments from the astrophysicists' and engineers.

Then there was a page in the book had been opened to many times. There was a date and the subject was "Time." They had passed through a wormhole, and the voyagers were not sure how long they had been in it as their capacity to tell time was lost. None of their time pieces were accurate any longer. With this new dilemma, they had to call an emergency meeting of the Mission Flight Committee to create a new way to measure time. Time is infinite, but it is necessary to measure and be able to base calculations on. This must be adjusted and ratified as quickly as possible.

The Commission had insights and thoughts on every subject, it seemed, had any of us ever given any thought to the idea that the Outpost was not using Earth "time." They were in some unknown time-space continuum. We were now living in a new creation that was adapted for their voyage from that day, forward.

It can be noted that the next entry was about two days later when it was documented that there had been no communication that had come through of the other two groups of Voyagers since they had entered the Worm Hole. It was also noted that more data on this subject would follow as voyagers from 621 would start tracking this void of information, to see if communication would be reestablished.

The Last Journal was Green, and it represented the starting day of their flight as they left earth. Date and time entered. Followed by the six assigned Mission Flight Committee Principals as well as Theologies and Philosophies, and a Master Engineer of Robotics and Computer Coding. This book recorded the daily routine and minor conflicts that needed addressing as they came up. There was a list that allowed for expansion, of the Voyagers that had started pairing off, or coupling, or held ceremony for their union. This was a very important part of the Outpost's survival and it had been discussed and reviewed before leaving Earth. Further into the journal were special community notations of how the whole crew immediately broke up and started working their appointed positions, in actuality, or by sketches or notes of what they would attempt first. There were also notes on how they would care and house the animals they brought with them. Starting seedbeds for the fruits, vegetables, trees, and shrubs that needed immediate attention. There were all kinds of notes and comments documented for historical records of the struggles and successes of the Outpost Community in flight and initial colonization.

Please notice that I mention the four colors of the Journals. This was part of the Commission's plan and blessing it sent along on this venture. White was the purity and honesty of the voyage, the red represented energy and ambition, the blue was the universe and travels, and the last color, green, was all-important. It symbolized our population and outpost growth and renewal. Everything on this mission had a place and purpose.

Luna took a breath and smiled. This is how our Outpost started, we followed these guidelines and directions to build and grow our colony. However, we had to learn how to live as one in this small community and grow and thrive. I read and reread these validating words of our pledge and commitment every day, as a reminder, and a renewal, for my life.

The focused Earth Commission sent our ancestors on this undertaking with devout and foreseeable knowing of what we would need to maintain, stimulate and defy human emotions and ego. Thus, creating the Mission Statement's three original documents, for our new colony to live by.

The Mission Statement includes all of the Outpost's population to adhere to healthy mental and emotional markers for sustainability and growth. This document solidified and still touches every part of our existence today.

Do these words, and commitments still hold value 100 years later? Yes, and even more so if we want to grow and expand our Outpost. Our ancestors lived by the directions in the Journals, and the ever so carefully worded Mission Statement. However, our colony has grown, in the domain, in population, creativity, and goals.

Let's look at each area. Our population has increased by 58 residents in the years since our colonization has been established on Gliese 581 d, not counting the 28 un-classified youths yet to be assigned to a vocation. We have built out quarters enough to house these new and upcoming families. Supply food, clothing, education, vocation, and exercise. We must adhere to community and appropriate allocation of duties for everyone to prosper and continue in the knowledge we are all one- "There is enough Love for all. Each of us must follow our obligation to our commitments for expanding the highest abilities in learning, creativity, love, positive mindset and intention. We all must follow our requirements to initiate, support, and motivate all others to their highest worthiness and innovation. With a monitored, yet growing population, we All participate in communal and societal meetings of import always. Keeping the primary focus on the Outpost as the foundation and the epitome of ALL objectives and topics.

The Outpost can celebrate, after 100 years of being on Gliese 581 d, in all areas of life, education, and challenging our residents, past and present to what we have created. By living within the guidelines of the Mission Statement we have expansions of sciences, such as our wings of biology and botany, that lends to current enjoyment and future utilization. We have built wings that express our human interest in the Arts and the human body and our health. We have built wings and areas of study for our continued stabilized community on Gliese 581 d as well as our continued searching the Galaxies for other life outside of Earth and our colony.

As we have grown, we have educated our new residents beyond what the initial voyagers envisioned. We have used artificial intelligence to broaden our thinking and creations for tools, housing, and food. Manipulated materials for longer space existence. Used our archives to keep languages our ancestors brought from Earth alive and relevant.

We are curious and anxious to grow. The Mission Statement supports these efforts. Our residents do not impede or challenge new ideas, nor do intentional harm to a fellow human or resources that are necessary for our survival. Let us use this and move forward. If there needs to be an explanation for a new concept or hypothesis, let it be presented and oriented in a positive learning platform. With collaborated thinking, we have gone past the stars, we can maintain ourselves, and we can dream and keep building and restructuring for future generations. My dream is a second living Pod substation connecting our Outposts, then on to the stars.

The Mission Statement is a TRUTH. It is a cohesiveness that gently guides us and expands the Love that each of us holds, allowing it to open and blossom. This commission has allowed survival and diligence to the mission, and each other for the last 100 years. This charter we have at our disposal doesn't belong in a dusty Archive, it is alive, and it keeps each and every one of us alive each day. The Statement expounds: "Prosperity- there is always enough, we hold the Contract of Love." "Do you believe in this Mission Statement? I do!"

My proposal, for consideration is that there is a review of our Statement, by all residents. Allow the 2nd and 3rd Generations to examine how our words, thoughts, and actions can be strengthened by the daily utilization of the confirmation of the covenant our ancestors made. Then, the second part is to put in place for the 4th generation, an introduction to the Mission Statement, and it can be anecdotal, historical, or taught literally. Each line, idea, or phrase. We are the 2nd Chance at Humanity. The colony of Gliese 581 d will not move into negativity or FEAR.

The three parts of the full Mission Statement follow.

"Thank you for your time and consideration." With that, Luna handed her presentation to Instructor, and went back to her seat.

THE END

PREAMBLE

The Commission was formed of outstanding progressive people from all countries of Earth and they decided to formulate and set into motion colonization on another planet. They were careful, and examined each aspect of the voyage and colonization they wanted to establish. It was 20 years in creation and planning. They had to go into history annals to decide where life interests advanced and where things went astray.

When the ancestors arrived on Gliese 581d, they had all the newest equipment, materials, computers, food supplies, with many years of stored history and data to assist the voyagers in their quest to colonize this planet. They also had a Mission Statement to help guide and ease some of the strains and burdens that were put on humans trying to survive in a strange environment, previously, but had failed.

The Leadership Commission must have constant impetus as how to keep the Mission Statement and Credo always in the forefront. To be thinking of all the residents constantly. These pledges could not slip away or be forgotten.

When the Mission Statement and Credo were referenced, all residents instantly knew in their minds and hearts the overwhelming gravity their assignment.

It was very easy for any and all the residents to lower their heads in reverence, and be proud to be a part of the new Outpost's Mission. The Credo and Statement strengthens their commitment to family, their leaders, and of course their ancestors that put this undertaking into action.

MISSION STATEMENT

The Mission Statement was strategically planned and sent forth as a blueprint for a new successful colony on another planet, showcasing humanity at its best.

The Outpost's Statement is a commitment to the discipline of always holding to one's self-correcting allegiance. May each new voyager hold to the highest good in learning, creativity, love, positive mindset and intention. Initiate, support, and motivate all others to their highest worthiness and innovation. Never impede or challenge new ideas. Never do intentional harm to a fellow human or resources that are necessary for survival. There is Enough Love for All. Let us use this and move forward. If there needs to be an explanation, let it be oriented in a positive learning platform. We do NOT want to move into FEAR or negativity. All of us must learn from our mistakes.

This Outpost has been chartered with an even higher ideology than any society before. This oriented philosophy demonstrates that humans have the capacity for this mindset and commitment to the Mission Statement to work well. All communal and societal meetings of import always will open in this manner, to keep the primary focus on the Outpost as the foundation and the epitome of ALL objectives and topics.

The Founding Commission that has recognized and chartered, The Covenant of "We are the 2nd Chance at Humanity," The abridged version: "Our Credo: Prosperity-there is always enough, we hold the Contract of Love." May this give clarity; helping remind each of the voyagers and their descendants of all responsibilities, and highlight their commitment to this Outpost.

Each event happening would help the voyagers to have a deeper understanding of the Outpost, and how each person is interdependent on all the others. The Mission Statement of Love with its tenets, will quickly realign the persons and put principles first.

From this day forward, we cannot forget to take in every sincere word that is part of our mission for survival and expansion. Thus, disallowing what was crafted so carefully for our existence to become faded ignored words on a monitor, being obliquely disregarded.

There continue to be serious considerations that must be adhered to by accepting the Outpost's Honor Contract. "Prosperity-There Always Will Be Enough, with the Contract of Love" and our adherence to the Mission Statement.

COVANENT

We may need to be reminded by continual review of the Original Statement to gain clarity for us to remain true to our responsibilities, and highlight our commitment to the Outpost- our ancestors recognized that 'We are the 2nd Chance at Humanity.'

We each will work with any of the Committee for realigning and recommitment to the truths of our Mission Statement so we can thrive and continue forward. We do not want to exemplify a failed experiment again.

The Credo is Prosperity: There is always enough. It is the sealed covenant of the contract of Love. The guiding premise is it is 'a second chance at humanity.

We work within our credo these three constants in Life: Change, Choice, and Principles.

We live by the ideology:

Motivate Through Positive Example

Support Ethical Behavior

Highest Good in Learning

Watch Over Maturation and Psychological Needs

Protect Emotional Wellness

Shelter Physical Needs

We aspire to what we want to create.

The Contract words:

There is no permission in any form to the following:

Never impede or challenge new ideas

Never do intentional harm to fellow humans

Never do harm or destruction to resources necessary for survival

Never use words, actions or activities of negativity, violence or abuse

We will not gravitate into FEAR or Negativity

This would include all of the Outpost's population and adhere to healthy genetic markers for sustainability and growth.

ABOUT THE AUTHOR

P S Morningstar is a retired CEO of an Identification & Security Company in Southern California that worked with many Fortune 500 companies and major Entertainment Studios. She has received awards in sales and quality, in addition to chairing exceptional fund-raising efforts for Non-Profits in the area. Her educational background in medicine and computing technology provided livelihood, yet writing has been her passion for many years. Her Native American heritage inspires poetry that is spiritual in nature touching the human heart. Her short stories are full of childhood memories that we all can relate too. Her initial book "Luna" describes the exploits of a young girl in the not too distant future recreating the elements of exemplary human ethics according to her ancestry from earth